Fire in the Morning

Fire in the Morning

Elizabeth Spencer

*All through the night Rome went burning. Put that in
the noontide and it loses some of its age-old significance,
does it not? Why? Because it has existed to the eye of
the mind all these years against a black sky.*

—Djuna Barnes, NIGHTWOOD

DODD, MEAD & COMPANY

New York   1948

C. 6

Copyright, 1948,
By ELIZABETH SPENCER

PRINTED IN THE UNITED STATES OF AMERICA
BY THE VAIL-BALLOU PRESS, INC., BINGHAMTON, N. Y.

TO

MY MOTHER AND FATHER

In appearance and personality, Daniel Armstrong bears an intentional resemblance to my grandfather, John Sidney McCain I (1851–1934); but no parallel in the circumstances of their lives has been attempted. All other characters and all the events depicted here are fictitious.

Contents

Part One

"AND consequently," the old man said, "I don't trust a one of them to cure calf, mule or pig, and for another thing they charge too much. And I'm saying that John Henry is your bull and if he gets distemper you can call Doc Jordan or whoever, but Miss Betsy is my sow and she's going to farrow smooth as she ever did. Using those rusty irons to alter that calf! And the pore little thing hollering and bellowing all night. I'm done with them."

"But what I'm telling you, Father," the young man laughed, "just because Doc Jordan is no good, that's no sign all of them are no good."

The old man bobbed his cork in the water of the branch. "I don't trust the tribe of them," he said. "I aim to get along without them."

Both fishermen had on soiled white shirts and gray trousers of a rough weave flecked in white. The old man wore a black bow tie and gold cuff links. His high-top shoes were caked in loam from walking through the wood and he sat on a cushion. His son fished upstream, a pole in each hand. He straddled an enormous oak trunk which had blown across the banks the winter before and had been sawn away almost to the roots.

Across from them, placed on a carefully cleared ledge of earth, a second cushion lay, deeply imprinted where someone had just been sitting.

The old man's cork jumped, slid and plunged. His skilled flick and lift of the line hardly rippled the marks of sunlight on the narrow stream. It was a little mud cat that swung toward him. He tossed it to his son to string.

"Son!" he called. "Kinloch!"

The fish flipped straight into the air where it caught the sun in a gleam of black, went skipping down the bank and was gone under

3

a small flourish of water. Kinloch felt the slick tail graze his fingers.

The old man regarded his son. "Don't get your feet wet." He began to wind his tackle around the fishing cane. "Aye dads, I been knowing for lo these years you can't catch fish. But when it gets to where a little old mud cat can get over dry land faster than you can—son, I shame to claim you."

Kinloch laughed in spite of himself. He gathered up the poles from where he had dropped them.

"Aye dads," his father continued, grunting with the strain of rising. "A little old mud cat. And now where's Ruth?"

He spoke as though her absence had not occurred to either of them until that moment when it became practical to think of her because they were going home.

"She went to meet Elinor, you know. I think I heard them up the branch just now."

"Well, you get them. I'll go along." He shouldered the three canes and gathered up his cushion. At a narrow place downstream, he jumped the branch. His vitality could be startling sometimes, even to Kinloch. The sunlight stamped his thick white hair.

"Be sure you invite Miss Elinor to supper."

"You know she won't come, Father. We've invited her a dozen times already."

"Won't hurt." He picked up the second cushion and moved away into the wood, manipulating the poles through the trees.

Kinlock twisted the string of fish around his fingers and struck off upstream. He followed a cow path which ran on a level with the branch, then swung a steep way upward to the crest of a limestone bluff. Sure-footed as he was on the slippery ascent, he would have walked in the same manner on the pavements of town, for unlike his father he was seldom mindful of things around him, giving any object his direct attention only when it figured forth a demand. He walked rapidly, his head down, his free hand open wide.

From the top of the bluff he looked down across the stream and saw

4

his wife. She was sitting on a shelf of rock with her shoes off and her feet in the water. The current, shallow and swift there over the white limestone bed, curled around her ankles. She was leaning back on one arm; her head, with its capping of short dark hair, was tilted upward. He did not call at once; instead he allowed himself the pleasure of standing silently and watching her until she should look up and see him. It had been eleven months since he had first met her, yet time and again when he looked at her she would seem completely new to him, and the wonderment of it would fill him, as it did now. "It is because she is strange to things here," he thought, "and different from them all." And he noticed how erectly, yet casually, her strong, light body rested against the rock and how smooth and still and undecipherable her finely-cut features could appear when she was not speaking.

Then she looked up and her face brightened instantly. "Look!" she called across the stream to Elinor Gerrard. "There's Kinloch!" She jumped down from the rock and waded straight across toward him on the slick stones. Her motions held the same quick, light quality as her smile. "You're going to fall," he warned. "Oh, no," she shook her head, laughing, and an instant later gained the bank where Elinor sat, putting on her shoes. He gave them a hand up the bluff to the path.

"Father sent word for you to stay and eat with us," he told Elinor. He wondered if Ruth noticed that he laid it on his father.

The visitor brushed at the mud on her slacks and pinned back her hair. "Oh, I've really got to get along home, thanks. Besides, you're going to be at our house tonight after supper. Justin is coming home from school and bringing a friend—some boy or other; I can't keep up with them, you know." She eyed Ruth appreciatively. "Ruth, you always keep so damn clean."

He followed them up the path, carrying the cushion and the little string of fish. Now he was watching Elinor. She made him feel watchful.

He helped her into her car and closed the door. She braced her arms against the wheel. The polish was chipping from her long nails.

"I'll see you tonight."

He shook his head. "We appreciate it a lot, but I doubt if we can make it tonight."

She laughed. "Now, Lock, if you'd had one thing on earth to do you wouldn't have been sitting out there catching those pitiful little fishes."

Her drawling manner of reply, her sense of the ridiculous always made him feel uncomfortable.

"Don't count on us, hear," he said.

Ruth waited for him at the gate. Had she been displeased with what he had told Elinor? Would she reproach him for it? He hoped not. He hoped that this would be the end of it at last—the end of this one thing that he did not seem to be able to make her understand. He threw an arm about her shoulders as they walked toward the house.

On the front porch his father sat and drummed his fingers on the rocking chair in time with a soaring recitation. "What-is-so-rare-as-a-day-in-June-then-if-ever - come - perfect - days - when - heaven - tries-earth-if-she-be-in-tune-and-over-her-softly-her-warm-ear-lays. . . . It's going to rain, son. You see the shape of that cloud? I never knew it to fail. Felix McKie put me on to that."

"Mr. Felix? And he's blind as a bat." Kinloch sat down on the second step from the top. He leaned back against two broad planks that ran up from the ground. They had been nailed there many years ago to keep the chickens from laying under the steps and someone had always been meaning to saw them off level with the steps, but nobody seemed to get around to it. Kinloch fitted there. The sweat of his back had stained the wood. He stretched out his legs.

"Time was Felix could see," his father said. "He remembers all the signs. I said to him this afternoon—"

"So that's where you were when I couldn't find you. Father, I wish you'd tell us when you go up there to visit. It's getting to be a long

6

way to Mr. Felix's house."

"Same distance it ever was," said the old man, peaceably provoking Kinloch toward the statement he did not wish to make.

But he did not have to say it. "Ruth . . . ?"

She turned in the doorway. "I'll have to change my dress to go to Elinor's."

"I told her not to count on us."

"She especially wanted us this time. Lance's sister is coming home."

"Who's coming?" his father asked.

Kinloch started to say the name but did not.

"Who did you say is coming?"

"Justin Gerrard," said Ruth. "Lance's sister."

The old man glanced at the two in turn, then looked out at the sunset again, sealing himself away from them with a sort of exquisite courtesy so beautifully executed that even Kinloch sometimes thought of it as old age's disinterested lapse from the present into memory.

And so they were alone. He looked at his wife. She had stopped in the doorway and now she met his eyes with a slight inquiring smile and no reproach at all, and what had at first seemed to be the beginning of a contest between them turned upon itself like smoke in the stillest air and diffused. He had the feeling that if he said simply and positively that they would not go to see Elinor and Lance Gerrard on that night or on any future night, that would make the end of it that he wanted. But then, he realized, he would lose what he wanted more: that she would be of the same mind as he.

"I don't like to go there," he told her, as he had told her before, except that he spoke almost roughly. "I don't like your going there. No good can come of dealing with Gerrards. It's best to stay away."

He rose as he spoke and went to her. He saw that she was still smiling, though a little shyly now because of the unaccustomed sternness in his tone. "But why, Kinloch?"

"I don't have any reason," he said. "And the best way never to have a reason is to stay away from them."

"She thinks it's just an idea of mine," he thought. "Well, I wish I could think that she's right." He reflected, relenting, that things were probably pretty dull there for her on the outskirts of a little town like Tarsus, when she had been everywhere, lived everywhere. She stood so quietly, as if waiting for him to tell her what to do. He put his hand on her head and stroked back the hair around her temple as one might caress a cat.

"But if you want to go, if you promised Elinor, go on then. I don't think I'll go, just the same. I'll drive you over."

"I can walk through the path," she said.

"And get mud on your shoes? No, I ought at least to go and speak to them, I guess. I'll come back for you around midnight."

A tension between families based on — suspicion?

8

KINLOCH drove Ruth in his pick-up truck that night to a house located not a mile away, yet he had to go through town to reach it, for the old road that had joined his home to the valley where Elinor and Lance Gerrard lived was grown up in weeds now and crossed by stout fences. There had once stood in this valley a mansion known as Walston Cedars after the man who had built it there. He was a South Carolina man named Marshall Walston, one who had managed to be at once both pioneer and citizen. He had purchased from the Indians a sweep of acreage that cupped around Tarsus in a half-moon toward the south. He had found the oval, grassy valley where three hills rose, just missing symmetry. The center hill was black from fire. Marshall Walston planted cedars on it, built the great white house at its foot, moved in and waited for them to grow.

The house faced town. Backward to the northeast a Scottish family named McKie settled in rougher land, and due north a mile away, Ernest Armstrong, Kinloch's grandfather, built a plain house on a hill.

The three houses formed a rough triangle. They were part of a section still known as "the-land-west-of-town," though in former days the phrase had held a greater significance. Then the land was populous and rich; from the valleys its hills sloped strong and high, knee-deep in resilient leaf mold that crackled under foot, guarded against erosion by chestnut, sycamore, beach, elm, oak and chinkapin, solid, muscular trees that had grown straining backward to the sky.

But all the former Walston land was now the property of the Gerrards, and most of its high hills were bare. It had been rumored for years that old Simon Gerrard had wished to rebuild Walston Cedars for his own home. Then just before the depression Simon's son Lancelot married Elinor Dudley and they had not lived in the Gerrard house two months before the carpenters were in Walston Gap. On a street in Tarsus the new bungalow might have appeared only moderately small; in the center of the broad green valley, it looked like a doll's house. In winter, when oak and beech trees along the Armstrong road were bare, the house was dimly visible through the outlying pines, but one must be expecting to see it to find it at all and it disappeared entirely when the thinnest rain clouded the space between.

Now the still waxing upsurge of half-tropical growth covered and re-covered the filtered view.

Kinloch drove through Tarsus; he passed by the courthouse square where Simon Gerrard's house, flush with turrets, balconies and dark stained glass bulked on one corner; he took the Delta road until just this side of Hangman's Hill. Here a drive branched off, proceeded sharply down hill, curved into a lonely place where the ground was always damp and cool, and squaring left broke into the open valley. Trees on the hill made a melancholy line of black, darker in the twilight than in the night time. The grass was tall and wild; the visitor looked twice to discover what he had come such a way to find.

But there it was, the sleek, expensive bungalow, and the many lighted windows in the living room were casting a bold sheet of light, quickly lost in the darkness of the bolder landscape.

Kinloch could remember wandering through the valley as a child, watching with respect to their stern and upright nakedness, the four charred chimneys that had stood there through time and weather until the construction company came to start the bungalow. Kinloch had never seen Walston Cedars, he reflected as he drove into the valley; and he had never seen its last owner, young Kinloch Walston, the man whose name he bore. But he knew the story of how the great house had burned one night and how his father, Daniel Armstrong, returning from the field just at dark, saw his own windows ablaze

10

with reflected light and began to run, shouting to his wife to save the children. She had gone to the edge of the bluff to watch and when Daniel saw his own window frames untouched by smoke and looked behind where the broad flames splashed over the sky, he knelt down in the empty house and thanked God before he ran to hitch up the mare and drive to join the town at the fire.

Out of the corner of his eye Kinloch could see Ruth sitting quiet and companionable beside him. Her white dress brought her clean-limbed body into firm outline through the growing dusk. She is scarcely more than a stranger here, he thought with tenderness, and what should it mean to her that Elinor and Lance Gerrard live where another house once stood? It means nothing to them, but in another way they are strangers here, too, strangers to this valley and to the-land-west-of-town. But why should that mean anything to me?

A rabbit bobbed to safety across the glare of the headlights and a minute later Kinloch stopped before the white picket fence. He had reached to take her hand and tell her that he would stay with her here tonight after all, if it pleased her, when at that moment the quiet length of road behind them was broken by the sudden blare of a loud horn and a second car raced across the valley, moving break-neck but without the look of urgency, under the simple fascination of speed.

On the very moment of stopping, a girl jumped from behind the wheel; her heavy blonde hair swung in rhythm to the opening, closing door. She put her hands on her hips, stretching and twisting her shoulders, as though to shake the long ride out of body and mind with a gesture.

"Come on, George," she commanded.

But the young man in the loud tie moved with a certain tenderness toward his own person, as if he did not yet dare question his good fortune at arriving still in one piece.

The girl kicked her high heel impatiently into the fence. "God, George," she said. "You're okay and your precious car is okay. I don't

11

drive *that* fast, George."

"Is that Justin?" Ruth whispered as Kinloch held the door for her to get out.

He nodded without replying, for the girl in question had turned her attention from George to them. She recognized Kinloch when he spoke and made a slight gesture toward him, raising her hand from the wrist. She went on straightening her dress. He was close enough to have touched her. He remembered the day she was born. Yet in the small interim between their introductions and Elinor's coming down the walk to greet them, Justin addressed her trivial comment to George and Kinloch spoke to Ruth.

Elinor's first remark to her sister-in-law was sharp. "You and Kinloch know each other, of course?"

"Sure," Justin said. "We spoke. Where's Lance?"

Elinor laughed. "Wouldn't be made to get any clothes on till five minutes ago. He's trying to decide now whether to wear shoes or not."

George thought that was very funny.

"You see, George?" said Justin. "I've been trying to tell you how Tarsus is. And don't go thinking we're a bunch of hicks till you see the rest of the town."

"O.K.," George said. "We met this man on the way down—damnedest thing, he was on his way to Tarsus, too—and you know what she said? She said, 'God knows why anybody would want to come to Tarsus.' How 'bout that?"

"Yes," Elinor drawled. "How 'bout that?" She was mocking George already, but he didn't know it.

"Oh, Lord, Elinor," Justin said, "you know it's the truth. Tarsus will drive you to drink, and it's about to right now. Come on, you all, let's go in."

"Don't tell me George drinks," Elinor said, holding the gate wide.

"I just this minute started," George grinned happily. "I like Tarsus fine."

"Ruth, darling." Elinor held out her hand. "And Lock. I'm glad you

12

all decided to come."

"I came to drop Ruth," Kinloch said, withdrawing. He spoke abruptly, almost rudely. "I got to be going on."

He got into his pick-up, backed and turned in a wide arc that carried him out of the drive, fender-deep in weeds. He thrust the accelerator low against the floor as he regained the road. Because what always happened had happened again, and the greatest stranger of all here in Walston Gap was not Ruth, not Elinor and Lance and Justin Gerrard, but himself.

THREE

KINLOCH met the main highway in a lurch of speed and turned the wheel away from town. For five miles he sent the pick-up hurtling like the wind, but at the top of Valley Hill he pulled out and stopped. He sat staring out over the treetops at the Delta. A few headlights streaked the highways and the low clouds glowed here and there above the towns. It was like looking at a map to a man born, as his father said, with red clay between his toes.

At last he straightened at the wheel, turned and drove back to town. In the square the pick-up jerked and rattled on the embedded gravel. The clouds were swift behind the white courthouse. Under the shadow of Martin's filling station, he jammed on the brakes and swerved left. The lone man in the street stumbled aside, thrashing his arms, but whether from anger or to keep balance Kinloch could not tell. It was only Ben Gardner, he saw, drunk so early, an unhired watchman of the square whose omnipresence was a source of comfort to the regular town nightwatchman.

Kinloch took the road toward home.

Yes, that was where he had found Ruth, he remembered, in Martin's Grocery and Garage on the last hot day of the year. The cotton truck had stalled at the gin and he had driven here for oil. Busses stopped at the filling station. She was sitting just inside the station door in a cane bottom chair. He had met her back in the summer when she came to work as secretary to an agent of the Farm Security Administration. What she ever did in that office was something he could never get at, he suspected because she did not understand too well herself. But then she was a woman. He was not exactly unaware that she had caused some speculation around Tarsus. He had heard his sisters remark on the "different" sort of clothes she wore,

14

and though he was not one to pay much attention he could see now that this outfit was probably brand new, or something special at least. He lifted his hat, but from the way she nodded, he knew she did not remember him. As he passed the time of day with J. T., he became extremely conscious that she was looking his way, but when he turned back to her, intending to remark on the weather at least, he realized that she was not seeing anything around her. The curve of her white blouse rose very still against her throat.

"What's she doing?" he asked J. T.

"Find out anything from her you're better'n me. Heavy Holmes and me got four-bits up on whether man, woman or child will get off the bus."

"Why don't you ask her?"

"That's what I say. Look. Heavy says, 'Waiting for a bus?' 'Yes,' she says. That's all she said. Heavy goes back on his heels a mite. 'Expectin' somebody?' he says. You know what she said? 'Yes.' I had to get back behind the stove to laugh when Heavy come on back. I'm betting it's a man. That gives Heavy two shots on the woman and child, but I figger I'm bound to win. She's not bad looking, you know."

Kinloch stared at him. She was most certainly not bad looking. But he only nodded and drove off with the oil. As he neared the gin he heard the hollow whistle of the bus driving into the square and he wondered who had won the money. He wondered a half-hour later at the little start he felt when he drove back with the oil can and saw her standing by the gasoline pump.

He put his head out the window. "Good evening, Miss Shaffer," he said.

She nodded again and in her brief smile he saw that she was tired.

"Waiting for the next bus?"

"Yes."

"Expecting somebody?"

"Yes." She turned away.

Kinloch opened the door and got out. He had a great deal of the

15

kind of patience required to win the obedience and affection of animals. And so he would work for hours training a bird dog to retrieve without bruising the dud. Sometimes he would be angry enough to lash the hide off its back, but he knew how to keep a punishment separate from his temper. He broke horses that same way. It took a long time, but when he finished he could ride deep. It might have struck him as comical—it would certainly have made his father laugh —to know that this was the thing that made him get out of the car to go to her.

"Excuse me, Miss Shaffer," he said, lifting his hat. "I didn't hear you answer me."

She faced him and he encountered her look for the first time. There was nothing either surprised or offended in her dark clear eyes. Perhaps poise and good breeding were her predominant characteristics. He classed them so, at least, although it came about that in the closest contacts of companionship or passion some part of her would elude him still.

"Pardon me," she returned. "I didn't hear you ask me anything."

"I asked if you were expecting somebody."

"Oh, that. Yes, I am."

He simply waited.

"My brother was coming today. He had planned to, at any rate. I suppose something must have interfered at the last minute. Or perhaps he missed connections somewhere."

Her voice betrayed enough to convince him that she was both disappointed and lonesome.

"Maybe he's telephoned you. Or wired."

"I hadn't thought of that."

"I'll drive you home," he said.

As they backed out of the garage he saw J. T. staring open-mouthed at him through the screen door. Then it was his turn to be surprised.

"Tell me," she said, "how much is four-bits?"

He shot a glance at her, noting the easy lift of her head, her white even teeth as she smiled and the quiet amusement in her dark eyes. He laughed outright. He recalled that just yesterday somebody in the drug store had spoken of how distant "that Miss Shaffer" was. And he laughed again, thinking that he, at least, could see how wrong they were.

In the following days, he discovered that he had been right in believing her lonesome. Her parents were dead; there was only the brother who had never yet come.

When Kinloch drove her to odd places around the town, he discovered for the first time that Tarsus was wonderfully rich in stories, that odd kind of exaggerated, half-accurate lore that small town people tell about themselves, repeat, and believe.

He told her only those things which would amuse her because he liked to stir her quick sense of humor, and the hours they spent together were much alike until one fall afternoon when they walked beyond the fringes of town.

"You don't know how lucky you are," she told him as they walked.

"Lucky?"

"Living in one pleasant place like this all your life. Knowing about all your relatives and your neighbors and their relatives. Disturbing nobody and nobody disturbing you. It's so peaceful and quiet."

"Peaceful and quiet!" he echoed, amazed.

They had reached the top of the grassy hill where no trees grew and as they advanced across it, he remembered that this was the hill where the house that Colonel Grierson burned had stood. The family there had fed breakfast to the soldiers and then Grierson took all the extra kindling wood and heaped it on the fire until the stove was covered with it and it burned and the house burned all on a dust-dry August morning. It happened and people still talked about it, because they had heard the old ones talk about it, but nobody was ever really convinced of it. Fire in the morning burns as thoroughly as another fire, but it has no efficacy in the memory which must evermore look upon it through a veil, unreasoningly conscious that here is something

17

which should not be. Even Rome is seen, in the memory of the world, burning against a night sky, and so the housecat derives its mystery from the sphinx. An afternoon fire leaves a red mark on the twilight. A fire at night—scarlet, wild, reflected—brings sleepers starting up in the absolute knowledge of fire. But fire in the morning is orange and transparent and the sun undoes it. People stand fully clothed, and they murmur and huddle. The men ask each other about business or farming. The family groups tearless and wooden among the uprooted chests, dressers, chairs and beds. Because he who is enemy or vandal is expected to take his prerogative from the night, and the spoiler who will not, troubles a vaster sphere than thought would choose to enter, and something unreconciled is here.

As they passed down the opposite slope, Kinloch wanted to tell Ruth this story also, but he did not. Yet later that very afternoon he came unexpectedly upon the spot where he had once faced his own Grierson and, lost in the compelling memory of that day, he knew a space, the first in weeks, that he did not think of Ruth.

They had walked on into wilder country beyond the fringes of Tarsus and, along the ridge this side of the creek, they found themselves in the middle of a forgotten graveyard where tombs were covered with honeysuckle and jackson vine and leaf mold caked the dim inscriptions.

Kinloch brushed a few of them clean enough to read the names. "All 1878," he remarked. "The yellow fever epidemic."

"So bad?" she asked.

"The town graveyard is thick with them," he said. "That's probably why they opened one here. Lea, Welsh, Anderson, McWillie, Hardin, Brandon, Featherstone. So few of them left in Tarsus."

"Moved away?"

"Moved away. Died out. But those that move away do come back, they say. 'Give them long enough and they'll come back to Tarsus.' Now surely you've heard them say that. Still I always have doubted it. People here repeat it to encourage themselves. What they mean is,

Life in Tarsus is best after all. And when one out of a hundred returns, they say, 'You see, people always come back to Tarsus.' "

"Where do they go when they leave?"

He laughed. "That's another thing about Tarsus. It doesn't care to bother about that."

"Oh, it's that way everywhere," she said.

"No. It's that way only in Tarsus. Look. They forget their dead."

"Only in Tarsus?" she smiled.

"Yes," he insisted earnestly, almost angrily. "That is something you must understand. And if you can't understand it don't ask me to explain it. You'll just have to believe that it's true."

He could tell that she did not see what he was trying to say, nor had he words to make it clear, so he took her hand again and led her to the edge of the bluff which had caved back a great way since the days the funerals were held. He bent back a low pine bough so they could see the open country again, brilliant, misty and faintly blue. The willows along the creek were green.

"Let's rest a while," he said.

She sat down on the trunk of a large fallen pine and turned her face toward the view. He settled himself crosslegged, facing the same way. They did not speak for a while. He sat wondering at the sudden mood that had fallen over him. How could she know what he meant when these last days he had been busy showing her dirty, incongruous Tarsus, as a romantic, if still incongruous, legend? When without intention he had thus told more than half a lie?

Even in this wide ring of sky and woods with the town blocked out behind them, there was a spot the image of whose memory distorted the grouped figures in the mirror he had tried to hold before her.

"Look, Ruth. Can you see where the creek bends just the other side of that field? No, you're not looking right. It swings out wide and leaves a deep hole in by the bank. Well, one Saturday morning some boys came to the house to get me to go swimming there. Have you ever met Lance Gerrard?"

19

"He's the tall, sandy-headed one who comes up town every after-noon?"

"That's the one. He was about thirteen then, I guess. I was twelve. Anyway, Lance was the head of the bunch that came by that day. I had a shepherd puppy named Pet. A little white dog with black ears. I had found him about a month before that, wandering around in the woods back of our house. I was crazy about that dog."

The incident he seemed about to tell her had started back at school. He had written a paper for English class and Miss Jamie had hacked him by reading it out loud. Girls were the ones who were always having their papers read out loud. He had written about the swimming hole he had found the summer before. There had been a Negro man fishing off the bank when he came on it. The Negro let him fish awhile and talked to him. Then the Negro went away and Kinloch took off all his clothes and went swimming in the water that was not muddy like the rest of the creek.

He was going down the school house steps after the last bell when the boys called him. There was a group of them and Lance was out in front.

"Come here, Lock," Lance said.

"What you want?" He let them come to him.

They crowded around him grinning. "Lock, you didn't really find no swimming hole, did you?" . . . "Show it to us. . . ." "Let's all go swimming tomorrow. . . ." "You could show us the way."

"I'll show you sometime," he said. He wanted only to be on his way. He had never played with these boys. He was one that brought his lunch to school because he lived too far to make it home for dinner, and that custom had set a line between him and them. They called him a "country boy." He and those like him would gather to them-selves under the big elm during the dinner hour to take out broad ham sandwiches and sausage and biscuit wrapped up in bread paper. They had no name for the other group and they rarely mentioned

20

them at all.

The next morning was Saturday. He was out hoeing up a flower bed for his mother when he saw them coming. For some reason he wanted to go to the shed and hide the hoe, but there was no time.

They stopped outside the front gate.

"Hey, Kinloch. What you doing?" Lance asked.

"Nothing." He stood a few feet behind the gate. His puppy stood beside him. He put his hand down and rubbed its ear.

"That's a pretty dog," Lance said.

"He's a full-blood shepherd," Kinloch said.

His mother came to the door. She called a welcome. "Won't you all come in?"

"We ain't got time," Lance said. "We thought maybe Kinloch could go with us."

"Where are you going?" she asked.

"Kinloch knows where there's a good swimming hole," Lance said. "He promised to show it to us."

Kinloch turned and looked at his mother. He was trying to see how she was looking at them, but she wasn't looking any way.

"Go ahead with the boys if you want to," she said. "You can leave the flower beds till this afternoon."

Kinloch was uneasy. They had never been to see him before. He was pleased, too, and his pleasure made him nervous. He ran into the house to get some lunch ready. He wouldn't let his mother put any sausages in. "I thought you were crazy about sausages," she said. "I'm tired of them," he said.

It was a long walk. Lance talked to him all the time. They all treated him with a special kind of politeness. He showed them other places along the way, places he had never meant to show a soul.

When he pulled back the fronds of the smaller willows at last and the clear deep water appeared, lapping in the breeze against the thick naked roots of the big willow, he felt the same as if he had made it all just so and now was ready to tear it up again in dividing with them all.

"Hot dawg!" yelled Jimmy Askew, ripping off his shirt.

But Lance held him back. "Wait a minute," he said. "Can't nobody go in till me and Kinloch goes in. It's Kinloch's hole and I made you all come."

Kinloch wriggled happily out of his clothes. That was the way he liked to do things too.

Their white bodies, surprisingly long, flashed into the water. The other boys plunged in. By noon the water was dim with mud, and long webs of slime, brought up as token of "reaching bottom," floated on the surface. The little dog tore in and out of the trees barking shrilly. He swam after the boys, splashed far out into the shallow part of the creek, and after a fit yelping himself hoarse at a treed squirrel, he spread his hind legs wide and laid his belly on the cool ground.

When the boys ate lunch, they broke off sandwiches and tea cakes for him to catch. Lance watched a while, then dug a piece of ham out of his sandwich and made to fling it into the water. Pet dived out, a proud, beautiful dive, paddled about snapping at leaves and twigs, and crawled out on the bank. Lance crammed the meat into his laughing mouth. He repeated the trick again, but the third time it failed. The puppy watched the false throw, then scrambled for the prize, his muddy feet smearing the boy's breast and arms. The others laughed.

"Get away, you son of a bitch," Lance said. He laid his foot on the dog's flank and sent him sprawling down the bank into the water. The boys laughed again.

"That's exactly what he is," Lance said cockily. "A son of a bitch. That's what I said."

Kinloch went to the water's edge and lifted the puppy out. "Here, Pet," he said. "He's tired."

"Ain't that a name for a dog?" Lance said languidly, tilting back on his elbow. "Sounds like a girl's name."

Kinloch stroked the wet black ears. "Pet can't help it what he's named," he said.

"You named him, didn't you?"

"Father named him."

Lance laughed. "You mean old Dan'l. My daddy calls your daddy Dan'l."

They lay about with full stomachs, pushing their toes in the mud. Keith Murphy was plaiting a skirt out of willow fronds.

Kinloch stroked the dog's head harder. "That's not his name," he said. "His name is—"

"Whyn't you say it?" Lance asked him. "Don't you even know?"

"It's Dan. Or Daniel." It sounded foolish.

"That's what I said. Dan'l. Just like old Dan'l Miskelly that cleans out the church."

Before Kinloch could answer, Keith Murphy leaped whooping between them in his willow skirt and began to dance like an Indian. One of the boys tripped him and he lay on the bank laughing as though he couldn't stop.

Lance hardly looked up. He stretched out more indolently than ever and propped his head on his palm. He punched a twig in a doodle bug hole. The dog crept over and sniffed at his hand. He caught it by the scruff of the neck.

"Say, look here," he exclaimed. His tone brought them up. They waited while he examined the dog carefully. He addressed Kinloch sternly "Wherebouts you say you got this dog?"

"I found him," Kinloch said.

"When'd you find him?"

"About a month ago."

"'Swhat I thought. That's exactly what I thought."

"What are you talking about?"

"I'm talking about this is my dog. Daddy got me three of them and this was the prettiest and it was exactly a month ago when we lost him. You right sure you *found* him, ain't you?"

Kinloch did not understand until many hours later what Lance meant by asking that. "I found him in the hollow down behind the house," he said. "He was 'bout half-starved. I took care of him. Anyway, I don't believe he's your dog."

"Why don't you believe it? It's so."

"Because if you lost him just a month ago and I found him starved just a month ago, that wouldn't give him no time to starve in."

"How do you know how long it takes a dog to starve?"

"I just know, that's all."

The boys had ringed closer. Lance got up. He still held the puppy. "I reckon I know one way to prove whose dog he is. Let's see which one he swims to." He pivoted and hurled the animal out into the water. Pet splashed up blinking and snorting. He began to swim. His black ears floated back in the water; his large anxious eyes were fixed on Kinloch's. The two boys knelt side by side, their arms outstretched. Kinloch slipped and fell. He caught himself on the willow limb. The dog swerved desperately to Lance.

"You pushed me," Kinloch cried.

"Okay, then," Lance said, twirling. "We'll try again."

This time he threw even harder. The white head swam deeper. Often before he went to sleep, Kinloch was to see great eyes, recognizing him, approaching him through wastes of water.

He couldn't ever remember the sequence of things at the last. Lance pushed him openly the next time. He struck Lance in the face.

It was after he struck Lance that the other thing was born. He did not know what it was. Though he had seen it before, he had never had to cope with it. Yet the thing had been in the wind since the moment Lance had fooled the dog with the meat. They had scented it and from that moment Kinloch's heart had beat in a strange way. He knew without any reason or expression to himself that they were working it up. And when it came they were the victims. Though his fists struck their flesh and the breath went out of him under their blows and though he still fought gasping as one after another just beyond his reach threw the dog the way Lance had done, he knew he

24

was fighting what he could not see and what he could not see was turning him blind.

Through slants of white and green light he saw his dog drown and when he ran away into the woods the wild weight around his heart still blinded his eyes so that he did not see the brush he ran through and falling before the thick black wall he thought he saw, he was surprised at the nearness of the ground.

A long time later he turned on his back and opened his eyes. He saw the clearest colors he had ever seen. Just above him each leaf on the sycamore tree hung separate from every other, measuring the trunk and branches against the immense sky. The tree grew in his mind, which was empty as the sky. He lay there with it until an ant stung him, and sitting up he saw his naked body. Next he discovered the cabin, only a few paces behind him. He must have been running straight for the side of it when he fell. It had looked black then, but now the unpainted boards were gray and pocked with the weather. At the bottom they had rotted into downward spikes.

"Thomas T.," he called, jumping up, for he had seen the fishing poles and he had some memory of thinking about Thomas T. while he was running away.

The big Negro man came out on the porch. He stood and squinted at Kinloch a while as though a strange calf had wandered into the yard, and then he bent double with laughing.

"Lawd, what that boy gonter do nex'? Buck nekkid. Buck nekkid, you is. Come here, chile, and put you on some of Thomas T.'s clothes."

He thought long and hard all the way home. When he got there, he hung around in the woods until they were at supper, then he sneaked in and changed his clothes. His face was not too badly scarred to keep them from believing him when he said he had fallen.

Monday afternoon he was too late to get in the stove wood. His father caught him by the chin. He asked no questions. "You've been in a fight," he stated. "You were in a fight Saturday, too."

"Yes, sir," said Kinloch. But this time he did not mind.

"Who was it?"

"Lance Gerrard."

He told his father everything.

"And did you win?" Dan Armstrong asked.

"Didn't anybody win exactly," Kinloch said. "Seem like he was worse beat up than me, though."

"When you've got to fight, fight hard," his father said. "Fight till you win or get licked."

"That's what I aim to do," Kinloch said.

"And listen." His father caught his arm. "There ain't a Gerrard living can throw an Armstrong."

Day after day, week after week, he fought Lance Gerrard. Years later he would wake in the night thrashing his arms; the muscles around his stomach would be corded tight. Life before had been a steady plane of wandering, hunting, fishing, working around the house. Now he had entered new ground, strange at first, but it took its own place, as the needle of the compass quivers at the point before it rests still and true. He felt some new tie with his father, undefined, but vivid.

And when the black car, so broad the road disappeared beneath it, drove up the hill one Sunday afternoon late in May, he knew who it was and he pretended not to hear his mother when she told him to run in and put on his shoes.

His father answered for him. "It's nobody but old Si Gerrard."

Simon Gerrard's thick shadow went squarely in front of him up the path to the steps. The thin shadow of the gold-headed cane he carried jerked short and long five times. Kinloch searched his soul carefully and could say he was not afraid. Yet he was mindful that two weeks before, Lance's collar bone had been broken in a fight worse than all the others.

Dan Armstrong went to the top of the steps and shook the visitor's hand. "Well, Si. It's been a long time since you came calling."

Kinloch went to fetch a chair.

The big man settled. "Too long, Dan, I realize. You folks who live on your land. I know there's always something to worry you, but all in all when you come right down to it, Dan, you've got the good life."

"Now, Si," Daniel laughed. "Every time I'm up town, I see you ornamenting the street corner."

"Have to snatch a minute from the store every now and then, Dan. No other time to see my friends. No time to go calling. You know, Mrs. Gerrard and I had started out to the car to come see you folks back in the winter, when bless me if Mary Helen didn't take that minute to fall out of the chinaberry tree."

"Well, dog the luck." Daniel laughed again. "Didn't hurt the little thing, I hope," he inquired soberly.

"Oh, you can't hurt those kids of mine," Simon said, very generally proud until he realized exactly what he had said.

There was a little silence in which Kinloch was conscious that his father wanted to laugh so bad he couldn't see straight.

His mother crocheted quietly. "We were saying after church this morning how dusty it's getting up in town," she remarked.

So they were off on that for a while and then it was still again.

Simon Gerrard spread his fingers wide and laid his heavy moist palms squarely down on the chair arms.

"I hate like the devil to bring this up, Dan, but I suppose you know how these kids of ours have been carrying on for the past two months?"

"I've noticed a few things between here and the woodpile, as the man says. Any subject among friends, Si."

"I don't mean I'm paying much attention to what Lance tells. I try to remember when I was a young one. Not going to let the old folks in on it, you know."

"I don't know about that," Daniel said. He reached over to muss Kinloch's hair in a rough caress. "I count on the boy here."

Kinloch watched Simon Gerrard's thick fingers close one by one over the wood. It gave him a curious sensation, almost like pain.

"What I'm saying is, Dan, I don't know much about the start of the whole thing and I care less. Let bygones be bygones, is my motto. But maybe you heard that Lance has been in pretty serious condition since this last round. He's going back to school tomorrow and he's not in any shape for another fight."

"As I understand it," Daniel said calmly, "it was Kinloch's idea to fight Lance until one licked the other, fair and square. Is that right, son?"

Kinloch nodded.

"And, as I understand it," he continued, "along about the close of that last go-round, Lance hollered quits. Is that right, son?"

"Yes, sir."

"So I reckon that's all there is to it, Si. The boys did what they set out to do. It took quite a spell, but it's over now and, you know, there's just one thing about it that really hacks me, Si."

"What's that?"

"All that scrapping and we didn't get to see any of it. Si, I have to confess I've been expecting you and I've had half a bushel of May peaches ripening on the back porch for the last four days. You come on back now, and I'll give you a sack full."

After the black car had eased down the hill, Dan Armstrong returned to his rocking chair and rapped out a little tune with his walking cane. He sang.

> "Oh, the goose chewed tobacco
> And the duck drank wine
> And the turkey played the fiddle
> On the pumpkin vine."

Then he began to laugh. "You know, Sally, why you reckon Si Gerrard felt like he had to get out that gold headed walking stick to come calling?"

Kinloch sat on the steps sucking a long reed of grass. The visitor had proved one thing to him: that the new bond between him and his father was not imagined, nor had it sprung from anything that had happened to him or that he had done. Something existed already, waiting to claim its counterpart in him. A new level unfolded beneath him and beyond that there were others, distance confused, presence actual, and only by seeking downward, he had found, could he know where he had once stood.

The "Southern" sense of tradition?

Now, eighteen years later, the water he pointed out caught the sun and shone like a purposeless mirror seen obliquely to reflect nothing, and even while he looked fixedly at it, Ruth's clear profile hung in the corner of his eye, recalling him to her.

"Go on," she said. "I'm listening."

"It's a long story," he said. "Too long to bore you with."

She turned to him in that light way she had of moving from her waist, her loose jacket falling open as though blown back by the wind. "You musn't think I'm bored. Don't ever think that. When I said that it was quiet here, I meant that I like it. It brings me close to something I've wanted all my life. You don't understand how things have been."

Her face was more intent and serious than he had ever seen it, as if the wind blew against it too, but harshly. He realized that he had been taken up with his own thoughts for too long that afternoon and that woman-like, she felt his mood to be her fault.

"No," he said gently, "I guess I don't understand. How have things been?"

For a moment it seemed that she could not make up her mind to go on, and at first her voice came hesitantly, as though from a distance.

"My father traveled—I told you that. He was a contractor. He built bridges, good bridges, they said. He went everywhere: Maine, California, Texas, Florida, and many times to the mid-west, then often back to New York between jobs. And we went with him. Mother and Scott—that's my brother—and I, always traveling. Mother was from

29

Louisville. Father had traveled as a contractor before he met her, and after they were married, he tried to settle down as she wanted him to."

. . . She could barely remember the yard of the house they had in Louisville, with hyacinths on each side of the walk to the front door. Whenever she thought of the yard, she could see herself as a child running happily up the walk and wearing a pink dress with a sash. The house she could not remember at all; there had been so many houses later on that all of them ran together in her mind. Because John Shaffer, her father, couldn't settle down the way his wife wanted it. When Ruth was five, Scott two years older, their strange life began. Six months of school for them here, the remaining three months a thousand miles away. Six weeks of summer in the cool Adirondacks, and the rest in the sweltering heat near the Rio Grande. In between these points of short residence lay the thousands of hotel rooms, and in between the hotel rooms turned the wheels of the baggage-laden touring sedan and forty-eight states went by like painted scenery being shoved across a stage.

Always overshadowing their lives was the mysterious company, which had the power to command them where to go next and did not even look to see if they obeyed, it was so sure of itself. Ruth never knew exactly what the company was. The childish picture she had of it—a castle like one in her storybook where officials three times as big as ordinary men sat at desks, working busily—still came to her mind whenever she thought of it. Because of the company, many unexpected things happened. Most vividly of all she remembered her first evening dress which she bought to wear to a school dance in Indianapolis, but which she actually wore for the first time at a buffet supper her parents gave three months later in New York. For a long time she had looked forward to wearing the dress, but when the hour came she was strangely afraid. She could recall how she sat alone in the bedroom of the apartment, walking back and forth, feeling the long skirts about her legs. Her parents and Scott had gone out to greet the guests. She knew most of them already. Would they introduce her again? There is the mirror, she thought; look into it and someone will look back. This is the room; it was flat as a photograph. She sat down on the bed. Suddenly, for no reason she could guess, there rose in her mind the picture of a little girl in a pink dress, pink socks to match and white buttoned shoes, running up the walk between rows of hyacinths and smiling all the way. She watched the little girl disappear into the house and, caught in an emotion akin to sorrow, she got to her feet and went calmly out to the party. She saw the faces of the guests light up when she came into the room. Her mother, fragile and pretty in her new black dinner dress, smiled proudly and held out her hand. So it is easy after all, she thought. She almost laughed aloud with a young, eager excitement, and turning, she looked into the eyes of a red-headed young man, and after that she forgot whatever had troubled her in the room behind.

But two months later, the Shaffers were on their way to Idaho, and New York and the young man with red hair shrank far into the distance and crying did no good for anything. . . .

"Were you so unhappy then?" Kinloch interrupted her, distressed. "Unhappy all the time?"

She smiled reassuringly. "No, not unhappy. Unsettled would be a better thing to say. We had good times together. Scott and I sometimes agreed that we were lucky not to have to live dull, uninteresting lives always in the same place. I wanted to talk like that for a long time, but he would lose interest. That was because he really felt that way and I was only trying. I knew, you see, that Mother was not happy. Not that she mentioned how she felt, but whenever they talked of saving money to retire and build a house somewhere, I would know the longing she had. Then, too, I probably think now that our life was worse than it really was because—because things turned out badly."

She pressed her hands against the rough bark of the fallen tree and looked away from his face, out toward the valley and the creek and wild Keystone Bottom beyond.

"We lost everything in the crash. The company went to pieces too. A little later Father died—in 1929, in the dead of winter, in New York. Mother was never very strong. She didn't know what to do, except go home. We came back to Louisville to live with her people there. It always seemed especially dreadful to her that it had all happened just a year before Father had planned to retire. She would repeat that one thing and it seemed to take all the hope out of her."

. . . They had stayed on in Louisville two years, living with relatives in an old brick house with frayed carpets and a crystal chandelier webbed in electric wires and hanging in a room nobody used. When you turned on the light in the kitchen late at night roaches scudded across the tables. Scott got a job as copy boy at the newspaper. He was too old for it, they said; it was just a shame that there were no more jobs, they added. Ruth went back to school. Late in winter, 1931, her mother took pneumonia. The house had grates for heating; it was always cold. By warm weather she was still in bed. She dressed to come to Ruth's graduation. She came down the stairs fanning with a little blue fan and smiling. She had worked on an old dress to get the length right. Whenever they admired her, she had to say something trivial. "You're sure it's long enough, Ruth?" She stopped on the stairs and turned right and left. On the newell post in an iron base sat a bulbous maroon glass lampstand, coiled with a sandy white dragon. When she fell she grasped the iron base and the light poured out of the red glass onto her face, blanching the make-up. Her lips were thin; even her cheeks were lined. It was nothing serious, they said. "You must go, darling," she said back upstairs in bed. "Run along with Scott." It was odd to remember that when they had come home from school the afternoon that their father had died, they had entered the apartment laughing and talking; but that night when they returned from the graduation, they glimpsed the house a block away through the trees, set among all the other old red brick houses exactly like it, and they began to run. . . .

32

"The day after the funeral, Scott called me into the parlor and said that we couldn't stay there any more. He said we'd both have to go to work. That there wasn't any excuse for people who kept on living with their relatives. He gave me half the little money that was left and asked me what I wanted to do. I had no idea what to choose. I tried to think, but too many things had happened. I couldn't decide. Scott got impatient. He said I should take a business course. A few days later he left and I entered a secretarial school there—"

"He *left?*" Kinloch repeated. "Left you alone?"

She nodded. "He knew what he wanted to do, that was all. He got a job in Richmond and went to art school at night. Now he has some students. He's always wanted to paint. He sells his pictures, too," she added with a touch of pride.

Kinloch knew what he thought of Scott Shaffer, but he checked the indignant words that rose in his mind.

"So you can see what I meant," she concluded, "when I said you were lucky to live all your life in one place in peace."

How different, Kinloch was thinking, how different from what I was about to tell her. Why, she told her whole life in ten minutes!

"Now," she was saying lightly, as if not wanting to bother him with so much seriousness, "you can tell as long a story about a dog as you want to. I'll listen to every word."

But in spite of her smile, he saw that there were tears in her eyes, and he moved quickly to sit beside her. "Ruth—" he began, and stopped, not knowing what he meant to say. He touched her cheek and saw how large and rough his hand looked against her smooth skin. "Tell you, Ruth—? Tell you?" What was the use, indeed, in trying to tell her what Tarsus and his life there were really like to him? Words always broke down for him under the real things that had to be told and those things depended perhaps on other things before them and so on backwards endlessly. But she was no part of that, he thought. She was completely unwoven with the materials that had formed him. She bore no crippling resemblance to anyone he had lived among. And the realization of this, coming at that moment, gave him a decision he had not dreamed of making so soon, and he asked her to marry him.

"Listen, Ruth," he warned her, for the quickness of her consent had alarmed him a little. "Listen to me. For all I said about Tarsus back there at the graveyard, it's more than likely that I'll be here always. It isn't just Father that keeps me here. Or if it is, it will be the same after he's gone. I'm afraid you don't realize—well, in a way that's hard to explain we are outsiders here. It wasn't always so, back before my time. Father doesn't mind. I've learned not to care. But you—"

She lifted her head from his shoulder and looked at him with a faintly puzzled expression, endearing, almost innocent, and said with the patience of someone explaining a simple fact to a child: "Of course, I'll be happy here, Kinloch. I don't care about other people. All I want is to be with you—" She paused, correcting herself. "With you and your father."

How close she came to his heart then he could never forget.

Returning to town, they passed back over the hill where he had remembered the old tale of the house on the hill. It seemed to him that many days had elapsed since they came that way. He looked about the bare hilltop where the late shadows lay. Again he felt the urge to warn her of the possibility of distress as vague in the future as the event of the fire was vague in the past. He heard again the glad shouts of the boys as blood wet his mouth where Lance had struck him.

"There was a house stood here once," he said.

He waited until darkness after supper that night, until he was lounging on his own steps again and his father was in the rocking chair, before he told him.

"My handsome young man," his father murmered at last, from an old song he sometimes sang. "Well," he continued, "we've needed a woman around the place for quite sometime."

Kinloch was annoyed. "I'm not marrying her just because she's a

34

woman, Father."

"If she's anything more or less than a woman, then it wouldn't do to marry her at all." ↜

Kinloch strained his eyes to catch his father's expression. There was a ribald streak in him, he knew, but there had been nothing of that in the tone.

He had opened his mouth to make a sharp reply, when he remembered that his father was growing old, that his wife was dead, his two daughters, both considerably older than Kinloch, had married and moved to town—he had never paid too much attention to them anyway. Kinloch was the strongest attachment of his life, an affection all the deeper by the pride that left it unexpressed, and jealousy, however passing and minor, might come even to him. Would inevitably come to him, rather, the most human of men. So Kinloch reflected, and he did not say "What do you mean?" And now he could not say it out of loyalty to her he loved, and in a similar loyalty to them both his father never gave him further opening, never even walked as though anything were to be spoken. And since, in her own way, Ruth was capable of the same thing, he found himself illogically caught between them.

He well remembered the incident which had first aligned them so— recalling his father as the prophet he could no longer question and defining her as the combatant he could not challenge—whether either knew their roles or not.

For several years past the Armstrongs had sold butter to some dozen customers in Tarsus and Ruth had willingly taken over the task of weekly deliveries. An order for an extra pound, forgotton the first time, had taken her back to Walston Gap late one afternoon. She stayed past supper. He became uneasy to think she might have had car trouble and took the short cut through the woods, hoping to meet her at every turn. He found the pick-up parked at a casual angle before the bungalow in the valley and drawing nearer he saw the three of them before he was seen. Ruth was sitting sideways in a cushioned wicker chair. Her legs were crossed and one foot was set in such a way on the green lacquered concrete floor of the porch that the high-heeled shoe and the fine curve of her ankle looked fitting there, neat as the tap of a polished fingernail on glass.

Dressed in slacks, Elinor Gerrard sprawling in a lounging chair, one leg slung over the arm. Her bright sandal swung back and forth.

Lance was stretched on the glider. He was slender and long and he was laughing. They were all laughing.

The long shadows coming down from the hills, the ragged length and breadth of the valley itself, the wild flourishing yellow-green grass (it was spring)—all set against the precision of the furnished porch. It was like finding a woman's fashion magazine in the middle of a swamp. Whether you thought it was ridiculous or pathetic, here was a mystery still and the how and why never touched the simple fact.

"Where have you been keeping her, Lock?" they asked him. "You all must come over real soon."

He was glad to have her away from them and to drive her out of the valley. A day or two later she went back again and after her third visit, he tried to tell her.

"People mistrust them," he said. "If I knew about anything positively cruel or dishonest they had done, I would tell you. But then that may be the very trouble, because there are plenty of scoundrels around that we get along fine with. But Simon Gerrard has covered his tracks so well that nobody knows."

"Are you sure there is anything to know?" she asked him.

"Even if that were true," he said, "they would still be mistrusted. They split people two ways. There are the ones who are afraid of them and they are the ones who copy them and admire them. And there are the ones who aren't afraid of them and won't stand to be treated the way they want to treat everybody."

"But how do they want to treat everybody?"

"They're highhanded, Ruth. That's Randall's word for it, and it's a

36

good one. Now you don't know what that means."

"Who says that?"

"Randall Gibson. My cousin."

"Oh, yes. I remember him." She sat idly turning a gold bracelet on her wrist. It belonged to his mother and he had given it to her. She did not speak for a while, and as often happened, he had no earthly idea of what she was thinking.

"But Lance and Elinor," she said. "They are friendly and kind. Aren't they? They're cordial to me."

"Of course," he said. "Because you—you are different."

She gave him a puzzled look. He recalled that this question of her difference to those around her had come up before and that she had not understood. She seemed to believe that all people were pretty much alike and that everyone she knew acted from the same good intentions she undoubtedly found in herself. One of her chief charms was that she won kindness simply by expecting nothing else. Whatever might develop beyond this she was not given to worrying about for long.

So the puzzled look vanished and she said lightly: "Oh, let's forget it. We could probably enjoy being with them. I'll bet you don't like Lance because you used to fight with him at school."

"Who told you that?"

"Lance. He was laughing about it just this afternoon. You see? It's all over and done with."

"I hope so," he said sincerely, and this she took as agreement and consent and because he had nothing further to supply him with an argument, he let it go.

And thinking, thinking as he drove this night of Justin's arrival, feeling the pressure of the unknown which he heard moving below like a buried stream, he wondered if his whole Gerrard myth were not, after all, false. Money, arrogance, talk, laughter—what evil violence is in them?

And what does Father think?

37

It began to rain. The wood he was driving through filled with the leashed sound of it and drops wandered heavy as mercury over the windshield. He stopped at the foot of a steep hill and looked up to where Felix McKie's weatherworn house hung above two high bluffs that each year washed back an inch or two nearer the wire fences. Close to the front gate the red soil had caved away, and the gap in the earth showed black in the night, ragged as the European bays he had drawn in school.

In one of those rooms, beyond one of those plain square identical windows, Felix McKie was sleeping the mysterious sleep of the blind. Felix McKie, the old hunter, blinded in a gun fight with Simon Gerrard's brother whom he had killed over some matter grown shadowy with the past. Felix was a Tarsus landmark now, for fifty years Daniel Armstrong's friend.

Could Felix McKie tell him what to think? Could he go and wake Felix McKie and tell him it was noon instead of midnight and ask, "What are the Gerrards?" And when he knew that could he ask next, "What is Ruth?" and perhaps what he needed to know all along was, "What am I?"

Midnight. He looked at his watch. Midnight indeed. Then Ruth should be expecting him. He turned around with some difficulty in the narrow road. A fence running along the margin of the wood blocked his free turning. The headlights caught a sign nailed to a tree: "Keep out. No trespassing. Simon Gerrard." Yes, he thought, Felix McKie might know, for the blind man's land had once stretched over the surrounding hills to join Dan Armstrong's corn field and Kinloch Walston's pasture.

The windows of Lance's bungalow were still broad with light when he drove into the valley. Through the gate, across the yard, even to the door he walked before he realized there was no sound but the rain. He called three times, then went in.

The living room was littered with glasses and choked ash trays. In plates here and there, a few uneaten sandwiches huddled and de-

38

spoiled each other. The curtains waved in the windows and rain blew in on the rugs and couches. He moved automatically to close them when he saw the foot: a heavy-soled brown and white oxford hanging in an absurd angle across the arm of a couch that had been turned to the window. It was that college boy Justin had towed home and all of him was lying like the foot was hanging. Kinloch tried to shake him conscious, but it was no use; he had passed out long ago.

They had driven her home then, he reasoned, yet feeling himself impelled to some sort of haste, almost as if the need of a pursuit and rescue were laid upon him. But no fleeing motors sounded from the drive and no call for help came out of the valley or beyond. Nevertheless, he ran to the pick-up and raced home. She had not come. Where had they gone? The Delta, Memphis, New Orleans even? He did not believe any of these possibilities, but thinking of them angered him just the same, so much that he did not know when he finally dropped off to sleep. When he awoke it was light. She had not come.

He pulled on his clothes and went out into the yard. It was scarcely dawn. His father was not up. The pick-up, splashed with mud, had the look of having come from a long trip. He was thinking that he must get in and drive to the valley again, when he happened to look down the road.

Ruth was coming out of the wood along the trail to Walston Gap. He thought at first she had had too much to drink, she walked so aimlessly into the road and her going was from one side to the other of it, unmindful of the mud. But when she saw him, her steps took direction. The ridge hid her for a moment in which he doubted that he had seen her at all, but she appeared again and her face, growing distinct, puzzlingly serious, somehow aroused in him a grave alarm. Was she ill? She was never ill. She came on steadily and stopped just in front of him. Before he could speak, she moved closer to him and stood leaning against him, her arms circling him. At the sound of her voice, he thought she was crying.

"It's such a long way, isn't it?" she said.

His anger fell away. He soothed her in all gentleness, while a gladness swept through him at the thought that something had happened to end their division and throw her whole back to him again.

"What is it?" he asked her finally. "What's the matter?"

At the direct question put to her, she stepped back from him, her hand to her face.

And while he waited for her to speak, he heard the sound of a heavy motor nearing and the splash of wheels cutting a path in the muddy Armstrong road.

Next chapter
gives "the matter"

FOUR

"WHAT was ailing Kinloch tonight?" Elinor asked.

"He hates to leave his father alone," Ruth said.

"Probably got him a gal over at the gravel pit," Lance put in. "After all, when you marry a woman ugly as a mud fence—"

She smiled.

"I'm ready to bet one thing, Justin," George said excitedly. "You hadn't met Mrs. Armstrong when you said there wasn't a good looking woman in Tarsus."

Elinor reached for a cigarette. "Said what, for God's sake? What's Justin said now?"

"It's what I was telling you about," George said. "There was this man in a blue coupe—Virginia license—Justin raced him all the way down from school. I kept telling her to slow down. When we were in the juke joint he came in too and said he was headed for Tarsus to see a beautiful woman. That's what he said, wasn't it, Justin? So Justin said, There isn't any such thing, not in Tarsus. I said, She means since she's not there. And she said, Oh, hell, George, I mean there never was, not in Tarsus. How 'bout that? Then she and the man started dancing to the juke box, middle of the afternoon, that's why we were late—"

"Pardon me," Elinor put in, "but what were you doing in a juke joint anyway?"

"That's what I was telling you. I kept saying slow down, and sure enough we had this blowout, see? It was a filling station too, see, and they fixed the blowout and we got our nerves calmed down. We like to turned over. God, I—"

"And I saved your life," Justin interrupted. "And you know what he said? 'From now on *I'm* driving.' After all that."

"Well, hell, Justin. I was trying to tell Mrs. Armstrong— Say, I hate to be so formal, don't you? All right to call you Ruth?—"

"I still think it's damned ungrateful, George. I'm still not about to get over it."

"Anyway— Well, who drove the rest of the way?"

Justin blew smoke rings. "I did. Of course."

"Anyway—"

"Well, get to the point," said Justin.

"This man, Justin," Elinor inquired, "was he the cutest thing you've ever seen?"

"I really didn't notice."

"Something's got into her all right," Lance remarked.

"I don't even remember his name," Justin said. She shook her hair back from her still, young face. Something had got into her, it was obvious, but her eyes gave no clue. Their gray-blue color was one-dimensional; their dullness interpreted nothing at all from the mind.

"Damn Yankee," George said.

"He was not," Justin returned. "I hope to tell you he was from Richmond."

"Well, he talked like one."

"Oh, Jesus," said Elinor. "Quit bickering. You sound like you're married."

"Maybe they are," Lance said.

"God, I hope she's got that much sense left," Elinor remarked.

"I don't know," Lance said. "Ruth and Kinloch don't squabble, I bet."

"Just give them a while longer."

"Yeah, if they live in Tarsus long, they'll have to start fighting each other," Lance said, mixing himself another drink. "Never saw the like of folks in this town."

"What's happened now?" Justin asked. "If it's not funny, don't tell it."

"Oh, it's all funny to me," Elinor said.

42

"Elinor goes to Jessie Mae Gardner to get a hem turned," Lance explained, "and comes back with so much gossip she has to write some of it down before she forgets it."

"Jessie Mae is my dearest friend," murmured Elinor. "We have so much in common."

"Yeah," Lance said. "Drinking husbands, for instance."

"And *I'll* be running for the barn next," Elinor said.

"Tell Justin that one, Elinor."

"It's Ruth's story. She saw it all."

"Tell it, Ruth."

"It didn't seem funny to me at the time," Ruth said. "I didn't know what to make of it. It happened one afternoon when I was walking through the alley by the Gardner's house. I had been to get some groceries. Houses are built very strangely in that section. There seem to be others facing the street, but from the back you can't find them."

"The bluffs," Elinor explained. "Go on."

"It was getting dark. I was nearly past the Gardner's when I heard a woman running and screaming inside the house. I couldn't make out the words. I stopped and waited. Not a minute later out the back door came Jessie Mae, absolutely naked. Ben—he's drunk all the time, Elinor told me, but for Jessie Mae's sake I do hope that this is not quite the ordinary thing—Ben was right after her. Fat as she is, she dodged him. She ran to the barn at first, but he stumbled to the door and leaned through it, looking in. She was just around the corner from him, not two feet away, pressed against the wall. I could see him decide she wasn't in the barn. He picked up a rake by the door and began to curse. Then he saw her. I began to think I'd have to call or run for help when he caught his trousers in the rake and fell. He was still blocking her from the barn and the house too, but when he fell she saw her chance. There was a white cow grazing in the corner of the lot. When he managed to stand up again, she—I've never seen anyone move so fast—she had disappeared. He walked slowly all over the lot. He came so close to me I smelled the whiskey on his breath.

43

He got so fascinated he forgot to call her or curse. Finally, as a last gesture—I held my breath for Jessie Mae—he stroked the cow's head very sadly. Then he struggled up the back steps and went into the house. I think he must have started crying."

"But where was Jessie Mae?" George asked.

"Oh, she was hidden behind the cow. They blended beautifully. I could hardly believe it myself."

Ruth could not help noticing that Justin did not join in the general laughter, but watched her narrowly while pretending to search for a cigarette. Because of the quiet good looks and collected, easy charm she had possessed all her life, Ruth had long ago become accustomed to the stares of women like Justin, who were ready to spring greedily upon a flaw. She would have felt no concern now except that she could not help wondering if it was Scott that Justin had danced with in the road house. Yet partly because she did not wish to question Justin, partly because of an evasive quality within herself, she did not ask. She merely hoped that it was not Scott. She had started a new life now; she did not want to be carried back into the past. So she did not find out, but for a full two hours listened instead, while the others chattered, to the story of George's life, which he seemed especially anxious that she should know. . . .

"And then?" she asked him for the twentieth time.

"Tha's' all there is," George said. He set his glass to his lips—the only motion he could not perform without taking thought—and drained it. "Tha's' the story of my life." He closed his eyes, smiled and slid heavily against her shoulder. Ruth settled his head comfortably on the arm of the couch and joined the others.

Justin glanced over the back of her chair. She had taken off her shoes and her feet were propped on the coffee table. "What's wrong with George?"

"George is tired," Ruth said. "He's had a hard life." She drew up a chair.

Lance yawned. "Ruth, you haven't had enough to drink. Here now,

44

come on. Give it to me. Just a small one. You won't even know—"

"What hit me," she finished, laughing and withholding the glass.

"For God sakes," Elinor said, "leave her alone, Lance."

"Well, I just wanted her to feel good. Ruth—"

"I feel fine, thank you," she said. "Do you feel fine?"

"You really want to know?"

"He feels like hell," Justin said. "I feel like hell. Elinor, think of something exciting to do. Just once. Four hours in Tarsus and I'm so bored already I could start calling people on the phone. Like the night it had been raining so long and we telephoned everybody in the book and said the levee had broken. There were cars heading out of here for the Delta all night long."

Lance laughed. "I can hear Justin now. 'This is your Cousin Mary Jane from over near Sunflower,'" he mimicked. "'Of course I'm not joking. I'm floating on the ice box right this minute.'"

"Did anybody ever know who did it?" Justin asked.

"They knew it was one of us," Lance said. "They always know it's one of us."

"Oh, let's think of something good to do," Justin begged. "Elinor—?"

"What are you asking me for? I'm not going to go projecking in other folks' business."

"Well, but you know people here. I don't know anybody anymore. People on the street—I never saw them before."

"You'd think she'd spent the last five years abroad," Lance said.

"All I think is I wish to God something exciting would happen. I wish somebody would come blow George's brains out. I wish some nigger would try to rape me so we could have a lynching. I wish—"

"I wish you'd shut up," said Elinor. "You'll wake up George."

"George dar-ling!" cried Justin. Barefoot, tall and lithe, she moved across to him and sat by him. "Is him got too much to drink and now him's all feepy? Well. It's fixing to rain, honey chile. Le's put him in the rain and he'll get all wet and then maybe he'll catch pneumonia

45

and won't live so long as he might." She shoved the couch across the waxed floor toward the open windows where the wind was blowing the curtains. George's hand trailed across the floor.

"Does he always pass out?" Lance asked.

"With the money he's got," said Justin, "he can afford to pass out any day of the week, any hour of the day he gets damn good and ready. But that ain't the reason he passes out. He'd act the same way on six bits and a pint of rot gut." She stretched and turned her arms in the wind. "Ruth, it's your turn. You think of something. No matter what. Just say it. All I need is a start."

"You might go see what Jessie Mae's doing," Ruth said. "She's the most exciting person I know."

"Wonderful!" Justin pivoted toward them in a wide dance step. She was young and for the moment at least, perversely pleased with herself for being young. She was younger than Ruth. "Come on, come on. We'll all go call on Jessie Mae." She snatched up her shoes. "Hats, purses, gloves, calling cards . . . everything. Oh, come on, Elinor. Get up, Lance." She tugged at his hand.

He slid further down in the chair. "Oh, hell, Justin. Act your age."

"That's what I say," said Elinor. "Jessie Mae's been in bed for two hours."

Justin flung the shoes on the floor. "That's the trouble with you. You sit here and sweat and gripe, but you want to be the way you are."

Lance dragged peacefully at his cigarette. "Deliver us from being the way you are."

She laughed scornfully. "You're lying and you know you're lying." She started toward the hallway.

"Now what are you going to do?" Elinor asked.

"Going to telephone Jessie Mae."

"Justin, if you make her mad she'll never fix another dress for me. Lance, stop her."

"Oh, let her alone," he said. "Chances are nobody will answer the phone."

She called the number. They could hear the buzz at the end of the line. "Somebody's coming," she whispered to them. "Hello. Jessie Mae? This is Elinor Gerrard, honey." She was an expert mimick. Elinor ran to the phone.

"Give it to me, Justin. Turn loose, I tell you. Hello, Jessie Mae? That was that fool Justin. I told her she'd wake you up. What?" Her voice turned serious.

Justin stood in the door. "Something's happening," she said to Lance and Ruth. "Listen to Elinor, won't you? Golly, it must be good. Oh, hurry up and tell us. When I said 'This is Elinor,' she said 'Thank God.' I swear. Oh, hurry up."

"Call you back in a minute. Yeah, well don't worry. Well." Elinor came back into the room. "Well by God, you sure hit the jackpot."

"What's ailing old Jess?" Lance asked, sitting up straight.

"She's running out on Ben, that's what. She's going to meet this cousin at Gospel Hollow on the Delta road. She was set to go in the car to meet him, but Ben came in drunk and got the car and now he's driving through town mad as a hatter, and she's got to get a ride from somewhere to make Gospel Hollow by midnight."

"Well, I swear," said Lance.

"I started to tell her to call Anse Slade or Roscoe Wright," Elinor said.

"Who're they?" asked Justin.

"Jessie's boy friends, they say. I don't know."

Lance sat with his hands dangling between his knees. He began to smile and his resemblance to Justin became marked. "Damn if I'm not for giving her a ride," he said. "Husbands ought to stick together, but damn if I don't think this is too good to miss."

"Oh, wonderful!" Justin cried. She squatted on the floor like a child and began cramming her feet into her shoes. "Just like old times. Call her quick, Elinor."

Elinor leaned on the door jamb and folded her arms. In spite of her excellent figure, sleek hair and definite mouth, she had a slovenly look about her dress and posture. Her voice slurred words without inflection, as though it were too much trouble to keep them separate.

"I'm here to tell you I don't want my brains blown out by Ben Gardner," she said.

"Well, stay here, then," said Justin.

"Elinor, we know damn well you're stalling," Lance said. "You always stall about everything. And the reason you stall is because you're so goddam lazy you don't know whether anything is worth the trouble or not. I'll call her."

She regarded him without resentment. "You're too drunk to drive anybody anywhere. And it's fixing to rain."

"I haven't had any more than you have," he said.

"But you can't carry it as well."

"Get out of the way of that phone. Move, I said."

She stepped into the room. They were silent while he called.

"Ruth doesn't want to go, I bet. You don't want to go, do you, Ruth?"

Ruth could not quite grasp their excitement. She viewed the town as they would have liked to view it, as though it were a neighboring village at some out-of-the-way resort. You went to the post office, the grocery, the filling station; you passed those who lived there the year round with a faint bite of curiosity that vanished as you drove past the last house and headed home. She could no more connect them with the scandalous tales that Elinor passed on to her, than she had connected the movie people she saw in Hollywood with the heroes and heroines of the dark theater and the screen.

"I'd hate to miss anything," she said politely.

Lance knocked over a smoking stand. He put his hand to his head.

"I told you," said Elinor. "You'll never make it through town."

48

"Oh God, shut up and let's get going. Are you coming or aren't you?"

"I'll drive. I can drive," Justin offered. "I don't feel a thing."

"Make up your mind, Elinor."

"Oh, I'm coming. I'd be scared to stay here by myself with George."

"Yeah, what about George?"

"To hell with George," said Justin.

"Well, he's your George."

They went out to Lance's car.

"Sit by me, Ruth," Lance said.

"You better be letting Ruth drive."

"I'm all right, I tell you. If you're going to bitch all the way—God!"

"What on earth?"

"A tree, darling. He can't even see a tree. Lance, for God sakes, let Ruth drive. We've got twenty minutes—"

"Anything, anything to shut your mouth. Here, Ruth. Oh, God, it's dead. You start it here. Now will you hush. Will you hush now."

"I won't say another word."

Inside five minutes they were at Jessie Mae's house.

"There she comes," said Elinor.

"There's a car coming," Lance observed. "Back there. Don't you see it coming?"

"Oh, I bet it's Ben!" Justin cried. She giggled wildly. "How perfect! If it would only be Ben."

"Hurry, Jessie Mae. Give me that damn suitcase and get in."

The woman's body was fat as clabber. Breath sobbed out of her. She came down on the seat with a plop.

"It's him, it's him, I tell you. He saw me come out. He's been driving by all night. I don't know how he knows, but he knows. See, he's after us. Oh, stop, stop. I shouldn't leave him. Poor Ben, he can't help it."

"Hush, Jessie. You can't go back now. Look, he can't even keep the car in the road. You'll make it. See, he's dropping back."

Rain fell thick out of the darkness, spreading wide into the headlights as though driven backwards through a funnel. The wet gravel swirled under the wheels but would not lift.

"Faster, Ruth."

"Where you going to live, Jessie Mae?"

"You don't remember my Aunt Willie that used to live in Tarsus? She lives in Memphis now. It's her boy, Tom Wilson, who's going to meet me. They've been begging me for years, 'Jessie Mae, come on and leave Ben and come to us.' But everytime I'd say, 'I can't leave Ben, Aunt Willie.' God knows I've put up with a lot. Everybody knows how Ben beats me."

"How does he beat you?"

"Justin!"

"We're almost there," said Lance.

Ruth watched the back mirror steadily. Dim lights raced behind, then vanished as the road turned.

"You know where the road to Gospel Hollow comes down the other side of that deep gully?" Jessie Mae said. "That's the place."

The gravel was heavy on the hill. It slowed their pace. Over the sheer bluff line that ran to the right of the road, a dim landscape was visible.

"Look up there. He's waiting."

"Do you see it, Ruth? Up to the right. There. Watch out for the edge."

"The suitcase, the suitcase. Quick."

"Oh, Jesus, he's coming behind. He's coming up the hill. Ben. . . ."

"Run, Jessie. If you go back now, he'll kill you sure. Run, you fool!"

"Is she in?"

"I can't see the car even."

"She's in. Oh God, it won't crank."

"It's got to crank. Pray, everybody. Ben's nearly here."

Headlights from behind illuminated their faces. At the crest of a sodden wagon road that angled into the highway, the hope of Jessie

Mae's rescue crouched dimly. Its engine ground, strained and whined dead.

"Let out the clutch, you fool!" Lance shouted out the window.

Gravel sloshed against their fenders.

Justin, on her knees in the back seat, peered through the window.

"It's Ben, all right!" she cried. "He's trying to get out. Back into him, Ruth."

Ruth switched into reverse. "Get your head out of the window. I can't see what I'm doing." She let out the brake. The front wheels skidded. How far back was he? Not yet, not yet.

"Hurry, Ruth. Quick, quick."

"I can't see, I tell you. Move out of the window!" She turned half around in her seat and the brake slipped into the arch of her shoe. The high heel caught in the rubber padding and before she could shake it free, they heard the smack of metal on metal.

"That got him," Justin said. "Oh, no, no! He's caught in the door! He can't get back in. He's turning the wheel. He's turning the wrong way. Oh Lord God Jesus Christ, he'll go over the bluff, he'll go, he'll go. . . ."

She screamed, a shrill, useless succession of noise that tried to assert its importance over the single calamitous sound which they now heard, unrepeated, without echo, gone and done with so much sooner than anyone would have thought. . . .

A few minutes later Lance scrambled out of the gully and rejoined them where they stood waiting beside the highway. Smears of red earth clung to his clothing.

"Stone dead," he told them. Headlights flickered through the rain and climbed toward them. The car pulled up. "Need any help?"

The friendly masculine voice calling out of the night communicated the first impact of guilt. They did not look at one another.

"No," Lance answered. "We'll make it now, thanks."

"So long, then."

"Pike County license," Lance remarked. "A long way from here."

"Why didn't you tell him, Lance?" Elinor demanded. "If that ever gets out you know how it's going to sound."

He did not say anything. They crowded back into the car. Ruth's hands were numb against the wheel. Kinloch. . . . What would he say? What was there to say?

"Where can we go to call?" she asked.

The three in the car with her did not answer.

"We've got to get an ambulance, a wrecker. Haven't we?"

It was as though she stood on a platform and asked rhetorical questions.

"Jessie Mae was gone when it happened," Lance said. "The car started just before Ben stopped."

"Well, let her go along and be happy while she can," said Elinor.

"The point is, she didn't see it happen," Lance said.

Ruth was struck by the cool, measured quality of his voice. The slur of drunkenness had vanished.

"There's something else," he continued. "It wasn't any Cousin Tom Somebody in that car. They came too near our headlights. It was Anse Slade."

"Well the dirty bitch," said Elinor. "Lying to us every step of the way."

"Word will get around," Lance said. "Anyway, she'll hardly be coming back to the funeral. She won't want to show face in Tarsus for a long time after this."

"Quit whimpering, Justin. It all comes of you howling for excitement."

"Ruth started it. She said call Jessie Mae."

"And if you hadn't slung that mane of hair in the back window it wouldn't have happened," Elinor said.

"Don't you dare blame anything on me. Don't you dare. Ruth was driving, wasn't she? Everybody knows Ruth was driving."

"You stinking little coward, you leave Ruth out of this," Elinor blazed. "It was you and Lance and you know it. It's always you and

52

Lance. So help me God if I have to swear on a stack of Bibles as high as Simon's house that Ruth was asleep on the couch with George, I'll do it and don't ever think I won't."

"And if two women could sleep with George on that couch, you'd be the other one," Lance said. "Or are you fixing to swear you were sleeping with somebody else?"

"Oh my God, Lance, I'm in it up to my neck. Hell, I married it. Once you've done that, there ain't nothing can happen that's not too good for you and you damned well know it. But I'm saying for Ruth that the only blessed thing that got her behind that wheel was not getting high as a kite like the rest of us. And if you touch her with a ten-foot pole—"

"But you can't go saying that I—" Justin cried.

"Oh, shut up, everybody," Lance commanded. "Shut up, shut up. Now look here. Elinor's right. Ruth's not to blame for a damn bit of it. Nobody is to blame, and nobody is going to start passing the buck. Ruth happened to be at our house. Justin happened to call Jessie Mae. Ruth happened to be the only one who could drive. Ben happened to see us leave. An accident is anybody's accident, or nobody's accident. So what I'm telling you is, the sooner we forget the whole thing the better for Ruth, the better for all of us."

"I'd rather not hide anything," Ruth said. "I've caused a man's death. Wouldn't it be better to say so now?"

"You had nothing to do with it," Elinor told her. "You know you had nothing to do with it."

"It wouldn't be right, Ruth," Lance said. "You've got Kinloch and the old man to think about, remember. Do you think for a minute they'd ever understand this?"

"I don't know," she said, miserably. "Oh, I don't know."

Somewhere they had shifted ground and what had at first seemed the only path now appeared as one way in a many-branched road, whose outlines were as vague as those of the sky and earth dissolving together in the rain.

An intolerable debate chased foolish circles within her head while they returned to the bungalow, nursed Justin out of the hysterics, cleaned their shoes, washed hands and faces.

At dawn she left them. They called after her to ride; she shook her head and went on, out of the valley, into the cedars, along the path. She saw leaves, branches and undergrowth slip into focus as the sun rose behind her. She came to the deep ditch where the bridge had washed away. One of the rotted beams had been used a long time as a walkway until the wood became loose and treacherous as sand. Now a strong plank had been laid beside it. But the old beam was in her way and she walked across it. The wood caved under her step. The slim dry center cracked. As she stepped on firm ground again, the beam doubled and fell, breaking apart on the hard scaly red pyramids of earth below. She walked on.

She had let them decide for her and she had agreed to do what they said. It was like Scott saying, Go to business school, and she went to business school because once somebody said it, that became the only thing possible. But there is more to this, she thought; there is more, if I could only think what.

She walked into an open space where two fields came together with a fence between. The path ran along the fence. The sun was bright on the dew-covered, soft young growth of cotton here, corn yonder. Compassionate, yet cool, disciplined, the light enveloped her, and long shadows crossed the path.

What have I come here and done, she thought in mounting horror. It was not supposed to be this way . . . it was supposed to be easy, secure. What have I done and what can I do about it now? Nothing, like they said? Nothing?

And midway across the field, she suddenly realized what she must do.

I will tell Kinloch, she thought and stopped stock-still. It did not matter that she had promised not to. She who had never done anything worth talking about, who beyond the few, bare, scattered facts of her past had never had anything to relate to him (to anyone, in fact, but most acutely to him) was now possessed of a thing. It was not a good thing, but it was hers. Its deformities demanded the greater regard.

Kinloch must hear it all, she decided, hurrying on. She must remember everything. She must make the story of it last a long time. She hurried faster. She almost ran.

At the first glimpse of the house through the trees, she dropped to a walk. The roof became of a piece; she saw the porch, the sagging window boxes, the front yard, fences, outhouses, plants, the pile of lumber where the weeds grew, chicken coops, gates, cowpaths, trees, hill, sky. She realized that she was thirsty, hungry, unutterably tired. This, then, was home.

"What's the matter?" he asked as she came up, and on that she could not answer him; she drew back, her mind floundered, she forgot what she meant to say first.

I've done it to *him*, she thought for the first time. He's the one who will have to suffer for it . . . more than I. No, I can't. . . .

But perhaps she might have gone on even then if the car had not come up the hill. When she saw who the man was behind the wheel, she moved away from Kinloch, out into the drive. He was beside her in a minute, sweeping her back from before the braked wheels.

She turned on him, pushing at his broad chest, twisting waist and shoulders out of his grasp.

"Nothing's the matter," she said. "It's Scott. It's my brother. Look, Kinloch, Scott's come to see us!"

Scott as a deus procrastinator

Part Two

U NDER the hot midafternoon July sun, Tarsus surrendered and became like a ghost town. Dust-ridden already, people in the far interior of houses choked and fanned when cars passed. Among the women there were those who did not dress all day, but pottered around the house until late afternoon in night clothes. Some ladies bathed three times a day and these called each other in between baths and talked about the heat, saying, "I de-*clare*—!" All the men gave in. Their hat bands turned greasy black; even on Sundays no one gave a thought to coats. Blind-drawn company "front rooms" gloomed invitingly and here the flesh cooled a minute, then ran slick with sweat. On Thursdays at dinner time all the stores closed. Through the long hours even the unheard motions of the store keepers were missed now in the intense stillness and there was only the sun, turning everything to dust, drawing apart gravel, leaves, wood, and all that moisture held close together.

On a Thursday afternoon in late July, Randall Gibson came walking into the square. He emerged from a street bordered in umbrella chinaberry trees and he made a diagonal path across the square, through the dusty weeds and swaths of gravel and pitted wheel tracks, past the iron fence around the court house and the little swaybacked shed matted with circus advertisements where the fire hose hung wound on a beam between two great wheels.

Randall Gibson was tall, bony and incredibly stooped. There was fortunately a quality about him which ignored or escaped or was utterly unconscious of his appearance. This he bore along with him, so that anyone watching from a distant window as he slouched across the square might have seen it sitting upon him. He did not bid directly for attention, but he won it an even surer way: by not bidding at all.

59

He made people observant. He had to have this. It was when the attention, the close staring, turned into some more definite thing—pity, admiration or disgust—which in the very process of being named invariably closed out portions of his nature—it was when this happened that he could not stand it. Once at somebody's open house—he was invited to everything and for rare intervals would go on a spree of attending—Miss Linell McIntosh, who had taught the Methodist Woman's Bible Class for twenty years, chanced to remark on the strange difference in certain denominational tenets. Her words for some obscure reason tapped in Randall a strong flow of idea, information and eloquence. Through the afternoon he talked, with poor Miss Linell embarrassed and thrilled by turns at this sudden religious spasm her words had set off in the young man. Here the guests were gathering to listen, here was Randall Gibson—Randall Gibson! Truly one could never tell!—quoting St. Paul, here was a lost sheep returning, and here was another star in Miss Linell's crown. When Randall stopped and lounged against the sideboard, half turning his back on them, Miss Linell rose nobly to the occasion. She laid her hand on his sleeve and said in a little voice they strained to hear: "And you believe this, Randall? You believe, Randall, don't you?" Her eyes, filling with soft tears, waited for his look. The atmosphere brimmed with her tenderness for him and all the staring company floated in it. Randall Gibson, after a certain play of deliberation, recited an obscene story about a priest—it was really pretty kind to do that, he reflected later, since none of them was Catholic—went to gulp down the remainder of the pecan rolls which he didn't care for especially, but which satisfied a sudden physical hunger, paid his respects and departed.

In years past when he was a young lawyer fresh from the university, he was sometimes invited to escort visiting young ladies to the picture show or to dinner at somebody's house. These he treated with a peculiar stand-offish courtesy, an incongruous kind of chivalry befitting to an old gentleman before a teen-aged girl. There were a few women in Tarsus who had thought themselves in love with him. The reason was always the same: deep down in him they perceived something dwelling which no one had ever understood before. This extension of themselves, transplanted in him, they claimed with a fierce possessiveness, until Randall, sensing the lift of the imprisoning net, would choose his moment to crush them. He had done this by indirect means and by direct ridicule. After all, nothing Tarsus thought of him could injure him so long as Tarsus could not define him.

After such pleasures he would go home down the street where the umbrella chinas grew, through the yard where the marble man looked out on him like a hunter, breast-high in weeds. He would enter the two-story house where the paint peeled in slivers like thin bark from the porch railing and the cobwebs in the hall stirred like oriental curtains at the opening of the door. From upstairs she would begin to call him, long then short, long then short, her voice going strangled and angry with the calling, and before she finished he would be in the big room just off the hall. It was fairly clean. There was only an iron single bed, a washstand, a table with a metal-bonneted reading lamp, and a long, low continuous line of bookshelves around the walls. He soared above them all even without standing straight, but the darkness soared above him and had most of the room considering all the space of blank wall up to the very high ceiling. He went about from basin to bookshelf to bed and the figures the leak stains had made on the wallpaper looked down on him, but they were too far above him to be seen until morning. Outside the window in the chill or sweet or stifling air were the scuppernong vine, the cedar trees whose limbs grew low and pressed on the ground like great webbed feet, the dripping hydrant, the wire fence baled in honeysuckle. He would lie on the bed and turn off the light while she was still calling him, just beginning to trail off, and he would stare up toward the figures on the ceiling which he could not see but which were: a monk aborting his aunt as she lay on a biscuit board, a great basket of hydrangeas with two round little faces among the blossoms, a naked bleeding man lashed by his ankles over the rump of a galloping horse, and, unmistakably clear, the inverted profile of old Daniel Armstrong, its forehead at the victim's thigh, its chin in his armpit. He would lie there flat on his back feeling the unseen cube of the room dip and reel slowly, for as a rule he was drunk, and what he thought about before he went to sleep may or may not have been anything important, or even connected, but not a soul in Tarsus could have guessed what he thought and therein lay his satisfaction and his strength.

He was seldom seen about in the mornings—perhaps he slept. In midafternoon he would come out into the sunlight, blinking and slow-footed as an old horse that has been stalled for a week. He would walk down the street to the square, the chinaberries crushing under his step like little fat spiders with their legs torn away.

Anybody in Tarsus could now have told exactly where he was going and what he was going to do. Possessive toward this routine, he had surrendered to them a fraction of his mystery in keeping it. He crossed the concrete gully to the sidewalk in one step of normal length and entered the Melrose Cafe, the only thing open on Thursday afternoons, sat down in his accustomed booth—second from the back—and waited without resentment while Joe-boy Snell brought him the beer he no longer had to order. Tilting the glass, he poured with meticulous care; the thin wash of suds rose toward his long dark forelock and in between were the big eyes. Who would come to talk to him this time? He did not seem to pay any more attention to the door than to the near-naked, fly-spotted girl who posed just above the mirror back of the counter, forever about to pick up a coca-cola. Less attention, really, since he often blamed her for his drinking; she made him thirsty, he said. She was stained across the face and neck where he had thrown beer on her one day; she looked so dry, he said. And once late at night he had recited a poem to her and the coca-cola: "Yet do not grieve; it cannot fade though thou hast not thy bliss. Forever wilt thou thirst and it be fair." But he never mentioned the door at all. Nobody in Tarsus knew how large it loomed in his consciousness, day after day.

First a couple of high school boys came through the door, but they did not count. They saw to it that the nickelodeon got underway with a loud cowboy lament, then they made for the slot machine. Next it was Miss Linell McIntosh who had tried to convert him. She had forgotten about the stores closing and she needed a loaf of bread. She picked her way around coming and going. Randall poured the rest of the beer into his glass and the door opened again. It was Kinloch Armstrong.

Randall greeted him with a flourish of his hand. "Well, Cud'n Kinloch."

"Cousin." Kinloch dropped his hat beside him on the seat. Randall waved for beer. The cowboy's song twanged and soared.

"Ah, Cousin," said Randall, "there is music here that softer falls than petals from blown roses on the grass. Music that gentlier on the spirit lies than tired eyelids upon tired eyes—"

Kinloch grinned. They were fond of one another. It was a friendship neither did anything about, or ever had. Sometimes they did not see each other for months.

"How is Aunt Cherry Bell?" he inquired. She was not really his aunt, the invalid woman who lived upstairs in the Gibson house, but she had been taken into the family by his real aunt, Randall's mother. She had come up from New Orleans to Tarsus for a week-end visit nearly forty years ago and what with the combined forces of hospitality, misfortune and duty, she was still there. It was Bright's disease she had now, but it had started with a broken heart and progressed through scandal and secret drinking at last to become bounded by four stained walls and a slanting view of what once was garden. She was losing her mind, they said. Perhaps, since his parents were dead, she was why Randall stayed on in Tarsus. He had treated her like a dog from the time he was a child, insulted her, mocked her, refused to come when she called. Yet here she was and here he was, and because she had a name and a story in Tarsus, she was like a single thin thread tethering him as citizen. Against one so small, it would be hard to stage a rebellion of dignity. Had Gibsons, respectable and always slightly older than their contemporaries, still been alive, Randall might have disappeared one day. Instead there was only Cherry Bell, a narrow ridge under the bed clothes in a room where her foot had not touched the floor in three years. The mention of her name usually made him glitter for a moment with a kind of savage semi-comic humor, so that the questioner wanted to laugh in spite of himself. Today Randall became simply morose.

"Cherry Bell?" he murmured. "Ma belle cherie. As a matter of fact, the last of Cherie's long series of misfortunes is about to befall her. I say the last because after this there will be nothing left to befall her but death, which I do not in any case presume to speak of as a misfortune."

"How's that?"

"A long story, Kinloch. Highly symbolic. If I were not in the backwash of decadence, I would tell you now. As it is, I have to be a little bit drunk. Yes, always a little bit drunk. I have hit on a new ambition, Kinloch, now that Ben Gardner is dead and gone. What is Tarsus, I said to myself, without a town drunk? There will be competition a-plenty, of course, but confidentially, Cousin, in my boundless ambition I aspire to this high title. It is six weeks today since I entered the race for it."

"How time goes," said Kinloch. "But it wouldn't be six weeks today, Randall. Ben Gardner died on a Saturday, funeral on a Sunday."

"Wednesday, Cousin. Funeral on a Thursday."

"Saturday," said Kinloch.

"Wednesday," said Randall.

"Saturday," said Kinloch.

There was a pause.

"Want to bet?" said Randall.

"Sure. I'll bet you."

"Kinloch, you never learn. I've won from you time and again." He smacked a nickel down on the table top.

"But this time you're going to lose," said Kinloch. He put down a dime. "I raise."

Randall laid another nickel beside the first. "I call."

"Well," said Kinloch, "I know it was Saturday he died because that was the night that Ruth went down to see Elinor and Lance Gerrard and decided to spend the night and came walking back home about sunup. Just as she got there her brother Scott Shaffer drove into the front yard and Nellie went out on a binge the night before and didn't come to cook breakfast and in all the stir we didn't get to church and didn't even know poor Ben had passed away till late that afternoon when we drove in for the mail and got caught in the funeral procession. It was hot and Ruth nearly fainted before we could get out of the procession and come on back home."

"Damn," said Randall. He shoved the coins to Kinloch. "I based my evidence on the stores being closed, hence, Thursday for the funeral. But I neglected the Sabbath. And stores do close then. And you are right, because I heard tell at the funeral how Ruth's brother got into Tarsus at crack of dawn and made Halpin Bramlett mad enough to kill him, waking him early Sunday morning to find out the way to your house. I laid off to ask you, Why in hell would a man coming all the way from Virginia pick daylight to land in Tarsus?"

"I don't know," said Kinloch. "He ran into some old friend or other over in Grenada and they got roaring drunk together till all hours and he knew if he went to sleep he'd have a hangover."

"Handsome devil," Randall remarked. "Ah, how the phrase would please him. No less than it would please Justin Gerrard."

"Yes."

Randall contorted himself in the corner of the booth, his elbows and wrists cracking on the table under their loose sheathing of flesh.

"How about that?" he pursued. "Justin Gerrard and Scott Shaffer."

"What do you mean, how about it?"

"Well, do they ride around in a car of nights, do they spend the week-end in the Delta, do they hang out down at Lance's? Where do they go to enjoy themselves, as it were? Not to the Armstrongs'. Oh, shame."

"You're telling me it's gossip by now, is that it?" Kinloch frowned. "All over town, I guess."

"All I know is what I hear."

"It's no affair of mine," said Kinloch. "They can do their courting on the sofa in old Simon's parlor for all I care."

"That's a new word you've got for it, isn't it? Though it might not be a new place. The sofa. And old Simon would come in looking for his *Jackson Daily News*, yank it out from between the cushions and go on upstairs to bed." Randall rocked with amusement the more he thought about it. "Of course," he went on, "Mama Henrietta Gerrard would just not see them. She would pretend—and really believe, mind you—that they were sitting there holding hands and think to herself how free the younger generation is becoming. She might even ask them if they didn't think it was a little cooler than it was last night."

"Now look here, Randall," said Kinloch. "I wouldn't give a damn what you said about them, if it wasn't for Ruth."

"Ruth," said Randall softly, his mood shifting. "The self-same song that found a path through the sad heart of. Alone, amid the alien corn. Entreat me not to leave thee, nor to return from following after thee. Only she doesn't follow you, Kinloch. You two go round and round in the devious maze of Tarsus, and at every sundown there you all are again, in old Daniel's house. Did you know, Cousin, I had a night of hellish sleeplessness after the day I first saw you with her. Why? Because I had been watching her ever since she came. Soon I found myself making a point of standing on the front porch to see her when she went into the court house to work. In the afternoons I would stroll to yon window to see her pass going home. The feeling she gave me then would be hard to name. It was something I like to bring on myself, to wallow in—some mixture of pity and nostalgia perhaps, with a touch of real fear thrown in to save my soul. And what brought her here? I would reflect, while thinking it was about time for her to pass by. What brought her here? I would repeat. Why, the government. Did you ever think about that, Kinloch? I would get me a laugh out of it, twice a day for quite some time in there before you came along. I had her first in a way, you see. But then she would come by, with her strangeness that cannot be placed even to the extent of calling her foreign. Her hair is too dark: it would make the fear in me grow and suddenly I would see the town, not just the little section of street visible there, but the whole town laid out before me—that tremendous universe bounded by Hangman's Hill and the creek, Keystone Bottom and the-land-west-of-town, and I couldn't think of hill or gully where she had the slightest business to be. I wished to go up to her and tip my hat and say, I beg your pardon, but you apparently do not know where you are: this is Tarsus. But she would go on by, straight legs, stiff back, dark hair and all, and I would be left with my beer. There are worse consolations, of course. But the *government*, Kinloch. The New Deal. Sometimes I would forget my fears for her and just laugh."

"I don't see what you mean," said Kinloch, unamused. "I don't see any connection."

"Between the government and Ruth? That's just it. There is no connection. No imaginable, no earthly, no conceivable connection. Note how one extremely well-turned item of life can, without even knowing it, give the lie to the whole monstrous machine. And this they sent to do a job for them in Tarsus, did they? Tarsus, mind you. Without even flinching."

"I still don't see anything very astonishing in it," said Kinloch. "Truth of the business is, she's the only worthwhile thing they've sent here yet."

"You and old Daniel and the 'truth of the business.' Confront me with that, I'm lost every time. Or is it that you always start a couple of beers behind me? But on one point you may agree with me, Cousin, if I haven't touched your stubborn streak, and that is that Tarsus can be an obsession too, no less than Troy; no less than Athens, Florence, Ireland, or Natchez."

"Why Natchez?"

"That was a mistake."

"You know," said Kinloch, "I've never been to Natchez."

"Neither have I. Drink to it." They drank. "I drink also to myself," said Randall, pouring more beer, "who am in my humble way the prophet of Tarsus. And the day the spirit sat down on me hardest was the day I saw you and Ruth together for the first time. I said to myself, He will marry her and she will marry him. Both."

"You knew more than I did at the time," Kinloch smiled. "Was this a vision or did you figure it out for yourself?"

"It was a result of two sets of figuring I have done—one about Ruth, one about you. I had them with me all along, but it was not until the day I saw you that the flash bulb in the vision went off and they photographed on one film."

"But what was the figuring?" Kinloch asked.

"Oh that." For a while Randall seemed disinclined to continue the subject. He shifted about in the booth, bumping here and there, and finally stretched his legs over the end of the seat. He sighed like a man with a little troublesome yard work to do. "Okay," he said. "I will tell you a story. Once upon a time there was a party at the school-house. Did the Baptist Sunday School give it, or the senior class? Was it Thanksgiving or New Year's Eve? Or did we have a new high school principal who thought he could do something about us? I don't remember. But all of us were there. Standing around against the wall. Not enough light or heat. Everybody with coats on. Then somebody brought more bulbs to take the place of the ones we had smashed out with slingshots the afternoon before and somebody fired up the stove and we played games. Directed by Miss Linell McIntosh who kept looking at the book. She never could quite figure that book out. God damn," he brooded over it, "I bet there wasn't a party given in

Tarsus while we were growing up that Miss Linell wasn't there with that book. And she never caught on. Well, the games ended in the usual mixup, everybody talking about something else and saying absently, What you reckon we do with these scraps of paper? Finally a couple of big boys went up to Miss Linell and started begging and arguing and teasing a little. What was it we called the game then? Conversation dates. There were all those dark school rooms around and all those girls. Lord, I was just at the age to think there were twice as many girls there as you would have found if you took count. Seems to me I was awfully conscious of breasts. There are two of them. Two. I would think on it with amazement. Miss Linell agreed to the conversation dates. She would agree to anything when they teased her. The little slips of paper went round again and the pencils. Now you were there, Kinloch, and I was there, and over in the corner against the wall was a little fat girl, new in town, loud, jumpy, dumb, pathetic. Her name was Milly Cabot. She had come with Miss Linell. When the boys started going around to the girls with the paper and pencils, that rowdy laugh she had been giving turned into a frozen, cornered smile. You and I—we knew better than anybody there. It would take too long a time to explain just why we knew better, but we did. I knew it and I turned around and started arguing Janice Askew into the fifth instead of the seventh. Did you ever know that I was watching you out of the tail of my eye? You messed around the stove for a while, you made a sudden move to cross the floor toward the girls. They used to get in a huddle for those things, you know, and the next look you had at them after they huddled, they all looked alike. But just before you got to them, you whirled around like you were ready to hit somebody and went back to Milly Cabot from whose warm side you glared out, not saying a word. You looked mad at all of it —yourself, her, us, Miss Linell and the existing order from whose implacable cruelty you had rescued the lady. I can see Milly Cabot now. She didn't say a word to you either. She chewed her gum in placid triumph and watched the couples go in and out. Oh, I was smarter than you, Kinloch. Both of us were smarter than the others who never know anything except what they see for the one time in the one place. But you and I see more than that. We see too much, but how will you have it? We did not choose to be the way we are. Where was I?"

"Damn if I know," said Kinloch. "I guess you're still telling about Milly Cabot."

"Yes, it is still Milly Cabot. Or Jesus Christ. Or heaven and hell. To you, that is. Kinloch, the trouble with you is that you ever and eternally think that you've got to do something about it. You aren't content simply to comprehend; you also have to act. The insufferable conceit of it! Even if you got drunk by yourself on a sweet April night and climbed Hangman's Hill at midnight and there was a full moon and a storm building up in the distant west, even if you stood there in sight of nothing but God Almighty and a stray dog and imagined that anything you did could alter the course of anything that exists, in that minute you ought to climb up on the old scaffold where your father sent two men to their death and hang yourself by the neck until dead. What happened to Milly Cabot? Don't think I don't know. Two years after that night she died while giving birth to the bastard son of a sawmill owner in South Mississippi. I found it out from a bootlegger in Mendenhall one summer when I was hitch-hiking to New Orleans. I ask you now, What earthly good did you do?"

Kinloch laughed. "It seems to me you did considerably more about Milly Cabot than I did, Randall. I forgot the whole thing years ago."

"Oh, I'm curious, you know. Have to know about anything that sets foot in Tarsus from conception to the grave. But you've never seen me do anything about it. I abdicate, I tell you. Confronted with heaven and hell, I choose neither. So I have baffled the devils and worried the angels. They are dreading the day I die because they won't know what to do with my soul."

"Maybe they will leave you swinging between heaven and hell, Randall, like the niggers talk about. Then you can haunt us."

70

"Excellent! Oh, wonderful! Kinloch, you are tracked on such simple straight rails that almost anything you say is true in a thousand directions you did not think about. I shall haunt Tarsus. Tarsus which has always haunted me. With those arrangements, I can go on keeping up with the course of events, and prophesying to my own satisfaction at certain remarkable moments like the day I saw you and Ruth together for the first time."

"Back to that again?"

"Because Ruth and Milly Cabot are the same."

"You're drunk."

"That has nothing to do with it, except that if I were cold sober I probably would not have told you the truth."

"Why, Randall, if Ruth had been there that night instead of Milly Cabot—"

"The other girls would have burned with little green flames while the boys stampeded her? I know. But that is irrelevant to the major points. Notice. In each scene we have as our dramatis personae: Tarsus, Randall, Kinloch and a woman who is a stranger. It is my guess that it would terrify Ruth quite as much to see Tarsus coming toward her as it terrified Milly Cabot to see them going the other way. But you and I know, I repeat, and we know that we are needed here to answer the call of some supremely human thing which is not so simple as loneliness. You go and I do not go and there I had better end it, because there the difference is already begun—the difference being that you or me or anything in pants would have made Milly Cabot chew gum that way, but for Ruth there was no one but you. And in order to name the reason why there was no one else we would simply tell about Milly Cabot all over again. It's like the picture in the picture in the picture."

Kinloch smiled, shaking his head.

"Am I right, Cousin?" Randall asked. "Or are you going to say that you married her because you love her? Which would be perfectly true, but which would not answer the question, Why do you love her?"

Kinloch's gray eyes flashed up.

"I'm sorry," Randall said sincerely. "You said I was drunk and you will be right very shortly."

"How is Aunt Cherry Bell?" said Kinloch at last, then remembered that he had asked before.

"Fine, thank you," Randall replied, also remembering that Kinloch had asked before, but choosing not to look as though he remembered. "Oh my God, what am I saying? Cherry doesn't know it but right now she is about to face a greater crisis than the day she and I and Simon Gerrard and every bootlegger in the country ran out of whisky all at the same time. I've never understood it. My theory was that Ben Gardner for once in his life got hold of enough money to buy all he could drink. That would sap us any day. Because Ben was reeling around the square bigger than life and twice as unnatural while everybody else in Tarsus was dry as a bone. Of course, I was suffering myself—that was before you could get beer like this—but Cherry! She could not understand. I was going to fix everything by luring Ben up to her room and just letting her inhale the fumes."

"Oh Lord, Randall, you didn't go around saying that."

Randall's mood of talkative animation vanished. He smeared his long thumb through a slosh of foam on the table. He heard Kinloch's question long after it was asked. "No. I didn't say so much about it."

"What's wrong with her now?" Kinloch asked. In a way he hated to hear Randall talk of her. He remembered her as she was in his childhood, a fair-skinned, bright-haired young woman, who one day walked out to her buggy after a visit to the Armstrongs and her back was straight and supple as a willow reed and his father turned to his mother saying, with a wry little smile on his lips, "She always did walk like a thoroughbred, didn't she?"

Randall again heard his question as an echo. "Damn it all, Kinloch, it's that statue out in the garden. The one she got from the old Walston place, you know. The Marble Man, I used to call it. Oh, have you seen the Marble Man, the Marble Man, the Marble Man. . . . It's got rabbit tobacco growing out of its ears and I haven't had the weeds cut since last fall. But she still looks at it through the windows. The windows are all she sees except the room, and all she looks out the window to see is that statue. Out of everything she might have had once, that strange chunk of stone is all she got. It stands for everything, do you know that? She looks at it and she can remember. I don't think she could remember without it. Like the bead on the rosary recalls the prayer day after day, until without the rosary suddenly you cannot pray. And *they* will take it away from her."

"*Who* will take it?" Kinloch asked, his voice as low as Randall's. He felt the strange prick of fear that Randall could sometimes bring to him.

The door flung wide, banging all the way back against the wall with a screech of the spring. Justin Gerrard stepped into the long shaft of late sunlight. The high school boys had just that minute hit the jackpot and were scrambling about the floor among a shower of nickels. She walked straight into them, her high heels cracking on the coins: she did not even glance down when one boy lost balance avoiding her and fell backward against the counter. Kinloch moved over quickly because she sat down so fast he thought she was going to land in his lap. She looked squarely at Randall Gibson who had not so much as lifted his eyes.

"You steppin' high today, Miss Justin?" he drawled.

She sat straight as an arrow, because she could do that well when she chose, and folded her hands together on the table. She had on a clean cotton dress, simply made, and splashed over with something tropical, either flowers or birds, of outrageous colors. Her eyes went down from his face to the glass of beer.

"I might have known it," she said.

"Don't let me shock you, Miss Justin," said Randall, lifting the glass. "When you get a little older, you'll understand."

She turned from the waist and addressed Kinloch abruptly.

"Where's Scott?"

"He and Ruth went for a long walk up the creek," Kinloch said. "Kind of a picnic, I think."

"Damn," she said. She dragged a cigarette out of an open pack on the table and bent for Kinloch's match. "What on earth did they want to do that for?"

"Just for the fun of it, I reckon," he replied.

She blew a straight jet of smoke. "I didn't know Ruth was so fond of the outdoor life."

"She doesn't care too much about it."

"Then why go?"

"To keep Scott company, I would think."

"And why didn't you go?"

Her voice utterly without inflection, she had been asking questions smooth on the heels of his answers. At this last their eyes met and though his reply ("Maybe I wasn't invited either") held the amused, tolerant, almost teasing tone of a man aged thirty speaking to a girl aged nineteen—the meeting of their eyes was something else again. It was not pleasant and there was nothing in it of the clean impact of sex.

She had been after him once. That was two summers ago. It was during the cotton-poisoning that he noticed it first. He and the Negro would poison until nearly daylight and then he would sleep until dinner time and late in the afternoon he would drive into town and have a coca-cola with the crowd at the drug store. He rather liked that season every year. Day and night got so out of order he would go about at hours when he was usually in the field thinking that he was not doing any work at all and after the grogginess from the morning sleeping got out of his head he would feel fit and lean as a good swimmer just out of the water. Then he began to notice that not only was she at the drug store every time he went in, which was to be expected, but also that she invariably contrived some way to make him remember that he had seen her there. It was not until one

74

afternoon when he stopped in the hardware store for some trace chains and met her walking by that he became certain of what she was doing. The hardware store was on the far side of the square standing between the undertaker's shop and a cotton warehouse. There was no need to pass it on the way to anything and no need for her to be in the vicinity unless, he thought, she wanted some hardware. But she stopped to talk to him and after that he was sure. Driving home, he asked himself in his own candid way, Now what does she want with me? From the tales he heard it would seem that she had every eligible male in a radius of twenty miles beating a path to her door along with several, so they said, that her mama did not consider so eligible. Simon did not consider them at all; he simply counted them with pride and boasted that he had to go around to the back door to keep from stumbling over them. Well, if she was anything like Lance there was more Simon in her than Henrietta and a roll call was probably to her greatest satisfaction. But he, Kinloch, was always absent. And that was it. A quorum wouldn't do and a mere majority carried its own insult. It had to be unanimous or it was nothing. He had been stubborn without knowing it. He swung the car into the Armstrong road and smiled. Now he could be stubborn on purpose.

But two nights later he was setting out to the Delta for his usual mild Saturday night call on a girl named Joy Kingston. She was a thin, shy, well-bred girl of a family that his father had once known intimately, and Kinloch had once had in the back of his mind that he would marry her some day. But he had known her for three years now since she got out of college and she was still the same pleasant good company she had always been and somehow her very good manners kept him comfortable in a position where she doubtless did not wish him to be at all. So the idea got farther and farther back in his mind until now if he thought of it, it would soon ease past him of its own accord.

When he went into the drug store for a pack of cigarettes, there was

75

Justin. She was sitting at one of the tables alone and calm as you please, which made her look even more remarkable considering that she was dressed in a white evening dress with a good deal of tan back and shoulders showing. She came directly to him. She was looking for a ride to the Greenwood Country Club. There was a dance and her date had called from the Delta to say that his car had broken down and she had promised to drive over herself. But Lance took a mean spell and wouldn't let her have the car, got in it and left for the Delta himself, pushing her out when she tried to ride with him. Whatever mad blaze of anger she had been in not twenty minutes before was gone and she even giggled a little when she told Kinloch. He would have suspected her of lying if the whole affair had not sounded so exactly like what went on among the Gerrards all the time. The most he could suspect her of was waiting purposefully for him. He gave her the ride.

From the moment she settled her skirts in the car, he was acutely aware of her express vitality. She was going somewhere—going, going, going. She even leaned forward a little. He caught glimpses of her ugly face and flat eyes, heard and answered the conventional things she said, but he understood that every emotion she communicated was the work of her body, that moreover she knew it too.

It was strange, off-key, almost formalized conversation. Because in Tarsus they had known each other always, they were greater strangers than two people who land next to each other on the train, having boarded it thousands of miles apart, having no common knowledge of anyone. Yet as though the very dust of Tarsus on the car were watching, they paid obeisance to the town in their unspoken agreement to converse desperately all the way.

Just before he turned into the grounds of the club, both of them ran out completely. They traveled the remaining hundred yards of highway and turned into the gravel drive in complete silence. It was when he parked the car and made a move to get out and open the door for her that he glanced up and saw her looking at him. He saw her full

76

scarlet mouth, half-sullen, and the light of the dashboard fell across her bare shoulders and slid fading down her bare arms toward the white dress so that she seemed floating and unaccountably without weight. He tried deliberately to amuse himself by thinking how much younger seventeen seemed to him than it did to her, but still he could think of nothing at all to say and the rather long moment in which she did not quite offer herself passed. She turned without a word and began to gather up her wrap and bag, but when she moved a distinct line of insolence flashed up from where the curve of her waist and hip molded the tight cloth, to the lift of her smooth brown shoulder. Then he really saw for the first time what they meant when they said Justin Gerrard, and he pulled her to him and kissed her almost insultingly because he was angry already, at himself who should have been knocking on shy Joy Kingston's door right that minute and at Justin for letting him know that any way you looked at it she was going to win. It was curious to remember that quite apart from emotion there came calmly to his mind just then a picture of Simon Gerrard standing on the street-corner with a cigar between his teeth—Simon Gerrard with the heavy slabs of flesh about his torso making his shirt bulge out below the armpit. His fingers moved down from her breast to her waistline, and out of an impressive number of men, only he found, in the subtle mixture of give and resistance her flesh offered, a definite revulsion. For the Armstrongs were of big solid bone, the skin over it showing the vein, inclined to blemish and roughness. At the worst this heritage could take on the sprawling irrelevance of Randall Gibson; at its best it was suited to the high eagle-like set of Dan Armstrong's head and to Kinloch's own manner of strong, steady motion. But about the Gerrards there was a thickness that had nothing to do with measurement, as marked in Lance's tall frame as in heavy Simon. It seemed that flesh, vein, muscle and bone, instead of finding a separate life and play within the larger, living body, each defining the other, were in them all matted and solidified together, affecting an imperceptible shortening or concealment of joint and

But in doing this he loses!

77

tendon, a layered depth of skin.

Before his mind's eye the picture of Simon Gerrard persisted. Quite suddenly Simon blinked. At that point even animal excitement failed and he released her, helped her from the car and walked her to the side entrance of the club. She went past him without looking at him or thanking him, already seeing some boy she knew, and as she moved up the steps her skirt made a sound like wind among leaves. The rustle and the scent of her perfume drifted through his senses, wakening them again as he drove away, calling him a fool.

Later, driving home through the night, he determined that there would be another time. He would not be the first for her, nor even the second, if you could put any store by what you heard. But she couldn't be more than seventeen. The thought pained him. But there would be another time.

He was in the immense horizonless Delta night and the Delta gives the illusion of the ocean—free, with an inscrutable face turned only to the sky—and yet is so different because it is profitable, crying Take me, take me, and passing most of the year in dread of too much sun or too much rain.

On Valley Hill he rose up out of the Delta and in one minute of driving that world was gone as completely as though it existed only in the longings of a mind tired of gullies, bluffs, curves, washouts. But the hills do their service. To one born and bred in them, the familiarity of their gully-scarred, pine-clotted ugliness, their rare passages of wild, rich, genuine wooded beauty, are sufficient after the lush, monotonous Delta. And by the time Kinloch drove into his own front yard that night he knew what he had known all the time: that about Justin Gerrard he would do nothing. The only way to violate her was to ignore her. She gave him other chances in the weeks that followed; she at last tried playing his own game and ignored him studiously in return, but even this evoked neither interest nor disinterest, and on this note she abandoned the effort.

One day in early September when she was getting ready for col-

78

lege by making daily clothes-buying expeditions to the Delta, he ran into her at the drug store fountain. She was having a coke with some strange boy whose dark, sinister look was something he would have to grow to, and when Kinloch tipped his hat, she looked just past his eyes and nodded vaguely, and he knew immediately that this was genuine, and that the game was done. But when he met her eyes through the cigarette smoke that afternoon in the Melrose Cafe, he remembered it all, and from the little angry tightening of her shoulders below her expressionless features, he knew she remembered too. Between them, like the flicker of a bird's wing, were the keen eyes of Randall Gibson.

"You well's to leave it alone, Miss Justin," said Randall.

"Well's to leave what alone?" she asked.

"The Shaffer lad. You well's to buy yourself a movie magazine with a picture of Clark Gable on the front, like I seen you do once, Miss Justin."

"Who made Scott Shaffer any of your business?"

"You did. You came trotting it in here, carrying it like a bone."

"Answer me one thing. Have I ever brought anything to you?"

"Obliquely, yes."

"Oh my God, that's the way you always do. That's the way you'll back up every time. Snatch up a few long words and then people will go away thinking maybe you're right after all. You think you're so different and you sit here and get the dry rot like everything else in Tarsus."

"Talking about me is something I do not object to; I simply deplore it as a waste of breath. Every time you talk about a person you assume he wants something and that something you think he wants is what you consciously or unconsciously attack. With me you are defeated before you start. I want nothing."

"It's a good thing," she said. "I don't know of anything you could get."

"Except more beer," he went on, ignoring her as he waved a

clumsy arm at Joe-boy Snell. "But it is easy to talk about you and every other Gerrard that ever came down the pike. You all's hearts' desires are simple one word things and they're written all over every one of you in letters a foot high. Yes, with Mary Helen it was marriage and money. With Lance it's liquor and leisure. See, they alliterate nicely. You don't do as well. Men and glamour. L'amour and gla-moor. At least they will rhyme."

"With a family like yours I wouldn't be talking about anybody's family."

"My family are all dead," returned Randall, pouring beer. "God rest them."

"You might wish she's dead all right, but she's not dead yet."

"I defend Cherry Bell," said Randall, "like a Southern gentleman. She is no longer able to defend herself."

"Don't think I haven't heard how she took that Walston man away from your mother. And your mother took old man Gibson on the rebound. And nobody could ever see why you all let Miss Cherry Bell stay on and be the star boarder. That's what they say. Or am I still wasting my breath?"

The surface of the beer quivered. Randall set down the glass and leaned suddenly forward across the table toward the girl who in her intensity had forgotten her poise and stuck out her face like a quarreling child. She recoiled from the hands that almost reached her. She had said too much and she knew it. Neither she nor Randall seemed to know what to do next.

Kinloch stood up abruptly. "You are going to leave," he commanded.

She gave him one look and slipped from the booth. At that little distance from him, she was able to settle her features and venture a quick shrug. "I was going anyway, thank you," she flung back. "Don't ever say I started it." This to Randall. Then she was gone, the high heels striking hard. The door banged.

Randall sat for a long time, his face buried in his great useless hands. He brought them down to the table at last and wrapped his fingers around an empty bottle. His thin mouth twisted.

"She stood up to me, Kinloch," he said. "You got to mark that down. And now that I've said it first instead of last, I can go on to pronounce that I hate her guts and the guts of every Gerrard who ever lived and I damn them eternally to hell. More than that, I damn them while they are still on earth because that will be worse on them. Maybe that has been the trouble all these years. They've been damned to hell before, too many times to count, but nobody has thought to damn them to earth."

Kinloch waited silently while Randall cursed them to earth in a speech that was long, deliberate and obscene. "You hate them too, don't you, Kinloch? I saw you look at her. You hate them too."

"Cousin Randall," said Kinloch, slowly, half-soothingly, "when I was a boy I had my first score to settle with the Gerrards. I settled that and from then on I determined to have no further dealings with them. Here and there, accidentally maybe, there have been times when that turned out to be impossible because Tarsus is not very big and we all move around in it. But there hasn't been any real meeting ground between me and them since I decided that until—"

"Until?"

"Until Ruth came. She made friends with Lance's wife. Now they're under foot again. I'm not blaming Ruth for anything. She just doesn't understand."

"And you hate them, don't you?"

At the repeated question, Kinloch felt a curious tightening in his spine which seemed to draw his head backward against his shoulders. He did not reply.

"Good God," said Randall. "I watch this town and the people in it with a wall of sawdust insulation around me that gets a foot thicker every year. Can't you see that it means infinitely more for me to say 'I hate' than it does for you? *You* are supposed to love and hate."

Kinloch said nothing.

"Listen," said Randall Gibson. "This has been coming on me since day before yesterday when Simon Gerrard stopped me on the corner. Don't think that little bitch could throw me like this. Not alone."

"What are you talking about, Randall?"

"I had begun to tell you when she came. Listen. There was the Walston estate, Kinloch, now fully owned and solely operated by—"

"Simon Gerrard."

"That big sweep of land, the only good land in the country really, whose timber and cotton yield and numerous tenantry for trade and just size if nothing else has given wealth, prestige and the run of things for these thirty-five years to—"

"Simon Gerrard."

"There was at Walston Cedars, the old house we never saw but have heard tell of all our days—there was in the garden by the house a group of three statues bought by old Marshall Walston in Italy back before the war. They were a shepherd, a prince and a minstrel. The shepherd and the prince were crushed under the fall of the right wing when the house burned. But the minstrel escaped."

"I knew that, of course. It's the Marble Man we used to play around in the front yard at your house."

" Willed to be in the garden at my house by Kinloch Walston, old Marshall's son. Because Justin was right about it. It was my mother, your father's sister, that Kinloch Walston planned to marry until Cherry Bell came along. In the strange affair that followed, Cherry Bell too was left alone, but he willed her the statue. I have often wondered why he chose the minstrel instead of the shepherd or the prince. Had she expressed a preference for it once? Did it have some sentimental meaning to them? For the answer to that we must know what Cherry Bell was and we may never know that anymore. She is all but dead, but she can still look through the windows at the moss-grown profile of the Venetian singer. Which Justin's mother now wishes to 'restore' for added grace to her own lawn, and the Garden Club will be so charmed—"

82

"Mrs. Gerrard wants to buy it?"

"Take it, Kinloch, take it. It is hers already—it belongs to the Gerrards. I thought they had long ago forgotten the statue, or scorned it, but after all these years, they suddenly remembered it again and can't wait a minute to possess it."

"But he willed it—"

Randall stared at him. He stared so long that Kinloch drew breath twice to question him, but did not.

"Then you don't know," said Randall. "I thought you must have known. Time and again I have asked myself, Does Kinloch know? Quickly I would say to myself, Of course. But some slower, surer instinct in me would always reply, No. Felix McKie and Daniel Armstrong could have told you, but they did not. As for the rest who knew, they had the truth by a patchwork of guesses and with the memory of that quiet crime's violent aftermath upon them, how could they tell where right and wrong lay? How could they speak of it except in whispers, if they spoke at all?"

"What in God's name, Randall?"

"Kinloch Walston's will, Cousin, was invalidated after his death through covert agency of the Gerrards who proved that the maker was insane. Three days after the trial, Felix McKie was covered with blood, lying in the doctor's office in back of the drug store with his eyes blown out. Simon Gerrard's brother was dead in the court house hallway. A hunted negro was shot down in Kosciusko and would have been lynched even in death along with his living wife and child but for Dan Armstrong, who ironically enough could not do justice to himself or mete it out in behalf of those he loved."

"But except for this talk of the will, Randall, I have always known these things. I know as much as anyone about Felix McKie, I have heard talk of Aunt Cherry Bell and Kinloch Walston, and I know more than most about the lynching Father stopped. Is that all? Or is it the will? What about the will?"

"In the original will, Kinloch, all the estate of the Walstons was

deeded to the only two people Kinloch Walston trusted and admired:
to Felix McKie and Dan Armstrong. And to their descendants."

The room could not have started more markedly if lightning had
plowed the dust-hung wiring from the four walls and thunder had
shattered the painted windows into the street. In the impossible
stillness Kinloch sat. It never once occurred to him to cry: You don't
mean that, or Say it again, or I don't understand. He could not now
quite recall his mother's face, yet when he came on the old dim photograph of her there was no need to say, Who is this?

"Do you hate them, Kinloch? Now do you hate them?"

Kinloch looked at him at last, not hearing him, not really seeing him
any more, but seeing instead a man from whom he wanted something.
He rose.

"There is a lot to be explained," he said, "and you've got to explain
it to me. But not here. Come with me."

SIX

WHEN Dan Armstrong woke up in his rocking chair that Thursday afternoon, it was his own snoring that did it. His white head came straight up with a final snort and the old black hat he had put over his face to keep out the glare toppled forward on his knees. He glanced around to chuckle at himself with whoever might be watching and since nobody was he laughed anyway.

"Aye gannies," he addressed the bird dog that sprawled sleeping in a dust bed under the walnut tree. "It's a mighty big fool that'll cut up too much racket to get his own nap out."

The old black-spotted dog opened his eyes, rolled his head upright on his crossed paws and cocked his ears brightly as a puppy.

"You're just as sorry as you can live, sir," Dan Armstrong told him. The whip-like tail thumped up a cloud of dust.

"You couldn't tell a potridge from a sapsucker."

The dog jumped eagerly to his feet.

Dan Armstrong fished in his pockets. "Take you hunting this minute, you'd break your back pointing a little ole feelark."

Wagging from the waist, the dog trotted to the steps where he caught the thrown biscuit with a smack of his jaws that sounded like a gar flopping. He swallowed the biscuit whole, then came and rubbed his head against the old man's legs and knees.

"That's all in the world you're good for—wolfing down biscuits," Dan said. "Don't come fooling around me. You stink." He stroked the bony head.

"Go on now." His tone concluded the conversation; the dog walked to the end of the porch and lay down with a grunt.

Dan pulled out his watch. Thirteen minutes past three on the dot and they were all gone. The daughter and that brother of hers for a

85

walk—Lord alone knew why, in this heat; the boy himself into town for something. He walked through the hallway where there would be a little breeze blowing if you could find it anywhere. The hall had been an open dog run in his father's day, but Sally had wanted it different. He turned into the dining room where the sideboard stood and the table, and the chairs lined back against the wall. The sideboard was cherry, high as his shoulder but without much depth, a little like the upright pianos so many ladies in Tarsus had in their parlors. In the upper part there was a long horizontal mirror and at each end of it, two small columns, scrolled and shaped like those for a house, pretended to support the flat top. Sally had got that with the egg money during his last term as sheriff, must have been '98 or thereabouts. As for the plain rectangular dinner table, it was just a table like it ought to be, taken down from the size it once was, covered for everyday with oil cloth that Nellie had wiped off before she left so that the smell of its dampness still hung in the air along with the scent of glasses scalded and dried, and ranged still warm before the mirror of the sideboard.

In the clean still kitchen, the negroid odor of Nellie was spread as evenly as soft butter on a slice of bread. Nellie had scrubbed; the floor was damp and long blonde streaks marked the dark boards here and there where more splinters had given up to the mop. The acrid smell of lye suds was somewhere about and near the stove was the scent of new wood ashes settling drily down into the old crud of the ash box.

Dan Armstrong went softly. It would be a shame to rouse up a quiet, new-cleaned, empty kitchen until someone came who meant business. All he wanted was to get to the safe. He opened one of the twin doors that closed the upper shelves. The doors were screened in fine wire, now black from long use and bagging near the knobs where many hands had touched. Along one shelf, bowls and plates in all sizes covered with other bowls and plates contained such scraps as wouldn't spoil. The old man lifted each covering dish a little way

86

and peered in until he found the right one. He took a knife from the safe drawer and cut a large wedge from the pound cake, wrapped it in his handkerchief which he knotted at the top like the dirty clothes.

Oddly enough, except for the neat opening of the safe doors, the firm slicing of the cake, all his motions among the dishes, knives and forks had taken on a fumbling quality. He stood uncertainly a minute, dividing a glance between the greasy knife and the sink. Then he wiped the blade on the corner of the handkerchief and put it back in the drawer which he closed as quickly as a little boy up to something.

For Dan Armstrong was nothing if not provoking. In the past he used to provoke Sally to distraction, but then he had given her the right and power to make him answer to her about most things. He had never seen fit to so privilege anyone else. It was going to provoke Nellie when she found the greasy knife; it was going to provoke Ruth to see the cake a quarter gone; it was going to provoke Kinloch that he had taken another trip to see Felix in the heat of the day without telling a soul. And since there was no one else to know, he may have even been trying to provoke God a little when he took the steepest short cut up the path. Even He, however, did not press to grasp the right that only Sally had possessed. And to Him Dan Armstrong could now say, as one gentleman to another, I'll be there shortly, Sir.

He got a little winded on the climb, so when he reached the spot where the trees gave way to a view of the pasture below he sat down on a rotting tree trunk to rest. Below him all green and smooth, dotted with clumps of jimpson weed and fringed in lean sycamores, lay Simon Gerrard's pasture, a lip of the acreage that had once belonged to the Walstons. The branch had cut a way near the hill and there was a pig wallow just below him. A couple of sows and six half-grown shoats were lying in the mud. The sun was very near and hot; the sycamore leaves looked closer than they were and imparted the feeling that if only one leaf stirred the sound would have snapped into terrific combustion all the absolute of bulging heat and silence.

The silence was heavy and enormous as a dream of space during late morning sleep in the summer while even the dreamer's tongue sweats like a dog's. Surely some little thing, trigger-small, was controlling, holding, while pulsing together with, all the vital mass of heat and silence that the hills enclosed into that pasture. But maybe the pigs would hold things down, because nothing on earth is to be compared with the inertia of pigs lying in mud and slime with the flies drifting around them on a July afternoon. Watching them, the old man felt his brain clouding, his head rocking in time with the white and gold heat waves. His eyelids lowered.

Then he heard the buzzing. He took it at first as the beginning of his own snoring, then he thought the flies were set on bothering him, but when the buzzing increased he felt compelled to have a look.

A minute later he was going at a great rate toward Felix's house.

The path led to the back of the house. If he had taken the dirt road around as he ought to have done, he would have missed the pasture and approached the sternly upright two-story house from the front. The McKies, an old-line Scotch Presbyterian clan, once populous there, had perversely faced their house away from town so that it confronted a terrain of scarred, uncompromising roughness, a mile or so of hills which jutted a tenacious triangle into the Delta. Except for the extra story, the house was of the same construction as the Armstrong place. But flowers, small trees, and grass did not flourish so well here, and the tall squared rise of the walls gave the front porch a foreshortened appearance. Here old Kinloch McKie, Felix's father, was wont to stand years ago, ensconced on legs bowed like a pair of hames, and greet the stranger entering his gates with a roll and thunder of Biblical quotation. So fitly did "ye" loose from his thick tongue, that old Marshall Walston used to remark that he now instinctively thought of Galilee as a Scottish lake and Golgotha as a prominent hill of the highlands. Old Kinloch was not above an occasional joke on sacred matters, and when a hard winter struck soon after the McKies were established and winds raked the hill, he christened the place Sheol and referred to it by that name all his days, preventing the curse that some might have feared by never even considering such a possibility. That was the winter of the sudden freeze after mild weather, when the big beams and planks of houses, contracting swiftly, popped as loudly as gunshot. Ernest Armstrong had rushed armed into the dog run, motioning his wife to keep hidden and shouting, "Who's there? Who's there? Show yourself, you coward, or be damned!" Marshall Walston had armed also and roused two slaves to search the house and grounds. But old Kinloch McKie had fired into the darkness when a shadowy form fled by and—he alone had no story to tell, being too hacked—had killed his own calf.

Intolerant the McKies could justly be called (sometimes, intolerable was almost as true), yet Marshall Walston, fighting to survive through reconstruction, had named his child of those times Kinloch.

Today Dan Armstrong found Felix sitting on the back steps filing a hoe blade. It was a strange sight to see Felix do anything like that because he never looked at what he was doing. The work went as fast as if he had both eyes to put on it, but it seemed, because his face would be turned to the sky or the ground or over his far shoulder, the business of some other man sitting there by him.

"Well, Dan," Felix greeted him just as he topped the hill, too far away, he thought, to call. Felix always beat him to the first words.

"Felix," Dan said, "run fetch a tin bucket and we'll make us a bee swarming."

"Bee swarming?" Felix said, nasal and high because he talked to the treetops. "Where 'bouts?"

"Down in the Ole Tuck pasture," Dan hollered after him.

He took Felix by the arm as they hurried out the back gate and down the path. Felix moved forward with fair certainty on his powerful, only slightly bowed, legs. He stretched his hands a delicate distance before his body, and over one arm a walking stick swung by its crook.

The two sat down together on the log above the pasture. Out near the sycamores in a dark brown cloud the bees circled and debated.

Dan commenced to pound on the bucket with his walking cane. "Oh, you devils!" he yelled delightedly. "Oh, you little honey bees!"

"They coming this way?" Felix shouted above the racket.

"They talking about it, Felix."

"What they doing now, Dan?"

"They've took vote, Felix, and they're for it. The procession is forming. Bees! Oh, you bees! Mind where you're heading, you hear me! Mind you cross that water! Mind you cross that River Jordan!"

Felix stamped the earth with his walking cane and laughed. "Preaching to bees. Preaching to little ole honey bees."

The pounding stopped. Dan sat down on the log and panted. He mopped his face. "Blowed," he said.

"What's happening now, Dan?"

"Blasted sons of grasshoppers. They took to that willow tree by the hog wallow."

The bees were settling now, forming into a pendulous mass shaped like an eggplant. Just below, one of the sows grunted, sloshed the mud and settled again.

"What'd you want them up here for anyway, Dan? You can't handle bees. Never heard of you meddling with anything less than hornets." He laughed high and shrill to the treetops.

"You'll never forget them hornets," Dan said placidly. "Forty years ago you and Kinloch Walston busted a hame-string making tracks away from them hornets and you let me walk right into the nest of them. I'd shame to remember it."

"But how come you wanted them bees now?"

"I don't know as I *wanted* them, Felix. I was just trying to see what I could make them do."

The two sat silent for a while. Each leaned on his walking stick.

"What's coming now?" Felix asked, cocking his head. He heard things before anybody else.

"Don't see a thing. Hold on here. It's a wagon load of corn. Simon must be getting low over at the south barn. Well, damn me."

"What is it, Dan?"

"Confounded nigger sitting on that wagon sound asleep as you ever saw. Dead to the world. Mules just grazing along in the pasture. Getting off the road now. Heading for water. Now if that don't show you the difference between a coon and a white man. Here I wake my fool self up out of a perfectly good nap snoring, and here we cut up all this racket for the bees and that nigger keeps right on sleeping. Yes sir, those mules are coming down for water right in there by the hog wallow. Going to spill Simon's corn if somebody don't watch out."

"Better holler to him, Dan. You wouldn't want Simon to lose his corn in the branch."

"I'm tired hollering," Dan said, fanning himself with his hat.

"What's happening now, Dan?" Felix asked, just before the crash came.

"Bless my soul if they didn't run that wagon slap into the bee tree. All that fine corn is spilling in the branch, mules tangling in the harness. Axle busted? Yeah, axle busted. Pigs jumping up."

"You mean the nigger ain't wake yet?"

"Oh, he's wake now. He's wake now all right, but he don't know what to do about it. Yelling at the mules and not turning a hand."

"What about the bees?"

"Biggest fool bees I ever saw. I told you that. They haven't even noticed that nigger yet. Biggest fool nigger I ever saw. He hadn't noticed the bees. Now he sees them. One must have stung him. Get those mules aloose, boy! Get those mules out of that harness and make tracks! Felix, I never saw a nigger in such a hurry. Well. That leaves the corn for the pigs. They know it, too."

The Negro boy rode out of the pasture, astride one mule, leading the other. At the very edge of the far hill he stopped, turning back toward the wrecked wagon, the corn and the pigs. Even at that distance, Dan could see the slow, blinking eyes go to the bees. Then

91

he kicked his heels into the flank and rode away.

The two old men sat peaceably. Felix heard the rapid fire grunts the snorts and squeals, the tearing shucks and breaking kernels. Dan watched the slight hypnotic rhythm of the bee swarm as it hung, breathed out, drew closer. Every now and then a stray one or two would float off a little way from the downward tip, falling like a drop of thick molasses, then rising back as though magnetized.

He got up. "Huh?" said Felix.

"Ought to do something about Simon's corn."

"You'll get your fool head amongst them bees, too," warned Felix.

There was a bordock tree a little way up the path. Dan picked up two green milk balls that had fallen and walked to the edge of the bluff.

"Watch me hit those crazy bees, Felix." Long ago, after the first year or two of his friend's blindness, he had given up trying to avoid reference to it. Now he was forever telling Felix to come see something, to watch, to look.

"I'm watching," Felix returned. He liked for Dan to forget.

The first throw missed, but on the second the big squashy ball spewed into the lower section of the swarm. The largest part was left to round itself up again.

"Aye gannies, I knocked the props out from under some of them," Dan said. A second later a pig squealed.

"I believe you," Felix said. "Are they mad?"

"Those that are mad, Felix, are pretty mad."

Three more pigs squealed. Dan chuckled. "Not doing a bit of good. Don't even make them lift their heads out of the trough. The bee circles down and pops the stinger in and the pig hollers and clicks his little old heels together and goes right on eating corn."

"Well, I declare," said Felix.

"You know, Felix, I wonder how many of them things can sting a pig before he gets bothered."

"Counting from the squeals, that's six already. Seven, eight, nine."

"Ten. (There's six shoats and two sows.) Eleven, twelve. (Old sows don't even kick, just grunt.) Thirteen. (More bees getting interested.) Fourteen, fifteen, sixteen, seventeen. (Divide what you get by eight and when the pigs leave the corn you'd know, wouldn't you?) Eighteen."

"Seems right. There's two more."

"Twenty."

Dan picked up a little stick and began to mark on the ground. Four marks, then tally, the way they counted votes on election night up in the court room with the stove red hot yet the room chill and the vote callers at the table shivering in their coats and calling and the vote counter just across echoing as he marked down: "Armstrong!" "Armstrong, three!" "Armstrong!" "Armstrong, four!" "Dan Armstrong!" "Dan Armstrong, tally!"

At dusk-dark the last pig skidded in the wagon bed and still snatching at corn on the way slid kicking through the broken wagon frame into the branch. Gorged, he hit the sand with an asthmatic gasp and toppled over on his side where he lay blinking. The others mulled among trampled shucks and cobs.

Dan Armstrong lifted his head. "Five hundred and thirty-nine bee stings, Felix, all told. That makes close on to seventy bee stings apiece."

"Never bother them pigs atall, huh, Dan?"

"Felix, I don't think them pigs ever saw one bee."

"I've always said there's nothing like pigs."

"Well, let's see what the biscuit says." He pulled out his watch. "Must be going, Felix." He stood up, rubbing his hands where the joints ached. "Wonder why Simon don't do something about the Ole Tuck house?"

He was looking toward a large negro cabin, empty, rotting and weedgrown, that stood half-concealed by the line of sycamores at the far end of the pasture.

"Can't get anybody to live in it," said Felix. "Never could since that day."

"Tear it down, I mean. You wouldn't think he'd want to look at it everytime he passes through the place."

"I don't know, Dan," Felix speculated. "Suppose if Si looked at the Ole Tuck house twenty-four hours a day hand running, he'd be reminded of anything but an old run-down nigger house?"

"They claim the Lord doled out a conscience to everybody. Don't they claim it?"

"The Lord doled out stingers to bees and then He turned right around and made pigs so thick-skinned and corn hungry they don't know they're stung. How many times a piece?"

"Nigh seventy."

"It's like I told you. Seven times seventy would be the same. That's what the Book says."

"That's forgiveness you mean, Felix. Seventy times seven to forgive."

"If you're bound and determined to get it right, get it all. Goes on to say if your brother sins that much and asks your pardon that much, forgive him that much. You trying to forgive, Dan? Did Simon Gerrard come say, I beg your pardon? S'pose he had. You'd have busted his brains out once with the handle of that big black pistol before the words were good out of his mouth. I know you, Dan Armstrong, and I know you well's to quit saying you forgive Simon Gerrard. You're a man too quick on the trigger to do such an unnatural thing; such a thing is enough to weigh you to your grave."

Dan looked down at his friend's face: the high bald forehead, the chin habitually tilted upward, the strangely unwrinkled skin where none of the business of meeting other eyes or seeing objects set in their place, color or size had left a stamp. In his mind's eye there flashed a picture of Felix as he stood once forty-five years ago in a swamp path taking careful aim at a squirrel. Then every steady fiber of him leaned toward, was balanced by, the keen sight of one sharp blue eye joining two points of steel with a bit of gray fur a

94

hundred feet away.

"A man has to choose, Felix. There are things more precious than any land they can take from you. There are things that land or lack of it don't start and can't end."

"So when you decided not to put a bullet through Simon Gerrard's head, you decided on this forgiveness. Because you knew you didn't aim to be fool enough as to try to live with hate gnawing at you. Being too honest for that, hating and doing nothing. But then a man can't live with forgiveness all his life either, Dan."

"You're holding forth on forgiveness, Felix, not me. I've been too busy living, happy enough, by and large."

"Aye, but I tell you, Dan, I have been free. That was a day for shooting. The man that aimed at me, hit me; and the man I aimed at, with the last ray of light the Lord was to give me on this earth, I shot and killed. Blind I am and by myself here worthless all these years, but I'm due to be blind. Wasn't blind or dead or shot nigh to pieces, I'd have to forgive somebody because I wouldn't fight, or be forgiven because I slipped up behind somebody. I'm not set on blaming you, Dan, or saying you were wrong, Lord knows, but I am saying that I'm a freer man for being blind than you are for seeing."

"A body has to do right as he sees it and not be too long about seeing it, Felix. So we both did that day. And so we stand by it, I as well as you."

Felix sighed. "Now Lord forgive me, Dan, for setting on you again. You and Kinloch Walston and me. It was for him and me and all the rest to see who the good men among us was. But for all your goodness there's a temper in you, Dan, and I'm ever fearing you went against it that once."

Dan stood silent, looking out toward the pasture. When he had come up the hill and sat on the log alone, he could have said if he had thought of it that even there no fierce memory had attacked him. He had dozed off, thinking simply that it was too hot.

"Once again, Dan, now that we've touched on it. Have you yet to tell young Kinloch?"

"Yes, Felix. I've yet to tell him."

"You aim never to tell him?"

"I aim to tell him sometime. But not yet."

"You fear there may be blood in it still?"

"I hope never again," he said with finality, adding, "They'll be waiting supper on me, Felix. I've got to be getting on."

As he passed down the path into the trees which shut off a view of the pasture, two men came walking down the road below by the branch. They cut across through the clumps of jimpson weed, passed under the sycamore trees and stopped before the rotting cabin. The tall, ungainly one took a seat on the edge of the porch and with an exaggerated sweep of his hand motioned his companion to sit beside him. It was Randall Gibson and Kinloch Armstrong.

They could not see the man on the bluff across from them, who was sitting with his chin on his walking stick staring at the sky above their heads. Felix had decided to sit there a while longer in the cool of the day. An hour or so later he would go and work his vegetable garden. Night made no difference to him. Presently, he untied the handkerchief from around the cake Dan Armstrong had brought him and finished it off in a very short time. He ate skillfully, scarcely dropping a crumb.

SEVEN

WITH one big foot Randall Gibson battered a decayed floor plank until he struck solid wood. He sat down and leaned his head against a creaking post that supported the sagging porch roof of the cabin.

"Now that this walk has cleared my head, Kinloch, I'm too sleepy to tell such a long tale."

"By God, Randall—"

"All right, all right. I'm going to tell you. But remember how it started and keep old Daniel off me. Remember you had to have it."

"Quit stalling, Randall, and begin."

"Beginning is the principal trouble, Kinloch. How shall one begin anything? That is why I suggested we come here, where this piece of land, this rotting house might serve as a touchstone for thirty-five years ago. Now I know that the events date infinitely farther back. Perhaps to explain Tarsus, Mississippi, on January 20, 1899, one must reach back in racial memory to the creation of man. No, I don't intend to do so. Let me as arbitrary as Shakespeare now. Begin with the great ones. Begin with the king. We know who that was. Marshall Walston knew it too. If he hadn't known what he was and how much he meant around these parts, he wouldn't have felt compelled to mount his horse on election night in 1875 and if he hadn't been up on that horse he wouldn't have got the bullet in his brain. Riding here and there, seeing that the maneuver he had dreamed of through ten long years of carpetbag rule was proceeding, correct in every detail."

"Can't you picture the court house square that night, jammed with voters, a-blaze with torches, while wagons draped in sheets and lighted inside—transparencies, they called them—drove round and round, the lights shedding an unearthly glow through the grotesque

97

enormous caricatures? In the jerk of motion and the flicker of the
lights inside, the faces painted on the sheets seemed to contort and
grimace, panicking the Negroes who had flocked to vote for Ames
and his black legislature. And if that wasn't enough, every moment of
quiet was smashed with the roar of the little cannon firing skyward,
time after time, until it blew itself up. Ernest Armstrong, your grandfather, was squatting behind the cannon they tell me, down low and
tending to his job where he ought to have been, but not Marshall
Walston. He rode and shouted, a commanding, regal figure, until the
shot came from somewhere inside the court house yard. Who did it,
nobody ever knew. Even Ole Tuck had no speculation to make and
of all Marshall Walston's cohorts and followers Ole Tuck, born in
slavery, yet owner still it would seem of this very house, loved
Marshall Walston best.

"Marshall hardly started in the saddle. He rode a little way across
the street, out of the glare of lights, and fell in front of the Episcopal
Church by the gate.

"The king is dead, long live the king. That king was Kinloch Walston but he never did know it. That was the big difference between
him and old Marshall. He had many of his father's fine qualities, but
he never had the knack of unconsciously playing before himself that
so delights the hearts of those who like their heroes.

"I never laid eyes on Kinloch Walston, of course, but I have lived
with him for many years and I have come to realize that he never
intended to bring the wrath of Tarsus down on his head. In the
twenty-four years between his father's death and his own, I suppose
no person in Tarsus was the subject of so much speculation. Marshall
Walston rode a black stallion; his son rode a little calico pony sometimes, a mule sometimes—hunting or to town, it might as well be the
pony as the mule. Marshall Walston was lord of the manor; from
Walston Cedars none went away empty and plenty went away more
than full. Kinloch Walston just lived there. When the long meeting
was done and the plans were laid, the townsmen would look about

98

for a leader and the first man they saw was Marshall Walston. Kinloch Walston never came to any meetings.

"Oh, I can see him walking through Tarsus. Medium-height, as tall as his father really, maybe taller, but stooped, intent, always leaning a little forward as he walked. He was not thin, but his shoulders sloped. At a time when handle-bar mustaches were the stamp of prominent men, his face remained smooth shaven. When he went past the men who whittled the bench before the post office, he nodded and bowed. But he did not call them by name—he couldn't and if he could have he still would not have done so—and he did not stop. In the first years there was only silence and a stare. Later there were whispers, and in times after that a burst of laughter, then in the long concluding years, silence again and a stare.

"If the men resented him for no particular reason they could name, except that he just ought not to act the way he did, the women were mad at him for a highly definite cause. You know women: they think marriage will fix anything. The like of the parties they gave him!"

"I remember hearing my father tell about the ball that old Mrs. Eustid gave for him. Miss Eugenia Eustid—old bitch, she flunked me in second year algebra—was young then and hopeful still. At that point Papa would laugh and say, 'You would never know it to see her now, but Eugenia was a fine-looking woman when she got diked out.' Then Papa would go on to point out how Mrs. Eustid had timed the ball so that Kinloch Walston could conveniently repay his obligations with a big Christmas party at Walston Cedars. This happy thought, it seems, was even hinted to him by Mrs. Eustid and her cronies on the night of the ball. He did not say yes or no, he merely nodded with a shy smile, and hopes ran high. When Christmas came, Kinloch Walston repaid his obligations all right. He sent the Eustids a ham from the smoke house and two gallons of Louisiana molasses.

"Personally I have always suspected that Dan Armstrong and Felix McKie put him up to that stunt. They would all three know how really funny it was, and they wouldn't laugh about it especially among themselves, the three of them sitting perhaps on the front porch of that big white mansion with their sock feet propped against a pillar watching the nigger boy go off down the road with the ham and molasses, and each one lighting up with that peculiar kind of dry superior humor they shared not through spoken agreement, but through likeness to one another.

"Papa didn't tell all that about them, of course. It takes somebody like me who never saw them together back in their old hunting days to come along and tell you with authority that they looked so-and-so and they shared so-and-so. But if it were not for somebody like me, who would speak of them when all who really saw them are dead? And even if everything I tell you is false, I will at least have testified to them, that they were to be loved.

"With my own ears I heard Papa telling his tales of Kinloch Walston and I learned then and there, young as I was, the horrors of humanity. Between my mother and Cherry Bell, he would sit in his armchair before the fire at night, and easy, polite and amusing as you please he would talk about Kinloch Walston, ten years dead, and it gave those two women hell. My mother—Beatrice Armstrong she was and the name did not forsake her—would sit quietly darning his socks while he talked. A good wife to him, you see. But the side of her face to the fire would get bright red from the heat, while her skirt began to smoke before she would remember to move back. On the other side of him, Cherry Bell, who in the firelight looked almost pretty again if I do say so, would crochet with a slim rapid needle flashing. Papa had her cornered, too. She had to stay in his house because there was no place else to go. Neither she nor Mama spoke. Neither looked up; oh, never, would they look up and meet his or each other's eyes. And never once would he relax the smile on his face or tighten his long discolored fingers on the cigar or drop for one syllable the paced, impersonal tone of a man just beyond middle age who has eaten a good dinner and enjoys the rememberance of things past. Time and time again, not every night but often enough, he sat there talking about the man whom both had loved and both had lost. What held those scenes together until merciful bedtime, I have often wondered. I think I know. Politeness is thin as a tissue paper wall, but the Mississippi levee and the dikes of Holland are nothing compared to its strength. Without politeness both women might well have taken up poker and tongs and beaten Cholley Gibson's brains to a pulp, then turned on one another.

"I, a nine-year-old boy, was the sole audience to this master comedy. I did not understand then, but so acutely conscious was I of the tension during such times that if I had known all that lay in the heart of those three I could not have remembered it more distinctly.

"When I did find out, it all added up to what I had known all along: that I, Randall Gibson, was not precisely a child of love.

"And ah, Cherry Bell. Under what star was she born? She had a flame in her, there's no doubt about that. I can imagine how she looked when she first came to visit her Aunt Lucy Gibson, my grandmother, that summer in the middle '90's. Her mother was dead and her father down in New Orleans got so absorbed in trying to wrest a fortune from the excursion boat business he was content that extended visits to relatives were quite the fashion of the day. Fragile, dainty, fair-haired she was, just made for the ruffles and bustles they wore then. She had a light, ready laugh and an erect, almost taut, manner of carrying her head and narrow shoulders, a manner that could make her seem at first glance every inch a lady. But on second glance did that very tautness communicate a constant disciplining of desire eager to be loose, and hint that under the last petticoat was a body only passion could relax?

"Just before she came, Kinloch Walston had decided to do a very sensible thing. Never lose sight of that quality of his: he was basically a level headed sort. Approaching his middle thirties, he determined to marry. He probably took an afternoon off to think over the possibilities and he chose Beatrice Armstrong, sister of his good friend Dan. A strong-built, quiet, dark-haired girl, she had studied him always from the background ever since she was a child. She had a beau, Charles Gibson by name, but she kept putting him off. When they teased her about him, she would blush, but she never giggled.

"The day after Kinloch Walston proposed she told Charlie Gibson to go away. Her happiness glowed within her, like a steady candle in a closed room. She grew quieter than ever, and her dark eyes intent on her sewing were wide and bright.

"Tarsus, of course, was enraged. Oh, how the women rared and charged! Beese Armstrong, and who did she think she was? Come to think of it, there might have been just a little touch of perversity in Kinloch Walston's choice. Somehow it's a mite like the ham and molasses, you see. An Armstrong. No boast and pretense about them, always small landowners, good people, sturdy stock. They live out from town. Their houses, plain, old and comfortable. No chandelier in the parlor, no silver service on the sideboard. No ugly cold high-ceiling bedrooms. No sets of Tennyson, Sir Walter Scott, the Encyclopedia Britannica; no Paradise Lost with illustrations by Dorè—all sitting musty and unused in the bookshelf. I have no fear of angering you, Cousin. You would not trade the cedar bucket on your back porch for all the plumbing in ten counties. You would rather be an Armstrong than anything on God's earth, and you mean God's earth, too, when you say it. In his heart, Kinloch Walston was one of you. Your mouths never watered at the thought of Walston Cedars and when you walked inside among all the really beautiful antique furniture under the lavish crystal chandelier, you never batted an eye. You have the respect of the Walstons and their kind as no one else can have it. And my mother, blood and bone, was one of you.

"But here is a question to baffle you. The wiles and coquetry of every good-looking and every not-so-good-looking young lady in Tarsus, aided and abetted by parental advice, had failed through fifteen consecutive years to ambush Kinloch Walston. Why then was Cherry Bell able to turn the trick? And here I point to Tarsus which, all unknown to itself, reaches the fullest expression of its essential nature

102

when a stranger comes to town. A stranger injures them. A stranger is the nail driven into the tree, and the whole pattern formed, forming and to be formed must adjust into abnormality. Only through long living, through absolutely essential passage of time does the iron give up to the wood and crumble like a bit of brown bark when the saw brings it to light.

"A bitter process. They with their materialism thwarted by too little money, their spiritualism cramped into Protestant sects, their desires toward a neighbor's wife, their bickering hatred toward some long-past, trivial incident, their fierce love toward their children whom they observe with satisfaction, urge even, to carry out their own pattern of hate against the children of the enemy at school, in summer play. But it is our own dirt, they are as good as saying. It is the smell of our own bathroom and it is dear to our hearts. God love them; I can't.

"But can you see how they meet the newcomer with the invisible sword drawn? At the sword's point they are saying, Become like us or begone. Still, take it all, it is not the strange newcomer that plagues them most. No, the unkindest cut of all is dealt out to them, offended souls, by the stranger who was born among them. Here you have the battle worth watching, for this kind of stranger has learned early to draw his own sword. You and I are a little like that, I more than you. Kinloch Walston was like that. I do not think he hated them, I say again, or meant to wound them so deeply. It may have started in him with shyness and shyness is only a step away from fear. His was at first a calm sort of fear—the kind of fear that will make a man drive around by Winona to get to Grenada when the roads are slick. They had figured him woman-shy, but they figured wrong. He was Tarsus-shy, something we both understand, and for all my vent of eloquence just now how can I say once and for always exactly why?

"At any rate, that peculiar affliction of his—or whatever you choose to call it—gave Cherry Bell, the stranger in town, a head start. She must have known her advantage not through reasoning, but the way women know things, through the difference in two looks, the contrast in two tones of voice.

"If only Cherry Bell had had the good sense to possess her soul in patience, or the patience to follow good sense. She had him, all right, but it would take him a while to admit it to himself, a while longer to admit it to anybody else because of Beatrice. She, poor girl, strove to look on the affair as a brief flirtation, his courtesy toward a visiting young lady. She was as quiet and peaceable with him as ever. She would never question him. It was for her men folk to come right out with what they wanted to know; for the women, never.

"Poor Cherry Bell, too. Like Cinderella, she had come to the ball and found the prince and like Cinderella, too, she dropped her slipper. There was the eagerness beneath the petticoats that maybe she didn't understand. Because I am perfectly sure she started it. Kinloch Walston would never have laid a finger on the dainty creature she seemed to be. All still might have been well if it had not been for the horseback ride with him one summer afternoon late, the return to Walston Cedars just as the storm broke, the forgetting that for lovers time doesn't behave in ordinary sequence.

"The night was all but gone when he drove her home. If she had done what he told her to do, given the sort of flat-tire or stuck-in-the-mud excuse that we give nowadays, there might have been speculation and nothing more. But night-shirted and be-candled, my grandfather met her on the stairs. He was a stern old fellow and she was his responsibility. Cherry Bell-like—God, I hate it in her—she stood there on the steps below him and lifted her little flower-like face and told a hair-brained lie. She said she had been at the house of her new friend, Henrietta Mathison. Cherry Bell-like, she went tripping over to Henrietta's house the next morning. It should have been easy to confide, at least partially, in Henrietta. Henrietta was such a good friend. Henrietta was so happy to help. Perhaps they laughed and giggled over the situation that morning. Perhaps Cherry Bell was encouraged to hint at telling a little more than she had planned, her heart

warming to Henrietta's teasing. Most certainly Cherry Bell was igno-
rant of Tarsus. Henrietta had taken her try for Kinloch Walston, too,
and not long before. She did not blurt the news to her family, nothing
like that. She went to her dearest friend, her friend of many years
standing, Eugenia Eustid. Before nightfall the town was in a pitch
of quiet ecstasy.

"Does Henrietta Mathison, now that she is Mrs. Simon Gerrard,
ever remember what she did to little Cherry Bell LaGarde? Did she
have it somewhere in the back of her mind, the shadow of justice's
righteous scepter, when she told Simon to serve me notice about the
treasured Walston statue?

"Kinloch Walston was enraged. All the stored temper of the suc-
cessful recluse poured out of him when her mistake turned the tables
and made his private affairs into public property. For that brief
interval he despised her. If I am not mistaken, there was always something he disliked about her, even when his desire for her was strongest. It is the same thing that has made me shrink from her ever since
I can remember. She got scared and stood on the stairs, lying wildly.
She could have had Kinloch Walston, anger and all, if she had stood
up to him, stood up to Tarsus. But face it, she could not. A legend—
God help me, she clings to it still—of the sweet young lady that the
mirror and all the half-observant crowd gave back to her, she believed. She got scared and, seeing the anger in his eyes, she thought
it was for always, her heart withered and she ran away to Memphis
where some more relatives took her in.

"Why couldn't she at one time or other have taken stock of her
inordinate passions and tried to master them? Or that failing, have
been honest enough to turn street-walker, can-can dancer, to run off
with the animal trainer in the circus? More power to her, I'd say then.
And years after Kinloch Walston's death when she came back to the
pitying bosom of my grandmother—there was a scandal in Memphis
too and her not-so-pitying relatives sent her packing—why did she
then have to hide the liquor she drank, explain every time my father

105

got her more that she felt a slight cold coming on, sit downstairs crocheting a dainty pattern long since gone crazy with the thread tangling before it was off the ball, her eyes too blurred to see it?

"But to get back. When she went away, Kinloch Walston came to Beatrice Armstrong. Master of himself again, he was fair enough at least not to ignore that things had gone wrong, but honorable enough to beg her forgiveness and place the matter in her hands. She refused to marry him. She would have gone through with it, I know, because she loved him still, but in her heart she knew that he had never really wanted her very much and that now he did not want her at all. She knew it even more when Kinloch Walston took his first trip to Memphis. His efforts to bring Cherry Bell back were unsuccessful. Rumor drifted down to Tarsus that she now had a wealthier suiter than he, a yankee shoe manufacturer, no less. Pastures were greener there, it seemed, and perhaps from such a distance Tarsus shrank comfortably in her breast so that her frail voice might rise in laughter as she told of its quaint, country ways between bird-like sips of champagne. Yet she saved the letters that came to her. I do not know why. How could her passion-swayed little heart recognize burning remorse and deep constancy except as words upon a handsome page? How could she tell that loneliness and the gossip of Tarsus were setting devotion in him with the permanency of words cut in stone?

"With Kinloch Walston dead and Cherry Bell gone from the Gibson house for good everybody thought, Beatrice married Charles Gibson. How did she feel when Cherry Bell returned to become a burden outweighing all the rest, and there were burdens enough already? I don't know what she felt, but I know she faced up to it. There are those who can face up to it, whatever it is. There are those who can't. Even with her father dead and the doors of Memphis closed to her, Cherry Bell for many years spoke of her residence in Tarsus as temporary. Perhaps she still thinks of it so.

"Kinloch Walston quit writing letters at last. He could face up to

106

things, too, but like the rest of his methods, he would do so most curiously. He went to the curious little war with Spain. He was really too old for anybody to expect him to go, but he had attended a military school in Virginia or the East—somewhere—and he got a commission easy enough. And got killed. One of the few.

"Only one who, like him, is a perpetual stranger in Tarsus can understand why he had to do that. His friends, Dan Armstrong and Felix McKie, had forgiven him as though nothing had happened. He had acquited himself honorably before Dan Armstrong's sister, and Felix McKie contented himself with speaking of Cherry Bell as a 'forward woman.'

"Was some forgiveness lacking yet? Did he feel that the personal enmity between Tarsus and himself would never be resolved except into more bitter things, and therefore did he have to go out and face the impersonal war to meet with finality, and so peace? He did not share the excitement and bustle of the others; he expected to die.

"But, oh, how he reckoned without his true enemy! Forever personal, Tarsus.

"They buried him here, cried at his funeral, decided they loved him after all. Soon there would have been the gathering of romance around him; soon Cherry Bell and Beatrice would have been looked on as characters in the oft-repeated story, bearing no relation to the women living at the Gibson place.

"For all I have denounced Tarsus, I am inescapably a part of it, and sometimes when I am very drunk, I come half-way to love it, convinced for a little while that they are all good or, even better, trying to be good. But however my emotions run, I constantly know that I understand Tarsus, and that in their own way they understand some reasonable facsimile of me which is not as far from the truth as I would like to think. I have made a rare admission and I shall regret doing so, but how else shall I prepare for what I have next to tell?

"I have postponed it long enough. I have been searching for a synonym, a revealing phrase, some historical framework, perhaps, or some adjustment to type. There is none. So I say simply, The Gerrards.

"I have gone to some trouble, you recall, to point out the hypocrisy of the town as it covers its every sin with the false veneer of respectability. But what shall we say when people come along whose violence and greed is open, who place no value at all on the respectable thing except as it serves their definite and always visible ends? Cherry Bell has at last become one of us; Kinloch Walston is a cherished memory to a dozen women who danced with him once in their youth. But should the Gerrards live in Tarsus a thousand years, the record of every friendly gesture will show the purpose as their own gain, while their every idle minute will be filled with laughter at our expense, contempt for us, or more often, simple disregard. And these are the people we have allowed to all but own us, all but rule us. Never a hand called. I cannot understand it. I will simply give the facts.

"Old Wills Gerrard, Simon's father, came into Tarsus after the war, around 1870, I think. He drove his family in from about thirty miles out in the country where they had been dirt farmers since anybody could remember. Old Wills was about sixty then; his wife had died six weeks before and already he had a bride, Lily, sixteen years old. He had left about ten children scattered about on small farms in that grubby clay section where you can ride or hunt a whole day and never see a house. There are still swarms of Gerrards out there; I heard Lance laughing about them just the other day.

"Old Wills never gave any reason for coming. He just drove into town. His wagon was held together with bailing wire and at every dried-up mud hole it looked as if the dresser, bedstead, springs, mattress, chairs, wash pot, kettle and God knows how much else would go sprawling out into the dust, all on top of Young Wills, the son, who was asleep on the mattress.

"Nothing significant in that arrival. Your grandfather and mine came to Tarsus in pretty much the same way.

108

"They didn't have anywhere to go or any money, so they spent the first week or so in an empty Negro cabin down in the hollow back of the post office. Here I'd like to be able to say that Marshall Walston found them and offered them work. But it didn't turn out that way. No, the McKies, a big family then, none of whom believed in working Negroes, would send one of their number into town early Saturday during cotton-picking time when the wagons were first rolling in, and he would mill around until he hired two or three country fellows who needed cash—the McKies hired Old Wills, Young Wills and Lily, and the Gerrards got their first Tarsus money that way. After cotton picking was done they took odd jobs around—helped at the gin, hired out for yard work, Saturday clerking and the like.

"They had moved into an old house next to the blacksmith's shop. In those days you could see Lily most any morning sitting in a rocking chair out in front of the shop, just out of kicking distance of the horses and mules. She would be shelling peas or stringing beans and talking a blue streak to whoever was waiting. In cold weather she moved in by the forge and talked old Mr. Turnipseed to death while he ground the forge harder and harder to drown her out. She was there so much, the men used to josh him about her. He was an ugly, seamy, taciturn old fellow, sarcastic with everybody and principally with Lily, but it was all lost on her. Or maybe she caught on but wasn't going to admit it, because she had to have somebody to talk to. If her men-folk were as silent with her as they were with the rest of Tarsus, she must nearly have gone off her head.

"A phenomenal silence they kept for the first thirty years of their life here. Nobody remembers a thing they ever said. If they were caught in any double-dealing, nobody remembers that either. They moved like ghosts among the crowds the momentous events of that thirty years gathered. They never took a side or a stand. Or were they already feeling themselves the only real people in a rush of spirits?

"The only thing people seem to remember about them, in fact, is the number of times they moved. Every time things began to calm down after an election, a race incident, some personal or family spate of violence, here came the creaking of the old wagon with the same old furniture and Old Wills, Young Wills and Lily moving again—always to a better place which on the inside would look as shambled within two weeks as the one they just left. Lily died in childbirth during the late 'seventies. She had had two before, still-born. After the terrible ordeal of her first labor, the doctor they at last called had forbidden further children, and after the second attempt she began to look middle-aged at twenty and she became as silent as they. But if Old Wills felt that he had had anything whatever to do with her death, he showed remarkable restraint. They named the new baby Simon.

"After Lily's death, Young Wills began to talk a little here and there. Perhaps both of them had kept up their silence to spite her. He was getting to be a good-looking young fellow, tall, remarkably like Lance they say, though he gave his best impression at a little distance away. They gave him a steady job at DeWitt's hardware store. Old Wills quit work to stay home with the baby and cook. Bent and rheumatic, he grew almost womanish looking. There was the softness of flesh suggestive of fat that all the Gerrards have and when he came out in the back yard to chop kindling, wrapped in an apron with an old red cap on his head, you would have to look twice to see whether it was old woman or old man.

"So there was nothing to predict about them, you see. Nothing at all. From the time Simon could walk, Young Wills had him working at the hardware store. Nothing wrong with that. Young Wills bought out the business when old man DeWitt retired. Nothing wrong with that. In fact, if people felt compelled to mention them at all, by reason that there wasn't anybody left in town they hadn't talked about that day, they wouldn't have found anything to say but good, hard-working folks. The salt of the earth, it seemed.

"Oh, you could wonder how much they were making at the store, laugh about how tight-fisted they were, warming themselves over one lump of coal all winter long, and laugh some more to learn they

110

wouldn't put money in the bank but hid it somewhere about the place instead. And again wonder how much of it they had.

"Nothing to predict, but after what could not be predicted had been accomplished, their silence through all those years is to me the central point of horror. For from the day the wagon first came out of the obscure hills beyond Keystone Bottom, from the moment the back wheels bumped off of the bridge into Tarsus, they had been watching. Watching through thirty years, watching everything, everybody from Hangman's Hill to the creek, from Keystone Bottom to the far borders of the-land-west-of-town. They were waiting for they didn't know what, without even knowing they were waiting. I sometimes imagine them during that period as two pairs of disembodied eyes, unblinking, sleepless, forgetting nothing. Simon was born with those same eyes.

"Kinloch Walston probably never exchanged three words with them, but they knew him. They held no grudge against him; that was not their way. But they knew all about the grudges Tarsus held; they perceived with uncanny shrewdness what every family felt about him and why.

"The day after Kinloch Walston's will was read, all the Walstons and near-Walstons (everything from sisters to second-cousins-once-removed), who had materialized in Tarsus, packed their telescopes and with faces more sincerely mournful than anything the funeral had prompted, caught the train for points east and north.

"Yes, they were the grief-stricken relatives, all right, especially when they heard old Lawyer Eustid read how somebody named Felix McKie and somebody named Daniel Armstrong had inherited the Walston estate, lock, stock and barrel. The house and furniture to those two as well, to be settled however they chose, and even an Italian statue in the garden bequeathed out of the family also to somebody named Cherry Bell LaGarde.

"Out of the passel of disappointed relatives, one stayed behind, quiet, hardly noticed at first, down at the Cedars. His name was

111

Marvin Strong, a half-brother, old Marshall's wife's son by an early marriage. Schooled in the east, a Pennsylvania lawyer now.

"In the middle of the afternoon of the day the relatives migrated, with the town settling back into its groove after this military funeral, a slightly disturbing thing happened—disturbing only because it had never happened before. The two Gerrard boys, who habitually kept the hardware store open until ten o'clock at night if only to sell a handful of carpet tacks, locked up soon after dinner and went home.

"Simon and Young Wills had been at the funeral. Had they felt the rambling course of thirty years begin to gather under them like a horse two paces before the jump? Or was their presence another entry in the books, in the long record of their instinctive espionage? We can be sure they took a long gander at the relatives, one by one. We can be sure they had marked Marvin Strong.

"On their way home from the store Young Wills—people called him that still, though the father was long dead—hailed an old colored man. The brothers dressed with considerable care in clothes nobody knew they owned. They rented a carriage from the livery stable, put a top hat and a coat on the colored man and set him gaping on the driver's seat with the reins in his hand. My father was sitting in the court house yard when they drove by going toward Walston Cedars. He said that the horses were flatfooting along when Young Wills climbed up beside the colored man, wrenched the reins out of his hands and, standing up, lashed the horses till they rared against the bit. He took them out of town at a smart trot. The last thing you could see, he was climbing back beside Simon, dusting off his clothes.

"I'm inclined to believe that everything was arranged that afternoon. So simple a matter should not have taken long. The mistake one is prone to make about such things is to suppose they must be very complicated, composed of good and evil so intermixed that the world turns gray. Maybe. Sometimes. But not this time. Young Wills and Simon Gerrard wanted to become owners of the Walston estate. They had to sin to get it; they knew it, and they sinned coolly and deliberately in the simplest possible way. They told Marvin Strong that Kinloch Walston was crazy. They told him that Tarsus people would testify to that fact. They probably made it clear then and there that they, the Gerrards, would be glad to buy the land when the will was invalidated. They probably talked prices. In view of the backstage aid they offered, it was little to ask—to let them buy the property. I suspect them of pointing out that they, the Gerrards, were the only people in Tarsus able to lay a good percent of the sum across the board in the form of hard cash. And suppose the Walston half-brother had gone about Tarsus in his blinking, hedging, lawyerish way to investigate financial standings. He would not have understood that the well-to-do if questioned casually will speak as though the wolf is at the door, and even the few near wealthy habitually make out that the cook at the poor house is putting on an extra plate for them right that minute. But everybody would tell you that the Gerrards had plenty salted away.

"Most amazing of all to me is the trial. For weeks in advance it was the talk of the town. Marvin Strong hired one of his law school pals from Memphis to come down for the case.

"And Tarsus, which had haggled and debated about Kinloch Walston through the years in growingly impatient tones, was more pleased with that answer than it would admit. So that was it all along. Kinloch Walston was crazy. How many had suspected it for a long time! Or had said to themselves, you remember that day—

"Dan Armstrong and Felix McKie joked about the very idea. But they were not really a part of Tarsus any more. As many friends as they had here, it was not the same as in the days when Marshall Walston bound town and the-land-west-of-town into one social, economic and political unit. Kinloch Walston broke the tie; in favor of McKies, Armstrongs and families like them, he disregarded Tarsus, never knowing that he was the touchstone for both. It was his sin, bringing on his own ruin and the defeat of his friends.

"Just how far the active scorn of Tarsus, developed in him by the

Cherry Bell affair, had carried him was scattered information until the trial forced the pieces together. The hand of the Gerrards was everywhere in this process, unseen; Marvin Strong and his Memphis lawyer would never have known where to strike pay dirt.

"The foolish things Kinloch Walston did! I understand him, I know why he did them, I do things like them and if I were at any sort of premium by reason of great possessions they would have no trouble setting me up as crazy as betsy bug. But in the literal minded court room, satire is lost.

"There was the note he sent to some hostess declining an invitation to a dance. 'It is a common knowledge,' he stated, 'that my excesses in the matter of intoxicating spirits are an outrage to the high moral character of Tarsus people. At present, I am being duly punished by a severe attack of gout which prohibits my walking and consequently my dancing.' That very afternoon he passed the lady's house walking briskly to the post office. Had Kinloch Walston ever been known to go to excess in the matter of intoxicating spirits? Very rarely, Dan Armstrong had to say.

"A carriage full of young ladies had the temerity to drive down to Walston Cedars one afternoon. Ole Tuck came out to say his master had gone hunting. On the way out they caught a glimpse of the master himself, reading in the garden. They stopped and called to him. Giggling, they cried as he approached, 'Ole Tuck said you had gone hunting!' He came quite close. 'Ole Tuck is a finer man than I shall ever be,' he said. 'I would advise you always to believe any statement he makes.' He tipped his hat. 'Good day.'

"They called the girls to the stand, one by one. 'I don't know how everybody else felt, but something in the way he talked scared me to death. . . .' 'He looked at us so *funny*. . . .' 'I didn't know what to think. . . .' So they chirped to the crowded court.

"And so it went—notes, encounters, passing an old acquaintance with a vacant stare, maybe somebody whose wife had talked long and loud about him and Cherry Bell.

114

"Oh, he had blazed a broad trail for them in those three morose years between Cherry Bell and the war. Only the Armstrongs and the McKies knew him still over that period and what did their testimony amount to since they had everything to gain by giving it?

"Cherry Bell again. The weirdest note in the whole proceedings was the manner in which they walked a tight rope over that affair. She could have explained it all, you see. Up there in Memphis, she had the letters he had written to her, letters that mentioned or even explained many of the incidents presented as evidence against him at the trial. Yes, Cherry Bell could have turned the whole trick. But the Gerrards—Lord God, Cousin, I forgot to tell you one terrifying detail—they sold out the hardware store *before* the trial. They were so sure. They knew and bet their bottom dollar that Cherry Bell would never bring public disgrace down on her head by sitting in the witness box. She wouldn't have let anybody touch those letters with a ten-foot pole. And everybody—my father, my mother, Dan Armstrong, gallant old Lawyer Eustid—everybody but Felix McKie who wanted to drag her into court by the hair of her head—all combined to protect her from the aforementioned public disgrace. As if the disgrace wasn't public enough already. Lord love them. The Gerrards had counted on them for that piece of chivalry right down to the ground. Her name was not mentioned.

"After the sale of the land, Marvin Strong packed his brief case back to Philadelphia laden with a wad of bills big enough to choke a calf. I always wondered if the Walston sisters, in the name of whose inheritance he had waged his case, ever saw any of the money. The roll must have looked pretty good to him all there together, just about enough to retire on.

"Three days after the sale of the land, while Dan Armstrong and Felix McKie were cooling tempers that the court room had so frequently overheated, and were laying saner plans in hope of another trial; before the town had fully recovered from the turn-about of finding the Gerrards of all people the big property owners in the county—just three days afterwards, all hell cut loose.

"Because in the middle of the big track of land—which Young Wills and Simon at first could do nothing but drive into and out of, staring at it, even getting lost during their second excursion, they say—right square dab in the commanding center of all they possessed was that which they did not possess. Just a forty acre strip of woods, farm land and a pasture where a road ran through. Mighty little. But, all things considered, just enough.

"Legally the land was owned by Ole Tuck who received it as a legacy from his old master, Marshall Walston. Ole Tuck was to be sole owner until his death, and that occurring, the property should revert to the original estate. Kinloch Walston had appointed Felix McKie as Ole Tuck's trustee. He may have done that as a kind of joke: Felix's distaste for the colored race was a standing argument between them. Felix and Ole Tuck used to have it, as they worked adjoining fields, Felix shouting and Ole Tuck grumbling just under being heard, in long rambling arguments. You would have thought they were fixing to fight each other. Each resented the other right up to the teeth, and each would have died for the other.

"Ole Tuck was pushing eighty when Kinloch Walston died. By that time Ole Tuck—surnamed Walston himself, of course—had a menagerie of colored Walstons running around his house and helping him farm. He had his woman—she was fairly young—and his daughter who had just got herself a big mulatto from Kosciusko named Jeems, other grown and even middle-aged sons and daughters who were likely to be staying with him between jobs or mates, and a near dozen more little ones and middle-sized ones, explained and unexplained, chasing about the house and wood. From this pasture laughing and shouting echoed into the hollows.

"When Ole Tuck came home from a day's service at the Cedars, the racket would stop. They would none of them look at him as he mounted the steps. He would tip his hat to his family as though they were guests. 'Evenin'.' The dignified chorus rose: 'Ve'y well, thank

116

you, sir. You all right?' 'Ve'y well.' He would then proceed through the front door and somewhere inside would exchange the black broadcloth outfit of his service for a pair of faded, patched, very clean overalls, that smelled of lye scrubbing and the cedar sprout they rub the iron across and his race. Dressed so, he came to sit among them on the porch, but he was still different from them. The play, shouting and argument resumed. He crossed his legs and watched, unmoved. They scarcely ever spoke to him until he asked them something, and when they did their voices were low, casual and sober.

"I think of Ole Tuck as holding tribal court on those afternoons; he knew, in a sense, that he was king and his subjects knew they were subjects. I've heard it said that good negro land-owners are rare. I don't know about that, but I know Ole Tuck was a good land-owner.

"But it would probably be better to his liking should I call him the impeccable servant. He was that. When Kinloch Walston was away from Walston Cedars, Ole Tuck would walk up to the house twice a day, morning and nightfall, to take a look around. Even after his master's death, he did it.

"On the third day after the sale of the land, Young Wills and Simon Gerrard, high-tailing with increasing courage through their domain, were brought up short by a new fence, knocked together in a hurry out of pine scrap, barring the road. Nailed across the middle was a Keep Out sign with the name, Daniel Tucker Walston, lettered below. That was Ole Tuck's full name, believe it or not, and the Gerrards must have spent a worried minute or two trying to think where this new Walston could have come from. When it dawned on them that Ole Tuck was the sign-painter, they jumped to the ground, kicked the fence out and drove through. But just around the next curve was a mound of brush, horse-head high, and that cleared away left an open space to the bridge, only there wasn't any more bridge. It was busted out clean. Yes, Ole Tuck had had his menagerie busy the night before.

"Well, some plain and fancy cussing must have rung through the woods and hollows that day. The cussing must have got louder with the pace of remembrances coming on that here lay the roughest section of the land, that the only other route from the north wing of the property to the main barns of the south involved a ten mile detour, that Ole Tuck had all legal rights to this pivotal point until his death.

"They looked for the old fellow all morning, but they couldn't find him. Official and smooth-faced as you please, they went to see Dan Armstrong, the sheriff. Dan heard their story and sent across the hall for Lawyer Eustid who was playing checkers with the county clerk and watching his own office door through the window.

Young Wills slapped his fine new gloves against his thigh while Dan gave the beetling old lawyer an account of what had happened.

" 'Well?' Young Wills demanded.

"Lawyer Eustid addressed Dan Armstrong. 'How long ago did Kinloch Walston open that road, Dan?'

" 'Ninety-two or three. Somewhere along in there.'

" 'Too late,' Lawyer Eustid said. 'Has to be in use ten years.'

" 'What do you mean, ten years?' Young Wills asked.

" 'English common law, sir!' cried Lawyer Eustid. 'I didn't make it. A road through another man's property has to be in use ten years before you can tell him he's got to keep it open.'

" 'But how—?' Young Wills began.

" 'How did Kinloch Walston get back and forth before that?' Dan Armstrong supplied his question. 'Oh, he used a little road not far away. Led through the corner of the McKie place. You might inquire about it from Felix.'

"Young Wills divided a glance between the two. He saw Dan Armstrong's eyes light with a desire to laugh; he saw old Lawyer Eustid's walrus mustaches twitch. Oh, he was a big landowner was Young Wills, and he was in old Marshall Walston's chair was Young Wills. He thrust out his chin. He wanted to tell them they dare not laugh at him, that he would ruin them if they dared laugh; but then perhaps he reflected that he had already done that very thing, or close to it, and

118

that still they laughed, without pretense or bitterness, simply because they thought it was funny. And maybe he remembered the back-breaking days of cotton picking, the humbling odd-job work, the long years behind the counter at the hardware store, the long dreams which were a cheat somehow because they had given what they promised, yet they had not told him about this—this ineradicable, genuine, superior humor in the eyes of men he was supposed to have crushed beneath his foot.

"And in the end, he said nothing, made no fine speech, just jerked his head for Simon to follow and walked out.

"Before they were out the front gate of the court house, Dan Armstrong was out the back unhitching his buggy and before his foot was good off the iron step, the bay pony he drove was burning the road for Felix McKie's house. It was January 20, 1899. It was cold and the white sun sent a heatless glare sifting through the bare trees. You know how the country looked—fields where corn stalks broke from the top and cotton stalks made black lines like cross stitching between the water-filled rows. A desolate country in the winter. During the long summers and falls we forget.

"Even before Dan Armstrong arrived Felix McKie had his shotgun unhooked from the rack. Felix had been spoiling for trouble since the Gerrards tricked the land out from under him and with grumbling and protest he had agreed to Dan Armstrong's plan for the peaceful gathering of further evidence to present in a new trial. Strained, un-natural events could not relax so easily, Felix felt, and when he heard the beat of hooves far down the road he knew that here was the sound he had sat two days and nights expecting. He ran for the gun.

"Together the two men visited Ole Tuck's house where the menag-erie faced them in solid ranks from the front porch where we now sit. They gaped and shook their heads at the mention of Ole Tuck. 'We ain' seed Mist' Tuck since early this morning,' his woman said. 'You all tore up that road last night, didn't you?' Dan Armstrong said. 'What happened to him after that?' A dozen of them there must have been,

119

little and big. They gave back the same inborn unrecognizing state. 'Naw suh,' said the woman, thick-mouthed as though she talked in her sleep. 'We don' know nothing atall bout no road.' 'Listen to me!' Dan Armstrong shouted at them like a preacher at a congregation of hard-hearted sinners. 'We're not aiming to hurt Ole Tuck. We're aiming to help him. There're folks after him, folks trying to get ahold of what he's got, folks trying to run you out of house and home. Mister Felix and me—we want to protect him, save him. You've got to tell us where he is. Who will tell us, now? Nora Nell? Harrison? May Chile? Johnny? Big Foot? Lou?' All silent. 'We ain' seed Mist' Tuck since early this morning,' the woman said again. The two white men looked at each other. 'I'll cover all the cabins on the north place, Felix. Ole Tuck's got some more family over there. You take this neck of the woods.' They turned to go. 'Mist' Tuck been low in his mind since day 'fore yestiddy,' the woman said, conversationally. Since the day the Walston place changed hands, though she would probably deny knowing anything about that either. And perhaps they didn't. Perhaps Ole Tuck hadn't seen fit to tell his subjects of the goings-on among principalities. Maybe he just told them to tear the road and bridge to smithereens and they did it without having to know the reason. Maybe he didn't tell them where he was going when he left home, after all.

"The two white men parted. Dan put a saddle on his horse and set off for the plantation's north wing; Felix went on foot into the heavily wooded hills that separated his house from Walston Gap. He was nearing the big house itself when he came on Jeems. Jeems, you remember, was the big, strapping half-white husband of Ole Tuck's daughter, Nora Nell. He was a strange one. Nobody in Tarsus would have him on the job. He looked too big and mean and white. You know the mistrust they have of light-colored Negroes. Kinloch Walston had let him work around the house at intervals for years. In the fall he would hire out in the Delta where hands count too much to bother with blood. Sometimes he would just disappear. Felix McKie despised him. He started and half-raised his gun when he came on Jeems that day. Jeems was down by the branch washing his hands and face. A soap-stone bank rose just behind him. His skin was the same gray non-color of the soap-stone. Against that gray skin, gray bank and gray water, the blood on his face and hands which the cold stream frothed and thinned took on a magnified hue of lavish, startling brilliance.

" 'You seen Ole Tuck?' Felix demanded.

" 'No, sir, I ain't been home yet.'

" 'You been gone?'

" 'Been gone since last Tuesday.'

" 'Gone and got into trouble?'

" 'Got in a little trouble up around Clarksdale.'

" 'They coming to find you?'

" 'No, sir. Ain't going be no more trouble.'

" 'You see Ole Tuck tell him to go to my house.'

" 'Yes sir.'

"Felix headed over the hill. He looked down on Walston Cedars. Nothing stirred. The valley was wide and cold; green shutters blinded the big white house. Felix shook his head and swung back around towards Tarsus. He should have known. Dan Armstrong should have known. The Gerrards knew—or guessed—or simply gravitated. One never knows which.

"Felix was nearing a little settlement of three Negro families on the outskirts of Tarsus when he heard the shot. It dawned on him then. He turned and began to run, cutting through the woods. From a distance he saw them pass on their way back to town. Simon was driving the buggy; Young Wills sat beside him, cleaning the pistol. Felix cried out from the hill, but they passed by, unhearing. Time enough for that, he thought, hurrying on toward the Cedars. On the front porch before the wide, high doorway flanked by shuttered sidelights, Felix found Ole Tuck lying dead. He was dressed in the black broadcloth he had worn to serve Marshall Walston and had kept on wearing after

121

Kinloch Walston told him he needn't. He lay with his fingers tight over the wound. Felix said afterwards it looked as if he was trying to keep the blood from spilling over the floor.

"An hour or so later, a little past mid-afternoon, Felix rode into Tarsus. He saw the Gerrards' livery stable buggy hitched at the court house fence. Folks who noticed him that day remembered that he never hesitated, never looked at anyone he passed. A whole covey of partridges can flush not two yards from you when you're on a deer stand with the dogs baying just beyond the bridge, and staring right at the birds you won't think anything. Felix McKie was feeling like that when he walked up the court house path. The Gerrards were in there all right, checking through abstracts at the chancery clerk's office, laying claim to their newly acquired little forty acre patch. Maybe Felix McKie could smell them. Maybe his eyes—hard, bright, intense blue eyes that we never saw—could look right through the walls. However it was, folks that happened to be milling around in the wide, intersecting halls said that he made a bee line for the chancery clerk's office, tightening his grip on the shotgun as he went, and they vanished into all kinds of offices so fast the doors slammed like one.

"Felix stood on the threshold silent as a conqueror, and when old Mr. Mosley looked up from the ledger and saw him, he started so his glasses fell off. That was when Young Wills and Simon turned around.

" 'Get your gun and come out in the hall,' said Felix to Young Wills.

"Young Wills got excited. He didn't understand. I don't reckon he or Simon either ever really understood that here was a white man avenging a Negro. They thought it was something else.

" 'Wait a minute,' said Young Wills. 'I don't know what you're talking about.'

" 'You killed Ole Tuck,' Felix explained. 'Now I'm going to kill you.'

"'Wait a minute,' said Young Wills. 'If that old nigger had acted up to you the way he did to me, you'd of shot him, too. Why, that nigger was wanting to keep me out of my own house.'

"'And keep you off his own land,' said Felix.

"'I went to talk business with him,' said Young Wills. 'He wouldn't listen. I swear it. That nigger spit at me, I tell you. You'd of shot him, too.'

"'I'll be waiting for you in the hall,' said Felix, 'and you'd better have some kind of gun in hand when you come over this door jamb.'

"He backed through the door and slammed it behind him. He walked down the hall a little way and waited, tapping his foot against an urn-like brass spittoon. The little sounds echoed, solemn with portent for want of a better omen, through the deserted hall.

"Way ahead of Felix at one entrance, the outside door opened and in came Jeems. Explain these bastard white niggers if you can. They stop me cold. They'll walk through the streets like a white man and they'll come do business with you just pushing the line of the way a white man stands, talks and moves his hands, and it's not something that makes me mad and arrogant, as much as it makes me plain nervous. There it stands and what is it? Because five minutes after he leaves you, he'll mix up with an honest-to-God nigger in a scrape that's got the stamp of the colored race marked over it from start to finish, but often pushing the line even there in an exaggeration of violence. I've sometimes thought that day and night may make the difference. A white man under the sun, and under the roving night a Negro again. But I don't know. I know that Jeems came into the court house like a white man. The folks in Ole Tuck's house had got notice from the Gerrards to be out and away from there by morning. While all the rest knew that trouble was on them and were lying low as they could, and that's mighty low, Jeems struck out to see Dan Armstrong. He wanted to see if there was room on the Armstrong place to move his family. As I said, he came through the door like a white man with a white man's reasons, but the next second he saw

123

Felix McKie standing, waiting, the gun half-lifted in his hands, and the tide turned in his blood. He remembered his meeting with Felix when he bathed his wound, and in one wildly illogical leap of his mind, he hit the notion that Felix was waiting to kill him, that Felix thought he had killed Ole Tuck.

" 'Before God,' he cried, hearing the strange sound of his own voice striking the high walls, 'I ain't done it, Mr. Felix!'

"Felix, grim as rock, his toe tapping the spittoon regular as a drum beat, fastened unwavering eyes on the office door. Jeems thought the eyes were on him. I doubt if Felix ever really comprehended that Jeems was there, or what Jeems was talking about.

" 'Before God,' he said tensely at the sound of his name. 'Shut your mouth and take cover or you're liable to get your brains blown out.'

"The office door opened. It was Young Wills at last, crouched and ready to flee before he could get past the threshold, gun in hand. Felix raised his gun. Jeems cast about the bare hall for cover and ducking suddenly, drew the hidden pistol from his clothing and fired in a panic of fear, in the middle of a backward leap toward the door.

"Felix fell sideways but just before he touched the floor, he jerked upright again like a puppet on a string, and gathered himself around the gun at his shoulder as though instead of holding it, it supported him.

"How he saw to do it no one ever understood. Jeems' bullet had cut through his eyesight. The spurting blood alone would have been enough to blind a man. But in his last glimpse of the world he had seen Young Wills start through the door. Could it be that the intensity of his hatred flared momentarily to supernatural proportions, possessed a life larger than his own, drew aim and fired while the man behind the gun felt himself shrinking smaller and smaller, a pigmy, less than a pigmy, in unrelieved worlds of blackness slipping down toward the only true sensation left, the solidity of the floor beneath his feet?

"When Dan Armstrong heard the news of Ole Tuck's death, he was

124

way down in the north section of the Walston place, down in the bottom land by Tillila Creek. He knew at once where trouble would come to a head, and he put down the road to Tarsus at a hard gallop. My father saw Dan Armstrong come riding into town that day, but he once remarked that whether you saw him or not didn't matter because it was as if he set off an electric current that communicated his arrival to all Tarsus at once.

"Dan found Felix in the doctor's office back of the drug store near death. The curving bullet had missed the brain by a miracle. Out of the still alien darkness, he clutched at Dan Armstrong's hand. 'Young Willis did it,' he whispered. 'I killed him for it. Get Simon, Dan. Get Simon. Stamp them out while there's time.'

"But when Dan came out of the drug store on his way to look for Simon, he confronted a growing mob, some mounted, some on foot. Not that one in twenty understood the issues of Ole Tuck's murder, though its aftermath had excited them to the pitch of colts before a storm. Besides, they had all the information that mattered: a Negro had shot a white man. It was Jeems they wanted. Somebody had already cooked up a filthy lie about Felix and Jeems' wife and was spreading it through the crowd. 'Get her too!' the cry was rising. Men in the front ranks were all arguing at once to Dan Armstrong, though he hadn't said a word. He started to push his way through them, to go on his own mission, but he did not. He looked over their heads not listening to them, then he waved them away like so many aggravating flies. Turning, he stumped himself on the bench before the drug store and quieted them down by simply making more noise than they did. His thick hair was as dark as yours then and in the cold it stood high around his forehead.

" 'Listen to me first,' he told them as the hush swept them. 'Listen to me and then maybe I'll waste some time listening to you. You want to hunt that nigger down?'

"Cries of 'Yes, yes!' and 'Let's go get him, Dan!'

" 'Well, let's hunt him down then!'

More shouts. The crowd fanned in and out.

" 'But listen to me!' They calmed. He spoke lower. 'You think you know a lot about this, but the truth of the business is, you don't know a damn thing about it. Remember that, if it's lynching you're after, and let it rest on your conscience. If you haven't got no conscience and it's lynching you still want, and you get there ahead of me, that nigger's blood be on your hands. But I'm warning you fair, if I get there first, that nigger's going to jail without a finger laid on him and there's going to be fair dealings. Felix McKie ain't dead and he can still talk, and there's going to be fair dealings. Furthermore—let me get through with this here speech, confound you!—furthermore, I heard somebody frothing at the bit to get at Jeems' woman, laying on her some farfetched concoction of iniquity straight out of your own heads. John Bramlett? You here?'

" 'Here, Dan.'

" 'Nora Nell cooks for your wife, don't she?'

" 'Yeah, Dan.'

" 'Been cooking for her for nigh six years, ain't she?'

" 'Yeah, Dan.'

" 'Good nigger, ain't she?'

" 'I got no complaints.'

" 'Good steady, church-going nigger, ain't she?'

" ' That's right, Dan.'

" 'You lynch her, I'll lynch you—all of you!' Shouts of laughter. 'I'll string you up on the bridge side by side! And the ones that ain't worth the trouble, like old George Thurston there, I'll put you in a croker sack and drown you in the creek.' More laughter. 'That's all I got to say.'

"He pushed his way through them toward the court house fence and his horse. He had put them in good humor, but he knew better than they how temporary the mood would be. There was a basic disagreement between him and the town. They liked him, respected him, but they figured him unsound. The county's rural population had cast the deciding vote for him in the sheriff's race.

"While they went off with guns and whisky to beat the bushes and hollows and get riled up at him among themselves so that by nightfall when his biggest trial came they faced him angry and not to be teased any more, he was off at a rack for the railroad station across the creek, because he bore in mind that Jeems was half-white and wasn't to be besieged in any cotton house or run out of the back door of any deserted cabin. Sure enough, the station agent reported seeing a man, black or white, he couldn't tell, creep up on the right-of-way just beyond the trestle and swing on to the three-forty freight heading east. The station agent's pleasant afternoon of dozing by the red hot iron stove was lost that day. Dan Armstrong set him down and put him to sending messages to every town and pig track down the line until his fingers were stiff on the key. About two hours after sundown the final message came through.

"Strange how Jeems died. Strange and pathetic. He had gone back to Kosciusko where he came from in the first place, got wild drunk in a Negro café, deliberately picked a fight with an old enemy and never drawing his gun again, plunged toward the knife that killed him. A clean slash with a crab apple switch. He knew, you see, without any argument of mind what Tarsus would do to him and, unable to find a pattern of action toward black or white race because he was neither, he knew he could not face the consequences of the ambiguous deed he had done, firing like a white man, terror-stricken like a Negro. They put him in a wooden coffin at Kosciusko and shipped him back to Tarsus. The station agent's son who bore the message to Dan Armstrong up town had taken care to spread the word as he went and long before train time Tarsus was pouring across the bridge toward the station.

"Early as they were, Dan Armstrong was there before them. He had busied himself in a variety of ways since he left the station that afternoon. For one thing, he had procured a wagon to haul the coffin and he was sitting in it now, calm as you please, the leather lines slack in his hands. For another, he had gone and found Nora Nell and the baby, because he knew the rising temper of the people, deprived of Jeems, might turn on her. He found her late and there was no place where he trusted her to be safe, so he put her and the baby in the wagon with him. She sat on the floor of the wagon bed, covering the child, her head bent down below the railing.

"Stopping at some odd moment during the rampant course of that day's violence, Dan Armstrong had done something else which takes first rank among the indices of his character. He had scribbled out his resignation as sheriff and shoved it under the locked door of the county clerk's office.

"He told no one. The paper would not be found till morning. Tell me how in the main stream of action, the man had time to weigh on delicate balances the conflicting calls of duty and honor, right and wrong, see his course clearly, decide and act upon the decision, while all the time as though some second man was making an identical shadow with his own, he was thinking and acting in the terms of the outer emergency?

"But perhaps I do wrong to set a man like Dan Armstrong into a common framework. Perhaps to renounce office and political ambition was no struggle at all, when his code demanded it. Not that he felt, as some might think, that he was duty-bound to arrest Felix McKie for young Wills' death. No, that was a challenged fight, over a definite grievance, face to face, and both men armed. But I wonder if he had determined to follow Felix's plea the minute there was time and 'get Simon.' Certainly if that was to be the course, he would no longer hold office.

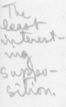
The least interest my supposition.

"You know the rest. You know how word spread like fire among the people that Jeems was not dead at all, that Dan Armstrong was cheating them this way. You know how they hurried, arguing among themselves, shouting at him, clinging to the methodically moving wagon, down the course of the road, how they gathered in a close-packed mob ahead of him on the iron bridge, blocking his way, while more and more came running down the long curving hill from town, shivering in the rising wind that whipped the torch flames in the sporadic silences of voice with a sound like blowing cloth. You know how he railed at them and denounced them and held them silent still after he ceased to speak, while he turned and wrenched the boards of the coffin apart with a crow bar, and, waiting dumb, they all heard the nails scream out of the wood and heard Jeems' baby begin to fret in its mother's terror-stilled arms.

"You know how he commanded the population of Tarsus, Mississippi, that night, something no man has ever done before or since, and how he made them against their will, by the sheer dominance of his tall frame, by the simple intensity of a simple command—made them file by the coffin and look in upon the face of the dead.

"The wild inconsequence of it, indigenous, more than a shade comical, considering that the whole role of Jeems began in a mistake and ended like a funeral in church where the congregation march by the open coffin after an oration on the deceased, in this case an angry and earthy harangue!

"And you know how it was over then, how they never laid a finger on Nora Nell, how they went calmly on up the hill, remembering how cold it was, eager to get home and build a fire.

"But there's one thing you don't know. Simon Gerrard was in the mob that night. God only knows why he came. He had taken cover after the shooting, jumped out the window of the chancery clerk's office, in fact. He was heard to stammer that he would get Felix McKie for it, by God, but somebody pointed out that he couldn't very well shoot a blind man and on that he was quick to acquiesce. He was mortally afraid of Dan Armstrong. But when the commotion started he had to be in on it. The Gerrards have always had to be there. They never take a side, they never put in a word, but they've got to see what's going on. When the long procession around the coffin began to pass Dan Armstrong and Dan Armstrong's pistol, Simon saw his hopes of mingling with the crowd melt under his feet. He tried to get away. The people blocked him, swept him forward. Dan Armstrong marked him. 'You, too, Simon Gerrard!' he cried. And Simon came. My father was near to him in line. There was a moment of perfect stillness, he said, when Simon's turn came and Simon stood by the wagon face to face with Dan Armstrong. Simon was scarcely over twenty then; he was pudgy and his round frightened face looked pitifully young.

"Dan Armstrong stood full height above him and slapped the pistol carelessly against his lean thigh. Simon shook to his eyebrows.

"'Why aren't you home with your dead?' Dan Armstrong demanded.

"Simon's jaw trembled to speak.

"'Go home!' Dan Armstrong thundered at him. 'Go home and sit up with the dead.'

"Simon went home. He did not walk, he ran. It was nearly a month before he put his head out the door again. They even told that the wife he had just married brought his meals to him in a barricaded room. Just as people were getting worn out with speculating about whether Dan Armstrong would call Simon out or not, Miss Henrietta Gerrard ran true to the form she's held ever since and collapsed from nervous fatigue. Old Colonel Mathison, her father, got worried and stopped Dan Armstrong on the street one day.

"'What you going to do about Si, Dan?' he inquired as casually as though asking about the price of hogs. Folks reported that the colonel didn't much care if Dan did take a gun to his son-in-law.

"'Haven't got time to waste it on nubbins, Colonel,' Dan said.

"So what kept him from it, we never knew. He did not try to run for office again after he resigned. He came into Tarsus less often than before. It sometimes seemed that he scorned Simon, scorned the land he held, scorned Tarsus, too. Or perhaps it was some subtle refinement of pity that kept his hand down, some perception of the inconsequential nature of circumstances, that made him see young Simon Gerrard as the victim of events. Dan never really wanted all that

Walston land, you know. It was Kinloch Walston he loved and with his death and Felix McKie's blindness all 'within one month, he crossed quite suddenly what most of us creep gradually and pain-lessly through—the dividing line that blocks the old days behind us, the bridge that burns behind at every step, the quiet river that leaps to flood tide when the bank is gained. There is no returning.

"The lovable and humorous kindness that we have come to regard in him as the essence of his undisputed manhood, began its ripening after January 20, 1899. Soon Simon opened the general merchandise store where he later forced all his tenantry to trade, and a few months later Dan Armstrong strolled into the store one morning and passed the time of day with Simon. So he seemed to have forgiven the past for what it brought to them both, and perhaps he really did.

"How indeed will you condemn him for not wishing to continue longer on an already too bloody path? Those days were dead to him; they had ended in a blaze of glory with Tarsus at his feet. As if in echo to his state of mind, Walston Cedars burned one night. Simon had planned to move into it soon, but Lance—or was it Mary Helen? —Mary Helen was getting born then, so the Gerrards never lived there. The Negroes had tales that Ole Tuck's ghost set fire to it; they talk about him still and not one of them would ever move into this house.

"But what did Dan Armstrong sit and think about when Simon Gerrard let the sawmills in and the big trees he and Kinloch Walston and Felix McKie had hunted among and camped under and used as landmarks came down faster and faster until the hills were bare to the weather and to the eye? What did he say to himself when Simon Gerrard commenced construction of the monstrosity whose balconied turrets crown our square like something Tennyson might have de-scribed during an attack of acute indigestion?

"I believe with all my heart that he is a great man, but what can we say? All he saved, after all, was a Negro woman and her child.

"He tried to save you, you see, waiting until you were wise enough

131

and old enough to understand what he did and why, and when you put things off they grow harder and time springs between the witness and the event. Perhaps he still plans to tell you someday. But the unscrupulous of the earth will always defeat him. Not because he does not know them for what they are or their deeds for what they are after the deeds are done, but because he is too great and shy a gentleman to force the measure of himself upon the future.

"I am the unscrupulous. I picked at my father for years before his death until the tale was out, swearing never to tell you. One rainy afternoon when Cherry Bell was in a drunken stupor, I amused myself reading the letters she kept locked in her dresser drawer. Now that the itch of the years is relieved and I have told you at last, I feel damned and sick and very old and I wish to hell for something, I don't know what."

It had grown quite dark, and after a long silence when he spoke again, Randall's voice was hoarse and low.

"I have thought of what it is like, after all," he said. "I told you that I could not place these people, this crime, but just now as I stopped talking I saw it for the first time, all of a piece. It happened in Tarsus, of course, but in Tarsus, oddly enough, at that unimaginable time before the name Gerrard was spoken here. It happened at the old Delbrook house, nothing but a bare hill now, out yonder way from town. Yankee soldiers did it—you've heard the story. But it is too easy to say 'soldiers' and stop there, not going on to say 'men.' Men then—I say it—the men stopped at the Delbrook house and spent the night and ate breakfast. There was not much to offer, but the Delbrooks fed them, even beginning to lose their first fear and pride and talk a little with these men, asking where they were from and were they kin to so-and-so.

"After breakfast Grierson got up from the table and went into the kitchen, his men following him. He put his pipe in his mouth and asked for a light. The old man—old Delbrook—took a little piece of fat pine and lighted it at the cook stove and handed it to Grierson.

132

X

That was when Grierson gave the order and before Delbrook could realize what they were up to, could cry out, the strange men in his house took the extra kindling and heaped it into the firebox and all over the stove, so fast that Grierson had just finished lighting his pipe when they were done. He tossed the little piece of blazing pine on top the pile, already turning to go, waiting impatiently at the door just long enough for the smoke to begin rushing up the dry frame walls— it was no fine house, but old—and for the spurts of red to follow, drawing upward from the kindling. Then he told them to let Delbrook loose and they all went out to the horses, while the old man ran to the well, shouting to his family to come and help at the windlass which creaked slow and contrary as usual.

"But Grierson was sure. The men mounted and he rode ahead of them down the hill and out through Tarsus to the south, with the smoke climbing into the clear August sky, and if he ever looked back, nobody saw him. But behind him the house burned; they couldn't stop the fire. In a very little while all the family could do was stand out in the front yard and look at it, unbelievingly, almost with curiosity, burning in broad daylight.

"Do you see, Kinloch? Do you see?"

"I thought of that once, too," said Kinloch. "Once last fall."

"Sometimes," said Randall Gibson, "you amaze me."

133

$\mathbf{D}$AN ARMSTRONG, coming down the dark path for home, stopped to listen. There was someone running on the path ahead, running, yes, toward him. He stood at the top of a rise. Below him, the path broadened, crossed the branch, and went on straight up the next hill. Here the earth was dark and firm. It was getting cooler now and the smell of dew lay heavy in the wood.

There she came, running faster down the hill, for what reason he did not know except that she did not run as though she was afraid, but long and smooth, and so as not to stumble looking down at her flat-heel shoes striking the ground. Her blouse, swan-white and moving against the dark wood, seemed almost to shine. He smiled and waited, because he knew that most things can wait to be got to and are perhaps easier for the patience. Then he liked the sight of her free young running. He liked to see her for once without her brother, because together—though he did not speak of it—they would seem to him like two feline creatures, making him and others around them act as clumsy and honest as good dogs.

He was reminded pleasantly now of one day long before the brother came, when she was new there and to be wondered at. That was the day that John Henry, Kinloch's part-Angus bull, got between them and the gate. She had gone to meet Kinloch in the field and when they headed for home, there was John Henry, grumbling and circling a little, on his mettle. They should have steered a wide path around the pasture, of course, and come up the far way, but instead Kinloch shoved her behind him and catching his hoe near the blade, swung it toward John Henry like a baseball bat. Dan hurried to open the lot gate. He noticed her watching Kinloch, who was moving steadily ahead all the while the muscles gathered and leaped out along his arms with the swing of the hoe. Her head was tilted back. He knew she was proud. She gave him a second level of feeling about the business, something he did not often entertain. She made him feel that in addition to driving a bull back through a gate it had got out of, which was a thing necessary to be done, that Kinloch principally, but he and the bull too, were all busy doing something for Ruth.

That was the woman in her and it was all right. But what in her was sending her at a run through the wood?

She jumped the branch without a pause and was on the hill with him.

"Daughter," he called from above. He did not want to frighten her. She drew up sharply, chin up and eyes wide, searching. If she put him in mind of a colt, it would be a colt just grown, out of the long-legged stage where the coat and mane mat easily, just into the sleek trim look, the first day of it, in fact, when you look out and see how the pasture which has seemed so enormously to surround the young thing has suddenly shrunk to no space at all, when the flying hooves cover it end to end and the fence stands scarcely breast-high against the gleaming hide.

She climbed up to him. "What's the matter?" he asked.

"Nothing," she said, catching breath. "I just came to meet you."

Touched, he caught her close to him. "I thought surely the patter-rollers were after you."

"You thought what?"

"I thought something was after you."

"Oh, no." She gave him her arm across the branch. Her skin was wet from running. "It's cooled off so, hasn't it?"

"You just running to be running, I reckon."

"I guess so."

"Kinloch come?"

"Not yet."

"How about the brother?"

"He's gone over to Justin's."

"So you were all by yourself."

"Yes."

He did not press to ask her whether she had been afraid.

NINE

EARLY after dinner that Thursday afternoon, Elinor stood by the staircase in the hall of Simon Gerrard's house and squalled for Miss Henrietta until the roots of her hair were damp from the exertion. There was no answer. For a minute she stared morosely up the ornate banister and seemed to see beyond the many upper rooms flanking the little dark halls which ran among them, other stairs into smaller rooms, turrets and the like, how much she could never get straight, nor cared to.

She shrugged and poked out her lower lip in a characteristic gesture of dismissal and, walking into the living room, flopped down into an overstuffed chair and kicked off her shoes. When the ash of her cigarette grew heavy she reached out for the smoking stand, but her fingertips just missed the handle and the ashes fell to the floor beside a torn slip, a pair of eyebrow tweezers, two bottles of red fingernail polish, odorous and gummy at the caps, and one white and blue striped play shoe.

She had lighted another cigarette from the stub when Justin walked in from the hall, barefoot and naked except for step-ins. She had a wad of nondescript clothes in one hand and seemed to have some vague notion of holding it in front of her breasts.

She was halfway across the room before she noticed her sister-in-law.

"Oh, Elinor. What are you doing over here?"

"Act like you didn't hear me screaming my head off."

"I was in the tub."

"There's supposed to be a package here for me. Miss Henrietta called yesterday. Said Simon brought it home. Mistake. Too hot to talk even."

137

"Isn't it?" Justin sat opposite her, dropping the clothes on the floor. "I just took a bath and look." She rolled dirt from her bare shoulder and watched the process reflectively.

"Date?"

"Uh-huh."

"Scott?"

"Uh-huh."

"Thank God that's one thing I don't have to fool with anymore. Not saying anything for married life, but thank God I'm not having to dress for a date."

Justin shot her a glance. "Tell me."

"I am telling you. It's what I'm doing."

"All right. You're telling me. Gimme a cigarette." She caught the pack and settled deeper into the chair. "God, this stuff is sticking me." She clawed at her back where the upholstery had rubbed, looked about and considered moving, then settled back again. She became fascinated by the sight of her breasts, touched her fingers to them gently and laughed. "Elinor, you remember how I used to run everybody crazy so scared I'd be flat?"

"Well, nobody's going to believe that now," said Elinor, caustically. She would have liked an inch or two more herself.

"I told Scott last night. He thought it was funny."

"Since you discussed your bosom last night, what will you find to talk about tonight?"

Justin stretched her lovely, golden tan body, completely unabashed. "Oh, there's enough left, I guess, before we get into politics and the weather."

Elinor's eyes went over her, head to toe. "God," she said at last. "Justin, you're acting like a damn fool."

"You're just jealous and you know it."

"You'll find out who's jealous when that little blue coupe leaves you with dust all over your sun tan oil."

"I'll think about that when and if it happens, thank you. Where are you going. Not leaving. I hope."

"I came to see about—" The front door banged. "Well."

Justin made a motion toward the clothes. "Well, say who it is, Elinor."

"Simon. What's he doing home at this hour? Oh, Thursday, of course. And Lance."

"Elinor? Hello, Elinor," Simon boomed from the door.

"Stay out of here," Justin called over the back of the chair.

"Si-*mon!*" Miss Henrietta's voice streamed down the stair.

"Lord help me," said Elinor, in a monotone to herself. "She was here all the time. Let me yell my head off, let him shut the front door — Stay out of here, Lance! Justin's naked as a jay bird."

"Elinor, I've seen Justin naked more times than it would do to talk about, and right now I want a cigarette."

Elinor called past her husband. "Simon, tell Miss Henrietta I'm here for the package she— Oh, my God. She's got him now and what's the use?"

"Not any use at all right away," Lance said. He threw the match down, then kicked it aside and sat on the floor. "Mama's after him about getting some kind of old statue at the Gibsons' moved over here on the lawn."

"Statue?" Justin asked, shrugging into a brassiere and slip. "What statue?"

"You know," said Lance. "That old marble thing over in Miss Cherry Bell's front yard."

"Oh, *that* thing." Justin's face took on the look of an animal with its ears laid back. "She's going to move that thing in the front yard? Like it wasn't enough to have this hideous house sitting up here for everybody to laugh at. Like it wasn't enough to have to go through asking people inside it. Now I'll have to drag them past that thing— it's awful. Mama! Ma-ma!" Elinor's calling was nothing compared to Justin's.

Miss Henrietta came. "My precious baby," she said, hurrying toward Justin. "What on earth?"

"That ugly old thing," fretted Justin. "That hideous statue. Mama you can't, you just can't, bring it over here. It's worse than the night you got out that set of mustache cups for dinner. It's humiliating, it's humiliating to me."

"Why darling," said Miss Henrietta in her thin wisp of a voice. "The statue is of Italian marble, way over a hundred years old. It was brought straight to Tarsus from Italy."

"Well, thank God, somebody had some sense about it. The Italians didn't want it; they had some sense."

"What the hell has the thing been doing in the Gibsons' garden all these years?" Lance asked.

"You'll have to ask your father," said Miss Henrietta. On her frail, lace-trimmed bosom her nose-glasses swung loosely on their metal chain. She zipped them back close to the little black button on her shoulder and smiled wanly. "Hello, Elinor, my dear."

Elinor forced a smile.

"Ask your father what?" Simon said. He came into the room biting the tip from a cigar.

Justin was still intent on her mother. Active, almost sturdy she looked now, the long lines of her figure under the clinging slip dwindled her mother's frailty into something absurd. Her bare toes pressed against the floor until streaks of white ran across them. "You're such a fool!" she cried. "A fool! Everytime anybody tries to say anything important you get vague. You won't listen—you won't ever listen. You won't listen—"

"You said that," Lance remarked. "She won't listen."

"What's all this?" Simon asked. "Who's a fool, Justin?"

"Not you, Simon," Elinor said. "Not this time."

Simon settled heavily in the chair Justin had left. He cast a glance at Elinor and chuckled. "Not me? Well, that's all right then. Go get some clothes on, Justin."

"Papa, are you going to let her move that God-awful thing in our front yard?"

"Talk to your mother, Justin, she's the one that wants it."

"What the hell do you think I've been trying to do for the last half-hour?" She turned back to Miss Henrietta.

"If you only knew how it upsets me to hear my baby use such language," sighed Miss Henrietta.

"Oh, God," said Justin.

"The fact is," said Elinor, "Miss Henrietta never would have thought of the statue in another hundred years if Scott Shaffer hadn't told her what a 'puffeckly marr-velous wuk of adt' it is. I heard him say it, not two days ago."

"Oh," said Justin. "Really? Maybe it's not the one I'm thinking about."

"Yeah," said Elinor, "you probably got it mixed up with the Confederate soldier's statue in front of the court house. That's the only other statue in town. You just got confused."

"Justin, *go* and get some clothes on!" Simon caught the chair arms and made a start at her. "Now," he said with finality as she thudded from the room. "Worse than coping with a balky mule from the front end."

"I *said*," Lance repeated. "If that statue is I-talian, and antique and star of the east and a joy forever, what's it been doing in the Gibson yard all these years?"

Elinor relinquished her chair to Miss Henrietta who accepted it with a murmur and a glance toward the ceiling so weary it seemed that she wished to impart how heavy life weighed on her.

"You'll have to ask your father, dear."

"What's that?" Simon asked from behind the newspaper.

Lance went through his question again, this time dogged and profane.

"Henrietta knows perfectly well why that is," Simon said. "The statue was part of the Gerrard estate from the beginning. Miss Cherry Bell was what you might call a good friend of the Walston fellow's.

He wanted her to have it, I understand. We hated to deprive the lady."

Everybody knew who "we" meant. Simon habitually referred to his business dealings in that manner. It was Young Wills he meant, though in later years it had taken on the ring of royalty.

"Like hell," said Elinor. "You never hated to deprive anybody, Simon, much less a lady."

Simon laughed.

"Miss Cherry Bell LaGarde," remarked Miss Henrietta, "was hardly what one would call a lady, Simon. I knew her—as a girl."

"Yeah, I know," said Lance, "Miss Cherry Bell and her carryings-on. Drinks like a fish. Dopes like a Chinaman."

"Anyway, lady or not, you're depriving her now, ain't you, Simon?" Elinor pursued.

"Hell, I don't want the thing. You can't do nothing with a half-ton chunk of marble. It's Henrietta who's depriving—"

"Simon," Miss Henrietta said as firmly as possible. "I have thought this through thoroughly and my conscience is thoroughly clear. Thoroughly. We are depriving no one. It is she who has deprived us. Through the years."

"It's a crying shame," said Elinor. "How she's depriving you. It's a wonder to me you've made it without the benefit of that statue."

Simon laughed again and flung ashes on the floor. "Oh deprivation! Oh degradation!" he cried heartily. "Oh hush, Henrietta, you know it's the truth."

"It isn't fair," sniffed Miss Henrietta. "It isn't fair for persons who don't understand to step in and criticize."

"Okay, okay," said Elinor. "I don't understand. I'm sorry. It just seems to me that poor old lady— Well, hell, what do I care?"

"Oh, Lord help us, Mama, let it alone!" Lance said. "Justin hates it, or did until somebody mentioned Scott Shaffer, Elinor is bitching about, Papa doesn't care and God knows I don't except I figure everybody is better off just leaving things alone."

"Lance, what are you doing over here?" Elinor asked.

"God, I don't know. What are you doing over here?"

"There was something—oh, the package, the package. Miss Henrietta, I'm sorry, I tell you. I'm sorry I opened my mouth. Listen, there's supposed to be a package here for me. You know, package? String, paper, stamps, mail?"

Miss Henrietta gestured wordlessly. Elinor glanced at the three of them, observed in what amused or offended or non-committal manner they said nothing, shrugged and walked into the hallway. The package was on the phone table. Been a snake, would have bit me, she thought.

"Oh, Elinor! You're going to *open* it!" The childish cry came from the top of the stairs. Justin leaned over the banister. She used the forbiddingly dark interplay of wall, rugs, tapestries and woodwork as a momentary background for her shining blondness and for the bright dress she wore that was printed in great tropical flowers. Then she scorned the dimness—she had never liked it, though it had time and again driven visiting children into inventing extravagant games about castles, outlaws and the like—and ran down stairs in a way to make most people cry out for fear she might fall. Elinor eyed her silently. Lance was right. Why, for Christ's sake, couldn't they leave you alone? But you couldn't open your own packages without one of them helping you with the string, reaching over to touch before you could get a hand in. Lance had said it, but he didn't know everything he had said. He was the same way.

"Oh, a negligee, Elinor! Oh, what a gorgeous color blue! No, no, it's a nightgown! Look—"

"Whatever it is, Justin Gerrard, if you don't turn loose you'll not be in any shape to see Scott Shaffer tonight." There was real temper in her voice.

Justin shied. "I just wanted to see," she complained. "What size is it?"

Elinor saw how her own hands, refolding the material, looked suddenly larger. Was it the wearing heat this worst summer of all, or was it the drip-drop of all the seasons, days and hours since she had come to Tarsus six years ago? Was it the Dudley in her breaking out? She had come close to striking Justin, of that she was certain.

She went to the door of the living room. "Lance!" She felt like ordering him again. Most of the time she didn't want to put out the effort. "Let's go, Lance."

"What was it, Elinor?" Miss Henrietta always came out very distinctly on the final syllable of that name.

"A gown. Aunt Ella sent it from California for my birthday. Two sizes too small and a month too late."

"Oh, was it too small?" Justin breathed. "Oh, Elinor—"

"I'm giving it to Ruth," Elinor said shortly. "Blue looks like hell on you, Justin." She walked to the middle of the floor and stepped emphatically into her discarded shoes.

Justin sulked, moving across the room to nowhere in particular. "All right, give it to Ruth and see if I care." Abruptly, she giggled. "And Kinloch's going to tear it to pieces first night she wears it."

Lance looked at Simon and they both laughed. They seemed to take a pride in Justin now as if they were noticing her for the first moment as a real person. Elinor stamped her foot into her shoe, but she had no effect. Miss Henrietta lifted her tired head out of her hands and murmured, "Don't be vulgar, darling."

But the two men had her; the little thread of humor had looped the three of them. Simon sat, the cigar poised before his heavy lips; Lance, mulling on his amusement, swung in the attitude of half-rising.

Justin giggled again. "Don't think I don't know what I'm talking about either," she said.

"Justin!" cried Miss Henrietta.

"Honey," Simon reproved in amiable curiosity. "What could you mean?"

"Oh, shut up, shut up," said Elinor.

144

"Aw, shut up yourself," said Lance, eyeing Justin with approval. "Come on. You started it. Finish it. If you don't finish it, so help me—" He made for her in a lazy, clumsy lunge. She side-stepped, giggling.

"Kinloch Armstrong, you mean? Oh, he just made a couple of passes at me one night."

"Tore your nightgown, huh?" Lance punched playfully at her face.

She caught his arm. "Strapless evening dress, thank you. The zipper held."

"What did you say to him?" Lance asked.

"What did I say? I said, Listen here, Kinloch Armstrong. Who do you think you're fooling with?"

"Did you?" Simon's shoulders shook. "Did you say that?"

"Sure. Don't believe it, ask him."

"It's a lie! A lie!" Elinor raged.

"For Christ's sake, Elinor," Lance said, in high spirits. "What do you care? You'll make me jealous, don't watch out."

"I don't care," said Elinor. "I don't give a God damn. I just know you, every damn one of you, and I can smell you when you're lying and you're lying most of the time, just like you're lying right now, Justin Gerrard."

"By God, Elinor, I don't care if you are my sister-in-law—"

"Justin!" cried Miss Henrietta.

"Oh, my God," said Lance. "Everybody was just joking, Elinor. Good Lord—"

"Well, by God, I—" Justin began.

"Justin! Lancelot! Your language! Correct them, Simon. Correct your children."

Simon drew on his cigar. "God damn it," he said, still amiable. "Don't you hear your mother? Quit cussing."

Lance and Justin reeled with laughter, children again. Elinor stood glaring. Lance saw her at last. "Let's go. We got to go," he announced. "Perk up, Mama. We were just carrying on about the old statue. We'll let you put it on the front porch if you want to. Won't we, Papa?"

Simon grunted. "Sure," he said. "Then I can hang my hat on its fanny."

Miss Henrietta sighed, clasping her son's hand. "Whatever I want," she half-whispered, "Simon, you children too, make it so ridiculous, ridiculous."

"There," soothed Lance. "I forgot it was from Italy. I just forgot."

"And it was Mr. Shaffer himself who said what a shame to leave such a lovely thing where the weeds grew around it. He said I would be doing the community a service—"

"Before God," said Simon, "Henrietta, I'll attend to it first thing in the morning if I have to tear the Gibsons' fence down and move it with my bare hands. But just do please have pity and don't say statue to me one more time. In the morning, do you understand? First thing in the morning."

"Yes, Simon." She held tight to Lance's hand, gazing up into his face as though from the bottom of a well, and that was because she was near-sighted. "My son, my baby boy. And Elinor. Is everything going all right, you say?"

"Yes'm," said Elinor, too loudly.

"Then hurry back. You're always welcome, you know. Justin, tell them good-bye."

Justin gave a little squeal. She ran toward the fire place and pulled something from among the tangle of stuff Elinor had noticed earlier. "My fingernail polish," she cried, holding the bottle aloft. "My new. I lost it."

Elinor had an almost overwhelming desire to know what shade the polish was, but her face had settled more than ever into its accustomed mask and she went out of the house without a word.

Miss Henrietta pulled aside the draperies of the bay window. There they went, down the steep winding steps, six sets in all, that lowered past the three terraces, terminating in a wide arc of pillared stone on the corner of the town square. They were passing the second terrace.

"Don't they make a fine-looking couple?" she inquired with a glance

146

at Simon, who did not answer, another at Justin, who was absorbed with her nails and polish on the sofa and did not answer either. Only Miss Henrietta felt the pressure of the silence and was compelled to consider her own question most politely. "I declare, they certainly do."

This family scene develops well.

TEN

"SON," said Dan Armstrong out of the darkness, "in the first place it all happened so long ago. Randall did some good guessing, all right enough, but it's a lot of confounded impudence nonetheless. Why did Si Gerrard show up on the bridge? Why did Jeems go back to Kosciusko? He went back to Kosciusko because he went back to Kosciusko. Impudence, impudence. And thirty-five years later, too."

"But the facts are right," said Kinloch, from the darkness, from his old place on the steps.

"The facts are right," said Dan Armstrong.

"The facts say that Kinloch Walston was no more crazy than you or I."

"Most folks knew that, time they got to thinking about it. There are other folks in Tarsus can figure besides Randall Gibson. Never make him believe it, but it's so."

"The facts say that you let Simon Gerrard live."

"Son," said Dan Armstrong, "it is no light thing to kill a man and a young man at that. If Si Gerrard had done me great treacherous wrong, I would have killed him for it. If Si had killed Ole Tuck or shot Felix or at least been the one who snatched away my rightful land, I would have called him out. But Si Gerrard just followed Young Wills, he was just on hand."

"He was a Gerrard."

"Gerrard!" Dan Armstrong cried. Kinloch could dimly see the big, age-bent hands gripping the chair as though his father would pull up straight to stand ten feet tall. "Gerrard." He sank back. "It means nothing. Then it meant less than nothing. Now— Through the years I have argued with Felix, You cannot hate a man, you cannot kill a man because of his last name."

148

"You say it, Father, but you don't believe it. If it was daylight you couldn't look at me and say it."

"Son, son. Listen. A McKie can do wrong. A Walston can do wrong. An Armstrong can do wrong."

"Then what made you say, when Lance Gerrard drowned my dog and I fought him, No Gerrard can lick an Armstrong?"

"Because in fair fight with clear wrong done no man living will ever lick an Armstrong. I say it again."

"But it is in you, Father. It is in you. If you had meant no man, you would have said it. You meant Gerrard and you said Gerrard. Say you meant Gerrard."

"Have it your way then. I meant Gerrard. But I did wrong to say Gerrard to you. Son, when you were a little thing hardly walking to the field to me I saw you would be living your life out here. One day you climbed a bob-wire fence to bring me some water. You got your pants caught and no sooner pulled them loose than it happened again. Loose again, caught again—it went on for quite a spell. I was resting by an oak sprout not five yards away and I laughed at you till my sides ached, but it got me, too, right hard the minute you made it through with not a drop of water spilled and looked up quick as a puppy when I called. I said to Sally that night, I said, Sally, the boy will make a man and just saying that, no more, makes it a hard enough row to plow. I said, Sally, we mustn't load him down with our burdens and mistakes. There'll be time to tell when he is old and settled as we are. We mustn't bring him up to feel cheated by Marvin Strong and a Memphis lawyer and the Gerrards. It wasn't my kind of fight and it won't be his kind of fight either.

"So I never told you, and I reckon what you're saying now all adds up to my doing wrong in not telling you. I didn't want to bring you up to feel like the underdog. First place, no dog acts as foolish because no dog hates as hard as the underdog. Second place, you really wouldn't be the underdog, you just might grow up feeling like it, hating like it."

149

"I know, Father, but just the same you wasted time. Underdog or not, I don't know—*they* would say it, maybe, I would die first—but talking about underdog is a waste of time. Because the main thing you fought against for yourself and me too was hate and how far you went towards licking it for yourself I'm not one to say, but as for me, keeping the past out was not enough. I saw them and I never needed to know about all the other."

"Not going so far as to say I've set myself to like them," said the old man. "Been surprised if you liked them. They go against the grain. Always will."

"Liked them? I hate them, Father. I have hated them all my life."

The taut pronouncement perversely drew a lighter voice from Dan Armstrong. "Time was I hated them. But blest if I didn't get tired bothering with it. It wasn't my kind of fight, this law swindling."

"I hate them," Kinloch repeated, freer now that he had said it at last. "I hate their thick necks and their smooth hands. I hate the way they set their heels on the ground walking. I hate them coming and going. One of the first things I remember was Lance Gerrard putting a nickel on the counter at the grocery store for some candy, and I hated the way he put the nickel down. One time Simon Gerrard spit out of the side of his mouth when I happened to be coming down the street and it made the dust spatter on my foot. I shook all over, thinking maybe his spit had touched me. Yesterday Justin Gerrard bought some gas ahead of me. 'Charge it,' she said to J.T. like he worked around the yard. And I hated her."

"You see," said Dan Armstrong, still light of voice. "It's like I tell you. It takes up so confounded much time."

And Ruth! The thought made him stand up straight as if to go right to her, then he waited, thinking, while the heat lightning quivered in the west and a strange sort of wind from no direction rose up under trees and bushes, pushing their lowest branches upward, as though the heat had gone on too long and the earth was heaving once and no more like a tired animal. She will understand now, he thought.

"Then there is the daughter for you," Dan Armstrong said. "She will come out a fine one."

It annoyed Kinloch that his father should think of her at the same time he did, yet it seemed in a different sense.

"What do you mean, come out a fine one?"

"You don't need all this. She will come out ahead."

"I don't know what you're talking about, Father."

"I'm talking about she was the start of it this time, running with Lance's wife. And you a grown man. The child must have her friends. Wasn't she the start of it now? Maybe not, maybe not." He coughed and in an ordinary way reached into his back pocket for chewing tobacco.

"I don't know," said Kinloch. He would have wanted to speak of her further; they had not talked of her since before his marriage, but even the mention of her name, the clear, simple, uninflected sound of it, commanded their separate loyalties.

"It's not the land you want, is it?" Dan Armstrong continued. His worn knife blade made a sliver of light in the dark, cutting through a corner of the tobacco. "All that land. I never had any use for it. So I told Felix. Like the fellow tried to give me a smoke house full of hog meat if I'd come out for him in the county clerk's race. Wouldn't venture to offer me money. 'Wouldn't be starving with all that hog meat,' I told him, 'for a fact. But then wasn't planning on starving anyway.' We got enough land to live on. There's a little twenty-acre strip twixt here and the upper branch would come in handy for pasture, but by and large there's enough."

"I don't want the land," said Kinloch. "What I want is Simon Gerrard. Simon Gerrard is a thief and a liar and I want it known, known to the world and known to his children."

"Son," Dan cried, bringing his walking stick down hard on the chair arms. "The world already knows Si Gerrard backwards and forwards, A to Z. As for tampering with his children—that's sinful, plain sinful."

151

"You're trying to tell me that's enough for you," said Kinloch with heat. "You're trying to tell me it's enough to sit here in your rocking chair and feel like you're on the right side while Simon Gerrard lives in his fine house and runs his fine automobiles and raises a bunch of snobs who wouldn't be caught dead with their hands in any of that dirt that's paid for every thing they've cried for since they were in diapers. Or speaking to one of those ragged tenants, black and white, who have paid hard cash or hard labor to Simon Gerrard's store for everything from overpriced work shirts to overpriced clevises. While all the time it goes on, one generation after the other, things the good people owned and had power and influence by, being used, used by them for nothing that's good, for nothing on earth really but to lord it over the ones who didn't steal and lie to get it. Has it been enough just to know you are right, all these years?"

"I'm not studying about enough," his father said. "I'm saying we've got along. Without giving too much time studying about that young fat boy, Si Gerrard."

Oh, yes, you licked him once, thought Kinloch, and you're remembering it right now. You licked him out in front of everybody. They all saw him shake at the sight of you and they all knew how silly he looked hiding from you for weeks on end. That's why you can call him "that young fat boy" and laugh a little bit under your breath. I've licked Lance and I've licked Justin, but I've never licked him. I don't know how it feels.

He said it aloud, or something like it. Deny it, he thought. Deny it, and lose before me.

"I deny it, in the main," Dan Armstrong said, again hitting his unspoken thought. "I might have had it in the back of my mind sure enough, but what I'm concerned about is right now, thirty-five years later, and damn it all, what in thunder do you mean to contrive for licking Si Gerrard?"

Kinloch strode to the rocking chair, bending in the darkness to make out his father's face. "I been trying to say," he said slowly, "that

152

thirty-five years later hasn't got a damn thing to do with it. Not a God damn thing."

"Mind your language."

"I been trying to say that it *is* now, the stealing and the lying, right this minute. It didn't wind up as long ago as yesterday and it's all set to get going tomorrow. All because there was a man you ought to have shot and didn't."

He felt the stab of pain in his own breast as the words came. The pain grew deeper when the lightning revealed his father's face to him, so near—in the daylight they would never have talked so, he thought, hating the darkness, hating himself for what he had said—and he saw his father's steady eyes gleam out from under the thick white eyebrows.

"What do you mean to do?" Dan Armstrong repeated, calm as before.

"With you against me, expecting me to tell you?" the son cried, though as a matter of fact he did not see the answer clear himself yet. He won't admit I hurt him, he thought. When I *did* hurt him, hurt us both, hurt us both again, and he won't admit it, won't argue with me, or refuse to argue with me, or lose his temper and shout at me, though he could—he has and he could—won't do it and I can't lay a thing to him for not doing it, not a thing because of his love and even that he won't express because of the unfairness.

A stronger wind swept through the trees and struck them. Kinloch, still damp with the sweat of the long day, shuddered. His muscles had been drawn tight for many hours and they ached in the sudden motion. He had an impulse he had not felt since childhood: to run and grapple with his father in mock roughness, a way he used to have of seeking forgiveness without asking for it, gaining for them both a welcome relief from too much embarrassing seriousness. He reflected, seeing the comic side, that it would embarrass them three times over to do a thing like that now, and in this relieved humor he opened his mouth, glad for the first time of the darkness, to beg pardon for

153

speaking harshly and say goodnight, when Dan Armstrong spoke.

"Son," he said, "it's God's truth. For the first time I can remember, I'm dead against you."

Although he had never heard or imagined his father speaking so to him, in such a tone where all the habitual lightness was as absent as the fire from cold ashes, he knew there was nothing more to be said. He went heavily inside the house.

Dan Armstrong sat for a long time in his rocking chair. He saw the lightning and the clouds and marked the wind as accurately as ever, but his heart was not in it. A few minutes later, when he heard the short startled cry from within the house, he rose and planted his walking stick before him with the resolute air of a man about to settle things once and for all. Of a man about to quiet his own dogs for foolish barking in the night, or of a man about to get the gun and fire a round of bird shot into his own Negro raiding his own watermelon patch. He took one such step, then stopped short, shaking his head. Bending slightly to listen, he heard Kinloch's feet tramp rapidly through the back hall, out down the back steps, beginning to run already before he reached the calf lot, but audible still on the long bare slope toward the wood, the branch and the hills. As the footsteps died he heard her begin to cry. The sobs, too, died quickly away before his straining ears, but not with the sound of stopping, but rather under the restraint of secrecy, hard-fought. He lifted the resolute cane softly to the crook of his arm and moved to the door. Here, too, his hand dropped. He shook his head again and returned to the rocking chair. He sat so quietly there and so long that Scott Shaffer, returned from his date with Justin Gerrard, passed him not an arm's length in entering, humming some jazz tune or other under his breath, and never noticed him at all. And for long after that late hour he still sat marking the lightning, clouds and wind of the storm as it tried to make and failed.

ELEVEN

FOR what seemed a dozen times the next morning Ruth woke and slept, woke and slept. It was hot and the sheet and spread clung to her body, bearing her down like deadly weights fastened about her as she half-dreamed, half-imagined herself trying to float, too tired to swim, in a warm, sluggish sea. She thought to throw back the covers, but her limbs were heavy and when she finally lifted an arm, it fell back, sore. Pain stitched across her shoulder. Bruised—oh, yes, he had bruised it. Slowly she turned her head on the pillow. He was gone. She had stayed awake till daylight, listening through every minute for his step, but he had not come. He had hurt her and he had not come back.

New tears filled her eyes and she closed them. The tears wet her lashes, sealing the tiny hairs together. Consciousness was like a tilted board her mind tried to scale, until slipping, failing, it fell back toward the dream and the dream was the sea. A small pain began beside her heart, like water seeping in. It grew larger and larger, filling her breast, another weight to try to keep afloat. But, of course, she was going to drown sooner or later, so why not abandon the slight thinking motion that was beginning to be as much of a strain as if the arms and legs moved in swimming. More of a strain, more. But the thinking motion that kept her afloat would not stop. She could not stop it. Undulant, the waves moved beneath her, never covering her, leaving her dry, pain-filled throat and torso under the hot sun. Below, down, down, there were coolness and pale green water for her eyes, and her hair would be no weight at all, floating soft as dark seaweed around her. But she could not think how to sink. Up and down, five times more, and then the wave came, the thinking broke off as smoothly as if she had written beyond the margin of a sheet of paper.

Her body seemed to capsize upright as she went down again into sleep. She thought that she had at last gone down into the depths of the sea, which was neither cool nor pale, but filled with a bright stinging glare. Here fierce creatures, shark-like, went searching for her as they swam by, and still she was alone. Now the creatures were below her. They saw her just as, powerless, she sank slowly toward them. They were converging upon her when suddenly she was able to move, to flee upward, shooting to the surface. Up, up; her head broke water, into the open. She gasped down the air. Sitting straight up in bed, her mouth open and panting like a hound, her eyes wide at last— she was awake.

"Dear God!" she thought, staring around and around the room, wondering at all the blessed, ordinary objects. She fell back into the pillow. "A whole day to be alive!"

When she reflected in exactly what day she was alive, she did not know but what she had rather dream. She sat on the edge of the bed, remembering the night before, remembering now only too well, and though every speech and action stood before her with the clarity of perfect meter, she labored under the annoying apprehension that this very clarity was tricking her eye away from the clues of meaning.

It had started so innocently. Elinor had brought the pretty gown, and finding no one at home had dumped it on the front porch in a white enamel box with a scribbled note, "Too small for me, but should be right for you." When she undressed for bed, Ruth stood looking at herself in the mirror and seeing how the pale blue set off her clear skin and dark hair, she decided to please Kinloch by waiting up for him. She had missed him lately what with Scott there and the two of them gone often with Justin, Lance and Elinor. She sat for a long time in the middle of the bed, hugging her knees and thinking, in warm confidence of his near arrival, that she had missed him a very great deal and that she would tell him so.

When he came at last, looking tired and worried, she went to kiss him. She was about to ask him what the matter was, but first she

156

stepped back and held the blue skirt wide.

"Do you like it?" she asked.

"Pretty," he said absently, and then, "Where did you get it?"

He had never asked any such thing as that about her clothes; she had never considered that he might this time. His eyes caught her and it was too late to dodge.

"Elinor brought it to me," she said.

He had been unbuttoning his shirt, but when he heard her he stiffened motionless, staring her down.

"It was too small for her . . . it . . ." How much had she said, trying to ward him away from the anger she saw building unmistakably against her this first time.

He waited until she finished, stumbling, then his voice came cold as ice. "Don't you think you've done enough already?"

She froze, stricken, tried twice to speak before the words came. "Then you know at last," she said. The wreck. But who could have told him? No, she could not ask that now, like a criminal cornered by the law. Adding to her confusion, she felt welling up in her unbidden a relaxing humility, a kind of peace. She repeated in surer tones, more gently, "You know at last."

He regarded her in dumb surprise. "Has everybody—everybody—known then, except me?"

He was not angry any more. She could not think what his words meant, only how his voice sounded, very weary and lonely. She reached out her hands and moved toward him.

"I didn't mean to do any harm," she said.

He drew back from her as though her touch would injure him. His features drew tight and hard again.

"No harm!" he repeated. "I tried to warn you. From the first day you met them, I said, 'Stay away.' Didn't I? I couldn't make you understand because I didn't know myself. But now that you know, you know what they can do, and will go right on shameless, laughing when they laugh, hearing their filthy talk over fine vittles, accepting

157

their cast-off clothes—"

On the word, clothes, he looked at the gown again. His eyes went all over it, top to bottom.

"But they've protected me," she said. Somewhere far back, the whole conversation had slipped from her grasp, but the minute these words were out, she knew they were the worst of all.

"Protected!" He repeated it twice, hating the sound.

Almost ready to cry, she held out her arms again and came nearer. "Let me explain," she begged.

He waited until she came close, then his mouth went down at the corners. He said, "Protected!" again under his breath and as he said it, he caught the flimsy blue material in one hand at her throat and tore it like paper, jerked it free, and hurled it in a wad toward the fireplace.

"You are mine," he said. His hard grasp twisted and wrenched her bare shoulder. "You are mine to protect and no one else's. You belong to me. Understand?"

"Yes, yes!" she cried, frightened. "I never doubted it, Kinloch. I never—"

"If you understand now, it's the first time you've understood." He shook her, crushing her naked down against his breast so that his big shoulders swayed and threatened above her like a tree about to crash. Pushing back from him vainly, her hands sought too for the familiar outlines of his body, but his muscles were ridged so strangely against her that for one wild moment she imagined that he was not Kinloch at all. She cried out once, in a frantic effort to see his face. Then she found it, found his eyes, and on that moment, it seemed, the door slammed, his feet were heavy in the hall, on the back steps, running down the hill in the dark, while she lay panting, sobbing uncontrolled at first across the bed where his final gesture had hurled her, like some hateful object thrown down in the moment of recognition.

Reviewing that dreadful moment when their eyes met, she bent her head to cry again, but there had been too much of that already, and she fought the tears and won, then sat with her hands folded, thinking soberly.

At least he knows, she thought. He knows what I have done. I should have told him when I first planned to, but I have explained that to myself too many times and in too many ways to give the right answer about why I didn't do it. All I can do now is tell him what happened the way I saw it. Tell him if he will listen. He must listen. He can't stay so angry forever. Listen to me? Of course, of course, he will listen to me. To Ruth. To me.

But there's no good just sitting here thinking about it, she thought, getting to her feet with a suddenness of decision much like Kinloch and Dan Armstrong. Listen at once to me. Now. She dressed hastily.

When she came out on the front porch she saw that the pick-up was gone from the yard. Perversely, during some odd moment of her fitful sleeping, he had come and gone. She turned bitterly and Scott confronted her in the doorway.

"Hello, darling," he said, catching her arms.

"Oh, Scott, I'm in a hurry now. Let me go." She forced a smile. He must not know.

"Let you go? Oh, no. But kiss me good morning."

"Confound it," said Dan Armstrong just behind him. "Kiss him or don't kiss him, but let me by."

Scott made way. "Feeling okay now?" he asked her.

"Of course. Why?"

"Mr. Dan here wouldn't let a soul bother you for breakfast. Said you went to bed with a headache."

She cast a quick glance to where the old man sat in his rocking chair, observing two chickens who were occupied among the petunias. "Shoo!" he cried, trying to punch them with his walking cane without troubling to rise. "Get away from there, you pecker-woods, you."

"Look, darling," Scott persisted. "Justin's mother is giving a farewell dinner for me Sunday night. From the way she cooed at me this

159

morning I think she fully expects me to be engaged to Justin before I leave." He laughed. He always took such an openly egotistical delight in side-stepping women and their schemes that you wanted to think him innocent and charming and the women pretty silly, after all. "It'll be dull, of course. But I said we'd be there."

"No, Scott, I can't go."

"Oh, surely you aren't feeling that bad," he said with a tone of dismissal.

"No, Scott, I'd like to, but I can't."

He faced her irritably. "But why not, Ruth? Why?"

"I just can't."

"God knows I don't especially want to go, but then they've been pretty nice to us as things go, I suppose."

"I know. I'd like to go. But I can't."

He grew exasperated. He did not like to be crossed. "What I asked you in the first place was: Why can't you go?"

"Is it so important?" She must get away.

"If it's not important, why won't you tell me?" he said, sulkily.

"Shoo!" cried Mr. Dan, standing now and beating on the edge of the porch with his cane. The chickens squawked and flew.

"Take me to town with you, Scott," she said. "I want to find Kinloch."

As they went down the steps, she paused and running back, she bent and kissed her father-in-law on the forehead. She felt as if she were telling him good-bye.

A premonition? Elementary.

160

So Kinloch ran into woods and hollows and gullies, through branches and past sink-holes, down eccentric paths he had grown up with, whose small changes were like changes in his own body or mind, so that he no more had to think about where to turn and what limb to dodge than he had to think what his own hands looked like when he woke in the dark. But on the narrow path, though there was no room, there seemed a second man running beside this first habit-obeying one, and the second man was having trouble about where to turn and the briars clung to him and limbs flew back and struck him, yet he reeled and kept apace. "What are you running for?" he said to the first man, who did not have these troubles because he knew his ground so well. The first man did not answer. The first man reached a sure hand into the dark and caught a limber elm branch and let it fly back into the questioner's face. But when the first man did that, something happened to his memory and he took the sharp plunge of the path down the bluff one step too early. He stumbled and rolled crashing through layers of dry leaves which whirled up around him, while dead fallen limbs broke under his weight.

Kinloch lay flat on his stomach. A flicker of lightning revealed the dark line of his passage down the hillside. The steep hill brooded above him. He did not move from where he stopped rolling, no more than he had tried to stop the progress of his fall. He closed the eye that was not looking into the earth. He was one man now, one man who had fallen down a hill in the dark. Black dirt was gritty between his teeth and against his tongue he felt the thick vein of a dry oak leaf.

"I almost did it," he said to himself, and with the movement of his lips against the earth, the oak leaf broke. "It would be a bad thing for a man to do, and something a woman would rightly bear against him through many years of tenderness, but my anger was up against her and if she had not looked at me, if she had not looked at me—" His fingers clutched deep into the loam, but he found no solid earth. "I hurt her anyway." Sharp contrition plumbed him. Should I go back to her now? he thought. But the thought did not stir him.

"But she ought to have told me," he said aloud. He sat up and spit the leaves and dirt out of his mouth. "If she knew all about what Randall Gibson knew, she ought to have told me."

Misun-
derstand-
ing!

But how did she find it out? Not the Gerrards, surely; they let sleeping dogs lie, for fear they'd have to feed them, if nothing more. Father, he thought with certainty. Father told her. With the picture of the talk they must have had before his eyes, he saw them speak of him, league against him in this matter.

No, he thought, rising. I cannot go back to her now. To her, or to him. He got to his feet and knocked the trash off his clothes and hair, cast about him for a minute, then set his course away from the waiting path, away from the-land-west-of-town, toward the far, less familiar reaches of the creek and Keystone Bottom, rampant in willows, cane and a thousand vines, unfarmed, half-explored, mysterious below its outward flouting of damp, bright green. . . .

"Kinloch," said Randall Gibson, looking up from his book as his cousin entered, "I've found a poem that you must hear. Not so much that you must hear, as I must hear myself reading it aloud. Listen.

Hardy;
neutral
Tones

" 'We stood by a pond that winter day,
    And the sun was white, as though chidden of God,
    And a few leaves lay on the starving sod;
        They had fallen from an ash, and were gray.'

"My God, Kinloch, where have you been? No, wait, don't tell me now.

162

" 'Since then, keen lessons that love deceives,
And wrings with wrong, have shaped to me
Your face, and the God-curst sun, and a tree,
And a pond edged with grayish leaves.'

"You see, Kinloch, there is something very rare in this poem; namely, the correct order of things. How would you or I do it, coming at it through the seven veils that so effectively protect that special little goddess, Poetry, from all our natural bent? We would say, all in rhyme and meter, that your face, this sun, this tree, this pond with grayish leaves, have taught, down memory's lane, keen lessons that love deceives. Exactly right, murmurs the young girl who just loves Poetry, and all she knows of a certain star is a damn long list of things that have nothing whatever to do with a star. But now this fellow, he's got it right. Objects do not go about teaching us little lessons. No, but when a man remembers those times which he cannot forget, he will forever find, too, implicit in the memory and not to be torn away from it, the physical objects of the scene—gate or bush or bed—in this case, face, sun, tree and pond. Present simply as they are, self-assertive and undescribed, 'shaped to me.' That is the heart of it. . . ."

Shaped to me, then, Kinloch was thinking as he recalled his wanderings of the night before, a 'possum's eyes gleaming up at me in the dark out of a sink-hole, and I fished him out and laid him, balled up and playing dead, by a rock covered with poison ivy and went away wondering whether 'possums caught poison ivy.

Later there was the sudden opening in the tangled, snaky brush of Keystone Bottom, so that I came silently to the edge of the clearing where the doe grazed and the wind was steadier with a little light coming on. When I saw her run, it seemed that I did not see a live animal anymore, but that I saw motion, nothing else but motion, like the wind, making a swish of leaves. And I wondered how on earth she knew I was there, and what I had done to frighten the pretty thing.

163

Has shaped to me my coming out of the last stout line of willows laced in heavy vines—which is fair enough warning never to go into Keystone Bottom—and seeing the water-grass and low, pleasant willows by the creek and, higher up, the bank where a Negro man sat fishing in the dim light that seemed to be running out of the current instead of the sky. On a bet with myself I yelled to him, "Hey, Thomas T.!" And he must have been asleep because he jumped up straight saying, "Naw suh, naw suh," before he started wondering who I was and made me out and laughed. Later on he said I had scared him because the law had been on him for grabbling a couple of times lately. "Thomas T., you don't never change," I said. "Naw, suh," he said, chuckling high in that way they have, "ain' change." He sucked at the line of an extra fishing pole and knotted the hook on and gave it to me, not stopping to ask if I wanted to fish. I took it and fished. "You done changed though, Mist' Kinloch. Yes suh. A sho nuff man, you is. You's fishin' too deep, Mist' Kinloch. Dey bites high t'wardjuh sun-up." A sho nuff man, I thought, adjusting the cork. I remembered the day when as if at some signal, though I looked the same and dressed the same, Thomas T. quit calling me Boy and Chile and said, quite naturally, "Mist' Kinloch." I looked up quickly with a laugh, thinking he was teasing me, but then I saw him pulling out a little mud cat and not looking at me, and I was ashamed for having showed anything, much less a laugh. I walked carefully before him that day and I was painfully polite to him. I didn't scuffle with him before I left and once, though my heart jumped, I asked him to bait my hook please while I strung the fish, and he obeyed. If there is ever a day you can mark to say that you became a man, that was my day for marking.

Has shaped to me the quiet, distilling, unthinking peace beside the creek, that ran as though through my veins for an hour, then began to break and slip away, like high water, receding. "Dere's a big ole grand-dad fish under that bank," said Thomas T. "I done sot a trot-line for him two nights this week, but he see that trot-line all the time

164

I'm sotting it, and he jes' lay back and laff. 'Fo' you come I set chere on the bank scheming how I gon' grabble dat fish come night, and when you come callin' Thomas T. I think to myself, Hit's de law again, hit's de law. Cain' get away with scheming without the law comes setting twixt your shoulder-blades." "What kind a fish is it?" I said. "A smart fish, Mist' Kinloch. I been watching since las' Chewsday and I ain' seen nothing but this mons'tus shadow setting back on his tail and rocking side to side. Might be a big ole bass, and might be a trout or a ole grand-dad catfish. Might jes' be a gasper gool." "In that hole there?" I got up. "Better min' out," said Thomas T. "Grabbling costs more than air fish can bring." I walked up the bank, took off my shoes, and plunged in up above the deep hole, waist-deep there by the bank with the sand bottom sloping steadily. "Better take off them clothes," said Thomas T., but I went on, wading deep and cautious, then swimming quiet, without a ripple, feeling around the bank for the dark recess where the fish lurked, knowing the hole's outlines by the coldness of the water. Then I dived. I could see him through the water, the long black shape rocking a little, then I saw him move, not gathering for speed like an animal but replete with speed already, shooting smoothly toward the outer water. My fingers touched the whiskers, thick as bailing wire, and then my chest blocked him; down and up, down and up, we went, the fish and I, and his slick black body was like one powerful muscle, lashing against me, stripped of the flesh. We broke water. Now it's your turn to suffocate, I thought, and as if in reply, he flopped and rolled the underside of his broad gills against my arm and ripped me with the fin. Thomas T. danced and slapped himself—"Ole grand-dad cat, like I tell you. What'd I say? Ole grand-dad cat!"—and strung him on a rope nigh big as a plow-line. It was a nasty little cut. I tore off the tail of my shirt to tie it, and lay soaking wet in the early sun, so tired I got my peace back for a while, then here she came with the coffee and big biscuits and sorghum and hot cake. She went on back to the house. "Where'd you get her, Thomas T.?" I asked as we sat on the bank, grubbing it down.

165

Thomas T. had always lived alone, with his long array of fishing poles, his little piddling garden, his clean-scraped front yard, and the chopping block in the back that gleamed all over with fish scales. Thomas T. laughed high, wide and handsome. "Lawd, Lawd," he cried. "Gettin' old, Mist' Kinloch. Too old to go visitin'. Way too old." So when I got rested and fed, the peace crept out of me again, like flood water seeping down out of the same rough crevices of the same old bluff and I went on home.

I reached the house while it was still early with nobody about yet, and with the sight I had the feeling for the second time I can remember: I am glad there's nobody about. And I took the pick-up and drove for a long way into the dirt roads of the hills, until I had to come back to Randall's. . . .

"If only he hadn't run God into it," Randall concluded, "like a second-string sophomore substitute. Well, there's something wrong with all of them and maybe that's the thing that really does it. Did you ever think about that, Kinloch? The one wrong thing, and the whole leaps into focus, explodes enormously into rightness."

"I looked for you at the cafe," said Kinloch. "It was about time for your beer."

Randall moved to return the book to its place among all the others in the long low shelves that ran around his bare room. "No," he said. "I got to stay here and see that the nigger girl keeps the shades down between Cherry Bell and the place where the statue was and isn't any more."

"But you can't keep the shades down for the rest of her life," said Kinloch.

"No," said Randall, "but, do you know, I have been thinking that since Cherry Bell can barely see who it is coming in her room, maybe she can't really see out the window any more and will never know her treasure is gone."

"But suppose she can?" said Kinloch.

"Then I don't know," said Randall. "I don't know anything to do for her. I'd stand out there and act like the damned statue myself if it would please her. The trim little Venetian singer with the smile on his lips and the mandolin slung across his arm." He flung a big hand into the wall so hard that a bit of plaster dropped from the high ceiling to the floor. He was moved to great pity, beyond a doubt, but whether for the invalid woman, the marble man, or himself who was neither trim nor little, it was impossible to tell.

"You ought to have met them at the front door with a shot gun when they came to get it," said Kinloch.

"Oh, I couldn't do it, Kinloch. Not me. Not Randall Gibson. They would think I was joking and walk right by me." He brooded.

"Randall, I came to ask you if you told me everything. If you left out nothing."

"Old Daniel should be able to spy any dropped stitches."

"I broke with Father last night. I can't ask him now."

"I thought perhaps you would."

"Did you tell me everything, Randall? I have been over it and over it, and there seems to me that there is one thing—one thing yet—I need to know. Do you know what it might be?"

"God damn it, Kinloch," Randall cried, turning on him, "can't you see I'm sick of it? Sick of this town, these people, this house, these books, this heat? Do you know what it is to have town, people, house, books, and sun all look exactly the same, not the same as something else, but the same as everything, the same as nothing, the same as myself. Why do you expect me to be interested in your theorizing today? Because I was interested in it yesterday? Why do you expect to find me at the Melrose Cafe today? Because I've been there every afternoon for the past ten years? Today I am interested in poetry. Ask me about poetry, Kinloch. It is the same damned thing as asking about the Gerrards or the weather or me. Do you know why that is, Kinloch? Since I am interested in poetry today, I will tell you. It is because nothing is my own, nothing is shaped to me. There is no corner of somebody else's privet hedge that is dear to my heart. There is no bank of cudzu vine down behind the town dump where I met my true love. And even the sight of my dear mother's little sewing box, God love it, recalls to me at what price she won the calmness to sit and turn my father's collars and, before God, it was not worth it. There is nothing my eyes meet to look on and claim single and precious and my own. Cherry Bell, who loves a chunk of rock, is infinitely better off than I. So I sit here dressed as I am dressed on any day, calmly reading a book. So you come in and your clothes are torn, there is dry sand in the folds of them and mud on your shoes and your arm is bandaged with a bandage that is so properly makeshift and you are worn out and red-eyed from whatever the hell you've been up to and you say that I ought to have got out the shot gun. Of course, of course. It is like coming on a pitiful cripple on the street and saying, Look, haven't you hurt your leg? You make me sick."

"I'm sorry they took Aunt Cherry Bell's statue, Randall," said Kinloch, picking up his hat. "As for the rest of it, whatever you're driving at, you can either tell me what it is, or go to hell."

"There is no choice," said Randall. "To tell you what it is would be impossible, and I am already going to hell." He bowed his cousin from the door of the room into the hallway. "I thank you for thinking you might suggest an alternative."

Kinloch did not hear the parting thrust. He had stopped at the front door and was staring down the street towards the square. Then he said "Ruth!" with an intake of breath.

Here Randall's curiosity was pricked all the way through his hauteur and he followed Kinloch onto the porch. Yes, there she was, coming from the square, and her steps hastened as she drew nearer the house where the pick-up was parked.

But Randall was never content to investigate only one-half of the view. He looked up the street as well and there coming down the walk from the Methodist parsonage was another woman—a fat, rapid, smiling woman. He divided a meditative glance between the two.

One moved, for all her haste, as if the world were large, too large, as if she had only just recently reduced it to a size where she was able to think about it at all. The other approached in the assurance that it was a small world after all; in fact, she often said so.

It was Randall's turn to exclaim. "Why, if it isn't old Jessie Mae Gardner!"

Then they were coming down the walk to Ruth, toward the place where she had stopped dead, leaning against an oak tree that had grown near the sidewalk and forced two blocks of concrete into a rough pyramid. She, too, had recognized the wife of the man she had killed.

She pressed her back into the terrible solidity of the oak trunk, waiting while the three, like arrows fired by an ambushed enemy, converged upon her.

Kinloch had vaulted the gate in his alarm. "Are you sick?" he demanded.

She shook her head.

"Milady seemeth pale," Randall murmured, joining them.

"We'll go on home," said Kinloch.

"Randall Gibson! Kinloch Armstrong! Ain't anybody in Tarsus speaking this morning?"

"As I live and draw breath," drawled Randall. "Mawnin', Miss Jessie Mae."

"Excuse me, Mrs. Gardner," said Kinloch. "I didn't see you till just now." He removed his hat.

"Better be watching for old friends," said Jessie Mae, cackling with disproportionate laughter. "You never know. Ain't that right, Randy?"

"That's right, Miss Jessie," Randall returned. "What you doing back in Tarsus, now?"

"Just come down for a little visit," said Jessie Mae, adding in lowered, confidential tones, "First time I been well enough to travel, you know."

"Been sick?" Randall inquired.

"Law, Randall, you ain't heard? So sick I thought I'd die."

"Malaria?"

Jessie Mae leaned closer. "Prostrated," she pronounced. "Prostrated with pure grief and nothing else. The minute I got word of Ben's death it struck me. I was flat of my back for a month before I could sit up to the table. Pore Ben! All these years I been warning and pleading: Neither God nor man can stop you from drinking, Ben, I'd say, but do pray have enough presence to stay from behind a wheel. And the very night, the *minute*, mind you, my back's turned for a visit to Aunt Willie in Memphis—been begging me to take off and come for five years, but I couldn't leave Ben—what does he do but run off in the gully." Her eyes swam in large, bright tears. " 'You shouldn't reproach yourself, Jessie,' Aunt Willie said. But on the very night I leave him for this little visit, you see, it ups and happens. I told Aunt Willie I reckoned she was right about it. But it ain't as if I didn't love Ben, I told her. You'd be prostrated too, I said."

"I was mighty sorry to hear about Ben," said Kinloch. "We all were."

"Yeah," said Randall. "The town ain't been the same since Ben left us."

"Excuse me, Mrs. Gardner," said Kinloch, "but have you met my wife?"

Jessie Mae's eyes, where the tears were now visibly evaporating, turned full into Ruth's for the first time. "How do you do, Mrs. Armstrong," she said chattily. "I've seen you round about a whole lot, but I declare I don't believe we've ever been formally introduced. I declare—" She turned to Randall in sympathy, shifting voice and gesture without a pause—"I heard all about Miss Cherry's marble garden-piece a few minutes ago, Randall, and I'm here to say I think it's a crying shame for Henrietta Gerrard to snatch it away from her. But, you know, as Annie Gayle said to me just now, it's the first time I ever heard of two women wanting the same man and him in marble

170

britches." She burst into a whoop of laughter. "She didn't mean no harm. Mrs. Gayle's the preacher's wife and all; she's just a good sport."

The two men laughed in spite of themselves and Jessie was on her way. "I'm staying back yonder at Brother Gayle's house," she called back. "Doing a little sewing for Mrs. Gayle. Can't nobody suit her like Jessie Mae, she says. Be here till week after next, I plan. So glad to meet you, Mrs. Armstrong. You all be coming to see me, you hear?"

"I swear," said Randall with a giggle a moment later. "Everybody in Tarsus has a pretty good idea old Jess ran off with Anse Slade the night Ben broke his fool neck, but I'm betting on her to lie her way through it to every last one of us without batting an eye. Flat on her back! I imagine she was, at that. Excuse me, Cud'n Ruth."

"If that's so," said Kinloch, "I wonder why she'd be coming back here at all."

"Easy to tell," returned Randall. "To get by with a lie like that must delight Jessie's soul. Though by now she probably believes every word of it herself. Anyway, if Anse Slade has left her, there's still that other one, Roscoe Wright, his name is. Works at the gravel pit, you know."

"Well, poor Ben," said Kinloch. "Probably the best one of them. All he did was drink and he never saw any use in trying to hide it. You remember Ben, Ruth. Used to always be standing around on the corner by the drug store. Ruth!"

He doesn't know, after all, she had begun to think from the minute he first spoke to Jessie Mae. Now with his words, "You remember Ben, Ruth," the open face and honest eyes turned to hers, it swept through her how utterly incapable he was of deception and she could not meet his look. Then it's all to be told, she thought desperately. Then I'm back where I was in the beginning, six weeks ago when I wanted to tell but Scott came, I wanted to tell but I couldn't, didn't—

She took a step toward him. The heat pressed heavier around her until she could see it crowding like black cotton before her eyes, between his face and hers.

"What is it?" he said.

"I forgot to eat breakfast," she said. Her voice rebounded into her ears twice, hard, and she fell forward into his arms.

"What is it?" cried the lithe, bronzed man in the blue sport shirt who leaped out of his car, half-pushing the blonde girl out too, for she was in his way. "What's the matter with her?"

"She fainted," said Kinloch, who carried her in his arms toward the pick-up. "A touch of sun, I guess. I'll take her home; you call the doctor."

"Take her home in that thing!" Scott Shaffer cried. "It's enough to put you to bed when you're in the pink. I'll take her; you get the doctor."

Watching, Randall felt his nervous diaphragm jerk with a convulsive desire to laugh. Are they going to start pulling at her, like two dogs with a rag? he asked himself.

But Kinloch saw the truth of it; the pick-up was unbelievably rough. He moved toward Scott's car. "I'll put her in," he said. "Be careful. I'll be on with the doctor."

Justin stood ankle-deep in dust and put her hands to her hips. "What about *me?*" she screamed at Scott Shaffer.

The motor roared. "Walk," he shouted, waving a hand toward the fretted white turret of her home, not a block away. "You go that way," he laughed at her, shifting into gear. Dust spewed over her, but she did not turn away or cough.

Now Kinloch was going in the other direction and his dust covered her. She turned slowly to where Randall Gibson stood laughing at her, leaning against the oak tree because he couldn't stand up for laughing at her.

"You laughed at me yesterday," he gasped, "and today you sent a truck and four nigger men to steal from me. But I'm laughing at you now, and nothing is going to spoil it. Nothing. And any man living will shove you out to let her in. Even her brother. Even her brother."

The hot sun poured through the settling dust, scalding over her golden skin and bright hair, casting ugly shadows down her ugly face. She did not even have to clear her throat. She just spit. A great wad of it, landing accurately in the shade before his feet. Then she walked away.

Randall bowed after her. "Did anybody ever tell you, Miss Justin?" he called. "You're getting more like your father every day?"

When Ruth opened her eyes, she was lying on the broad leather seat with her head in Scott's lap. She saw his face. The blue sky skimmed above them, nothing but sky and a few white clouds. Maine . . . California . . . Florida . . . Texas . . . Nebraska . . . ? She closed her eyes. Then the car lurched over a hole in the road, the dust came boiling up and she remembered. She looked up into his face again and thought (her decision completely reversed now that uncertainty and fear had returned again) how grateful she should be to him. Twice now he had come just in time to save her from telling the terrible secret.

He looked down and saw her open eyes. "Feeling better?"

"Yes." She started to sit up; then, though they were well out of town, she thought of Jessie Mae's fat smiling face and Kinloch with his look of concern for her, and she lay back, unreasoningly fearful that she might have to see one of them standing beside the road or driving along abreast of them.

"Scott," she said on the impulse of a sudden idea. "Are you still going to New York on business?"

"Leaving Monday," he nodded. "I meant to tell you."

"Scott, can I—can I go with you? I need to get away for a while . . . the heat . . . I need a rest, I think."

"Sure, Ruth. Be glad to have you."

"For two weeks," she said, half to herself. In two weeks, Jessie

Mae was planning to leave; two weeks away and she might be able to think what she ought to do, it might no longer seem important to do anything at all.

You're running away, a small voice within her accused.

I don't care, she thought. I'm confused; something is going on and I don't know what it is. I've got to get away.

THIRTEEN

"I'VE lived in almost every section of the country," Scott Shaffer said, pushing back his plate and lighting a cigarette. "But I have never realized until these last few weeks everything that is meant by the South—the deep South, I'd better say."

From the end of the table, every one of Miss Henrietta's beads flashed at the mention of the South. "Really? Can't you tell us what you mean? We hardly think about these things, you know."

"For instance," the guest said, dividing a glance between his thin hostess and Simon, who hulked spaciously at the head of the table, "the central fact in your society—something I have never encountered before—appears to be the preservation of a quite authentic, if modified, form of feudalism."

"Is anything wrong with that?" Miss Henrietta inquired nervously.

"Oh, no. Indeed no. In fact, I find it quite distinctive, even charming, I might add, though the word is often indiscriminately used."

And you're nothing if not discriminating, Elinor thought. The bastard is sure laying it on thick, she thought. She saw Justin's inattentive eyes move to where his brown hand with the cigarette lay among the crystal. He's stalling her, she thought. He's making her mad enough to die. She wants him out in that blue coupe with it raining like hell and the radio playing soft music and then they can go somewhere and park. He'll finally go, time he's tormented the soul out of her, and he'll turn on the radio and park too, but none of it's going to do her a bit of good. It's not going to keep him here or bring him back. She's pretty good, too, and maybe this is the first time she hasn't got to first base. Unless she really did cross paths with Kinloch, like she was lying about last Thursday. That was the day I warned her about this. I had my say. I didn't expect to head her, just wanted to have my say.

"I think you can see, Mrs. Gerrard," he was saying, "what I mean by feudalism in this section, provided I may consider Tarsus as typical of Southern society."

"Lord, yes," Lance put in with a grimace. "Nothing if not typical."

"Well then, surely it would take no one long to see that Mr. Gerrard, large land-owner that he is, stands in the same relation to the townspeople and his tenantry as the overlord of the medieval times stood to the villagers and the—ah—lower classes. It is a continuation of the aristocratic tradition. What was it Benét said? 'The tropic empire, seeking the warm sea, the last foray of aristocracy.' " The brown hand lifted to gesture around the room where candlelight mercifully concealed the dark pile of paneling and woodwork that in the daytime weighed down upon bright ornaments such as painted china plates, vases, cutglass bowls and the like, and seemed about to crush them all.

"Well," laughed Miss Henrietta after the brief embarrassed pause that bothered Scott Shaffer not at all, "we hardly ever think of ourselves as *aristocrats*, but as you say—"

Simon broke in heartily. "I'm not saying a thing about the middle ages at that, but I do call to mind what Jamie Perkins said many years ago to my brother Wills. Saw him out in front of the store one morning early. Wills had spent the night out at a dance and didn't take time to go home and change clothes. All diked out, you know, when Jamie Perkins come by. 'Wills,' said Jamie, 'never had occasion to notice it before, but dressed up like that I swan if you don't look like a damned high class fellow.' 'What the hell, Jamie,' says Wills—quick as a flash, he was, you know—'What the hell, Jamie,' he says. 'I *am* a high class fellow.' "

Lance grunted. "Jamie Perkins must have been running for something."

Elinor studied her husband and her eyes narrowed. With that look on her, and she had it often when she studied him, she took on an Oriental appearance, especially when her black hair was drawn back

176

straight from her forehead and knotted firmly behind, as it was to-night.

You needn't act like you don't care, like you don't give a damn, she addressed him in her thoughts. I've seen you do it before and it's mainly for my benefit because you know I'm sitting here seeing slap through all of it, and you know the way I feel, but you also know the way you'd like to feel, the way you'd like it to be with this bunch of yours, you son of a feudal lord, and that's where you're mixed up, mixed up all the time, and that makes marrying me the biggest mis-take you ever made, but even that mistake wasn't quite big enough to overtrump the mistake that's inside you in the first place, so that you'll go on and on, wanting to leave and not wanting to leave, wanting to believe what Scott Shaffer says word for word like your mama, yet knowing all the time that Scott Shaffer is sitting there listening to himself lie and not even having to think about what lie is coming next, it's so easy. And the only thing left to do is come out with a crack like that last one, enough to square you with me, you think, enough to give the wink to Scott Shaffer, but not enough—no, not ever enough to come to grips with Simon or unshade the light for scorching Miss Henrietta's little wings.

"My family," that lady was saying, "came to Mississippi from Vir-ginia. Mathison. Oh, there're many of them left in the Old Dominion, as they say."

"Why, there's a family in Richmond. I remember now," Scott nodded. "Another distinctive Southern trait, Mrs. Gerrard. The con-sciousness of lineage. How about your husband's people. Also Virgin-ians?"

"The Gerrards," said Miss Henrietta readily, "were among the ear-liest settlers of the state. They came over from Georgia, from the country near Savannah as far as I could tell, though it's just mighty hard to find records going back that far. The writing and all, you know," she added vaguely, while Scott Shaffer silently agreed.

"I don't know," Simon rumbled in somewhat deprecating tones

177

though he was obviously pleased with the subject. "Henrietta looked all that stuff up. Business, you know. I never took time to bother with it myself. I tell you what I always figure now: if a fellow's a good, straight-forward, honest fellow, it don't matter to me who his folks are or where they came from. Now don't you think that's right? Of course, all this other business is nice to know, but Henrietta took the trouble to dig it up."

"I was thinking of Justin, Simon."

"Of Justin?" Elinor was forced to exclaim.

"Why, yes, dear. My own father, was an officer in the War—" she smiled at Scott—"you know, of course, what we mean by *the* War. But I thought it would be so nice to find that both sides of the family were represented. That would make her doubly eligible, you see."

"Eligible for what, Mama?" Lance inquired, mystified.

"Why, honey, for membership in the U.D.C."

"My God!" Justin came to life crying, as the entire company exploded with laughter, Simon's base rocking in the background, Justin's shrill giggle cutting through and Elinor simply shaking till tears ran down her face. Miss Henrietta regarded them with anxiety, then her thin mouth grew pinched and she moved her dessert spoon a fraction of an inch to the left on her empty plate.

"My God!" Lance echoed, gasping. "Let's change the subject— quick. It's too much—"

"I really don't quite see—" Miss Henrietta began stiffly, but Scott, as if he had raised an acute nose to the social situation, chose not to hear her.

"Oh, let's not change the general subject," he said. "Elinor hasn't contributed her bit. Come on, Elinor. I must hear about Delta folks before I go."

"I don't know anything to tell about Delta folks," Elinor returned.

"Oh, really, now," Scott Shaffer scoffed. "Your family are Delta folks. I understand they are remarkably different from those of the hill section."

178

"My family lives in the Delta. But so do a lot of other people. I don't know what you're talking about by saying Delta folks. I don't know if there is any such animal."

"Oh, hell, Elinor," said Lance. "Tell him about planters and niggers picking cotton and all that stuff."

"What he said was, Delta folks," said Elinor, fractiously. "That's just like asking about Mississippi folks or Southern people or American people or European people. People! Hell, we're all people. And look at us."

"Elinor's people," prompted Miss Henrietta, "are one of the most prominent families in the Delta. The Dudleys are owners of a very large plantation near Leland. There is a town named for them. My daughter is much too modest."

"Town!" Elinor cried. "What it is is a general store with a couple of gas pumps out front, a nigger Baptist church and a white Baptist church, a post-office about half the size of this room and an open shed by the railroad which keeps niggers waiting for the train from getting wet provided the wind isn't blowing. That's the town of Dudley. Then you go on down the road a piece and there's the Dudley mansion which doesn't look too much different from a house about a mile up the road which was ordered ready made from Sears Roebuck. That's the town of Dudley."

"And how did your father happen to settle in the Delta?" Scott pursued.

Across from Elinor, Justin yawned and stretched rudely. There was a leashed, animal impatience in her movement and Elinor smelled perfume, laden with the warm scent of her body.

Elinor put her elbows on the table and leaned across toward Scott. "You really want to know, don't you? You just dead to know, ain't you?" He met her eyes with a faint flicker in his own and she grinned. You better recognize me, you bastard, she thought. You better let on you know that I know what the score is every minute. I don't make the score, like you do, or try to do, but what I do, I do better than

179

anybody else I know. It's an easier job than yours, but then you got to put it down that you're going to slip up someday and slip up hard, but I'm not going to slip up. I've been at it a long time and I'm not going to slip up.

She tapped a cigarette on the tablecloth and lighted it with a man's high-elbowed gesture. She slung an arm over the carved back of the mahogany chair and blew smoke through her nose.

"The Dudley estate," she said, "has been in the hands of the Dudley family for a grand total of thirty-three years. When Daddy got hold of it, it was mainly swamp with a few acres of deadening not even turned into new ground. There were a couple of hundred acres under cultivation down by Quiver Bayou, but we always figured that had been a natural clearing since before the deluge, or else the Indians did it, because nobody worth a plugged nickel had ever owned the land since the Indians pulled out and went wherever they went.

"Daddy came by the place accidentally, if you really want to know, Mr. Shaffer, and bought it sight unseen. He had him a little grocery store in Rosedale at the time and one week night when he was about to close up, in comes this Chinaman named Wang Tu Jones. Don't ask me where he got the name of Jones, that's just what people called him and maybe he finally believed it himself or maybe it was really his name, but he was a genuine Chink and the funniest thing about him was the way he loved to play poker and the way he could win. The night before, he had won a deed to a six hundred-acre tract of land and it was fire in his pockets, it was ache to his soul because now he guessed he had to farm it and he didn't want to farm half as bad as he wanted himself a little grocery store likee this one. Daddy picked all this out of him while he was tying the string on a sack of rice.

"Now two weeks back Daddy had dropped in on a live-stock sale over near Leland. They had a few horses up for trade. A lot of the ground in the Delta is black, it's so rich, and when the grass comes up on what land isn't already disked, it looks greener than any grass you ever saw. Horses take to a spring day like that was—you know how

180

horses take to the weather. Well, here was Daddy, who didn't want to buy a damned head of anything, he was just there because he still couldn't keep his eyes off the Delta. He hadn't been out of the hills many months.

"All of a sudden, while different ones were showing gaits, Daddy looked up from where he was leaning on the rail and he saw a girl on a three-year-old bay filly come riding into the ring. Everybody started looking then, because there weren't any women around—no, that ain't the reason; they would have looked anyway, by God—she was a pretty little thing—the girl, I mean—and she was Ross Morgan's daughter from over on the river near Greenville, and she suited that filly like hand in glove. Daddy stared and stared, and the third time she went around, she tightened her seat, brought the reins in and the crop down and she came beating by the inside curve straight toward him with the black dirt flying in the prettiest rack he'd ever seen.

"The crowd at the fence cheered as she went by and this young gelding hitched to the rail rared back and broke his reins, but Daddy just stood there and gulped until here she came around the curve and at him again, chin up with the dirt flying, and this time he couldn't stand it; he threw his hat in the air and yelled.

"He couldn't get over the feeling he had, but when he saw the filly auctioned off without too much regret, he figured it was the girl that had done it, and he figured if he saw her close up he'd be all right again. He went and got himself introduced. She had looked like the boss of creation on that horse, but standing on the ground she surprised him, she was so little and helpless, and the feeling got worse. It grew out of size for his chest and it got into his throat and his eyes—"

"How in hell do you know how he felt?" Lance grumbled.

"I'm remembering how I felt about you, darling—and he couldn't do a thing about it. The next weekend he was over to call on her where she lived in a big white house—the real McCoy, Mr. Shaffer; you'd be surprised—by the river. That visit was his ruination, though, because from the minute Ross Morgan, just being friendly, asked him what he

181

did for a living, he began to sweat. That was when he got the idea that on the day he was able to look Ross Morgan in the eye and say, 'I'm a planter, sir,' on that day Ross Morgan would begin to size him up as a son-in-law.

"It was just an idea, of course, because anybody that rasseled with cotton all his life would be more than happy to see his daughter marry into the grocery business, but planter sounded like a mighty high-stepping word to Daddy then and he grieved and lost sleep over it and harassed the Lord about it until first thing you know here came the Chinaman.

"Daddy figured Wang Tu Jones was lying when he said he hadn't even laid eyes on the six hundred acres and he figured there wasn't much to recommend it as farming land, but he had got converted in a hard-shell Baptist revival meeting up here around Peloosha before he left for the Delta and he wasn't going to quibble with the Lord. So Daddy and Wang Tu Jones swapped property right there over the sack of rice and Daddy left the Chinaman to lock up and walked out the door with the deed in his pocket.

"That's about all there is to it. He married Ary Morgan and finally more than trebled the Chinaman's land. You see, he believed then and still believes—whenever he remembers it—that he and the Lord walked out the door of the grocery store together, so six hundred acres of brush and uncut timber couldn't resist the two of them any more than Ary could. I guess that's as good a way to look at it as any."

In her last words, the habitual drawling boredom that had lifted a little during the course of her story returned to her voice and she propped her chin on her elbow and snuffed a half-smoked cigarette among the cake crumbs.

Scott Shaffer smiled indulgently. "You can't keep the romance out, can you?"

"I told you exactly what happened," she said. "You asked for it."

"And do you ride?" Scott inquired.

"Yes. I ride."

"But not so well as she?"

"As well, but differently."

"Differently? In what way?"

"In a way less feminine, I suppose. She probably swayed at the waistline. I lean to the horse."

"You've always been a little jealous of her, haven't you?"

The smooth line of his mouth, formed so like Ruth's, yet by the consciousness of itself so unlike her, mocked across the barricade of crystal.

"The boy with the ready-made answers," she said.

"Oh, for God's sake," said Justin. "I don't even know what anybody's talking about." With the air of having had patience with them all for too long, she shoved back her chair from the table and at the positive command of her rising, they all rose also.

Dawdling across the hall toward the parlor in the wake of the others, Elinor paused in the gloomy recess by the hat tree and pinned up a stray lock of hair. She stood gazing in the small oval mirror, not especially conscious of the face that looked back at her but caught instead in a pleasurable inertia to the present that the reminiscence had provoked.

"Quit primping," Justin said, shoving in by the mirror. She had come down stairs with a raincoat over her arm. So they are going for a ride, after all, Elinor thought.

Justin extracted a comb from somewhere about her and cocked her head to the mirror. Elinor watched the heavy blonde hair spring silkily into place under the comb. She saw reflected the carefully made-up face where the eyeshadow slanted provocative and vague toward the elusive hint of rouge and the full scarlet mouth. It had taken a good hour to prepare that face. Elinor experienced a little stab of pity.

"Look, honey," she said. "There are plenty more fish in the sea."

Justin's pale, depthless eyes set on her sister-in-law's face from out of the mirror. "I'll get you for this," she said. "You've all been against me, haven't you? You and Ruth and Lance, sitting around against me and looking at one another when Scott and I so much as have our backs turned. Don't be trying to make up to me now."

"Don't you be trying to blame your foolishness on somebody else," said Elinor, her usual attitude toward Justin (which had long since evolved as the only possible one) returning. "Nobody made you put all that lipstick on, but anybody can tell you it ain't going to do no good. No good at all."

Justin faced her, drawn up within some curious off-brand of courage. "It's not over yet, bear in mind. Until it is, you can go to hell, Elinor Gerrard."

Elinor smiled. The cursing Justin did was frequently over-sized for her, though she was growing up to it rapidly.

Scott came into the hall. The family crowded about him, repeating good-byes. From the door he looked over their heads to Elinor and doubtless remembering their contest at the table, he waved a hand. "All the best," he called.

Elinor saw Justin take a quick note of the glance that passed between them and knowing what the girl thought, she laughed aloud and straight at her, until the swift sound of the rain through the door and the closing door shut them apart.

Whatever she has to take she deserves it, Elinor reflected. She's been asking for it every breath she's drawn since they pinned the first diapers on her, and the only thing to have pity about is that it isn't any worse than this. That little bit of having pity for her is just exactly like the long spells of sympathy and hope I used to have for Lance, but he's like her, only he once had one foot forward as though he was about to take a step and he hasn't even got that now, and they both stem from old Simon, and the downgrade gets them in different ways. Of course, if I'm going to give them down the country, I have to include myself, because I knew it, I knew it all along. . . .

She lit a cigarette.

"Quit mooning in that chair, Elinor, and say something," Lance said.

"I'm enjoying myself," she replied. "Why? You want to go?"

"I thought maybe I'd wait till Justin gets back," he said. "If I'm not mistaken she had a bag of tricks up her sleeve tonight and I want to see how things turn out."

Simon said nothing, but he settled down to read the newspaper, column by column. Miss Henrietta had gone to bed with a headache.

"Yeah," said Elinor, "and Simon will be right here with you. You got more curiosity than any set of folks I ever saw in my entire life. You got to be in there looking or you'll perish—dry up."

"Aw, dry up yourself," said Lance. "You can sleep in the morning."

"I can evermore do that. Any morning you name. Someday, Lance, there's going to be something Simon wants you to do that can't just as well wait till after dinner."

"That's the morning I'll fix my own coffee," he sneered.

"That's the morning I'll go out before day and kill a brace of quail for your breakfast," she returned.

"I'd like to see it," he said absently, getting up and beginning to prowl about the room.

He's about ready to start drinking, she thought.

. . . And I left the Delta for this, for a simple life in the hills, in the bosom of the leading family of Tarsus. But it's not Delta or hills that divides folks. I said that to Scott Shaffer and I meant it, too. I found it out.

I well remember the day I first admitted to myself and to all concerned that my eyes were as wide open as a tom cat's at midnight. That was the day of the big storm. Lance and I were still living over here; we hadn't built the house yet. I was sitting in here in the living room reading and heard it begin to make, way over beyond the-land-west-of-town, a real July hot-weather storm. The wind blew short, hard and uncertain first against one set of windows, then another. Down in the square a man was driving three head of calves home from pasture and they went wild and dashed up on the sidewalk in front of the drug store while he yelled and ran after them, the wind

185

flattening his hair and pasting his clothes to him as though you saw him swimming under water. The sky was black toward the west, but bright and pale blue back the other way and for a minute while I stood at the window, too amazed to remember to be scared, the dividing line between the clear part and the clouds looked like it was right over the house. During that minute every tree and shrub and every single grass blade turned a crazy electric green, the terrifying color you imagine a man might turn when they shoot the current through him in the electric chair.

The sight threw me so hard I nearly jumped out of my skin when they all came pouring into the room from every direction—Simon, Lance, Miss Henrietta, and oh Lord, Justin, slamming into the house like the dogs were on her, straight from playing with some high school kids. "Is it a cyclone? Is it a cyclone?" she kept saying, pulling at Miss Henrietta, who buzzed around closing the windows. Lance and Simon were standing side by side at the bay window, with their hands locked behind them in exactly the same way, looking out, though the crazy green color was gone by then and it was allover black. Justin couldn't get their attention either, so she hopped on me. "Is it a cyclone, Elinor?" I told her to shut up, that if the house blew down she wouldn't be any deader than the rest of us. So she began to bawl, and right then the first over-due flash of lightning came, ugly and so close it popped in your ears, and Lance and Simon shied back from the window. "We're right under the turret in here," Simon said. "Where's the best place?" Lance asked. Both of them were talking so low and quick you'd think the police were casting a cordon around the back garden and closing in. "The dining room would be better," said Simon. The whole house shook in the wind and thunder, and next thing I knew they were out of the room like a shot. Vanished.

Well, I came walking and walking steady, by God, through the door of the dining room and there they were. Huddled a little off-center from the middle of the room, away from the corners because lightning might strike the corners, away from the windows because

good descrip-
tion of male
Gerards
and
light-
ning

there the big tree might fall, away from the side board because so much metal attracts lightning, away from under the chandelier because wind or lightning either one might unsettle it from the ceiling. In fact, it seemed that the one spot of comparative safety in the entire universe was a spot about six inches square between the dining room table and the French doors and they were all trying to get both feet on it. Old Simon was sitting on a straight chair right on top of this wonderful place and Justin was huddled in his lap where she sobbed at the wind and flinched at the lightning, and Lance stood just behind pressed against the rounds of the wood. They had crowded Miss Henrietta off their private island of blessing, but she was trying.

Clearly, they had beat me to it and moreover were damned glad of it. They looked up when I came through the door and I knew all of them—Lance too—had not even thought of me until right then when I found them grouped as though all ready for a nice family pose to be taken, and frightened as bad as if the photographer were aiming a shot gun at them. Outside the big elm tree bent low down, then whipped straight, leaves stripped backwards along the limbs. I waited till the next batch of thunder died away, hearing how it carried from downstairs to upstairs, exploding in every over-furnished room, shaking the balconies and turrets.

I gave them a minute to say a word and when they didn't—even Justin watching me now with bleary eyes—I delivered one long look they ought to remember till the day they die, picked up a candle stick from the table and marched back to the living room where I took my seat and read my book. When the roof off somebody's garage from down the street blew into the bay window, I didn't even know what had happened, and I vowed I wouldn't turn around. Lance came and stood in the door and looked things over, then he looked at me and I looked at him. We never said a word. Pretty soon I began to read again and after that he went back to where they were calling him from the haven in the dining-room, asking what had happened.

From that day on the game was up; but you can't pack your grip because your husband's scared of lightning. You can't get a divorce because your father-in-law's got so much money your husband doesn't have to go to work. You can't claim incompatibility when your husband doesn't believe any of the things you've never believed either, and if you've always had a honing towards those things you've never believed, it's not his fault he hasn't got the honing too. (You get the honing from your folks, I guess, and it's for the things they really do believe in, though you'd never say you believed in them, too; and Lance's folks haven't got any idea what things I'm talking about.) And I can't charge mental cruelty, because it's my own mind that's doing it to me. I could charge infidelity, of course, because I'm as sure of that as I'm sure of the difference between black and white, but there's never been anything flagrant or extended, and besides I've got enough pride not to want to throw it all away before a courtroom.

And here I sit, just like I've sat for six years, counting off the whys and hows while I rest on my backbone chain smoking, deciding nothing.

I wonder what makes Ruth decide to do things? I wonder what made her know she wanted to marry Kinloch, for instance? Ruth and her butter business. It makes me want to die laughing just thinking about her sometimes. I always did think there was something a little bit comical about her, way back before I got to know her, when she would come to the front door with her little basket of butter, looking so pretty and fresh and business-like and before it was over I'd have to sit down and help her make the right change. Then after she left, I'd go around for an hour saying to myself, "So that's who married Kinloch Armstrong," and somehow I couldn't figure it.

But soon afterwards she got to coming around to see us right often and I still couldn't make head nor tails of what she was really like until the day she came flying in, middle of the morning, with a croker sack. "I can't do it, Elinor," she said, just like that, walking in on me in the kitchen. "Can't do what?" I said, putting side meat in my turnip

188

greens. The cook was having a baby. Then I saw how the croker sack was bulging and swaying around in mid-air and thin little noises were coming out of it. "Oh, no, you don't," I said. "If there's anything in this world I've got no earthly use for it's a dozen baby kittens." "Just eight," she said and smiled in that way she has that always tickles me, as if to say, "I know that I don't look quite natural selling butter by the pound and carrying a croker sack full of kittens and driving a pick-up truck and being married to Kinloch Armstrong, but it's really all right, you know; it suits me just fine." "I saved them," she went on. "Kinloch found them left by the side of the road to starve. He said the only thing to do was throw the poor things in the creek to save them misery, and I promised to do it for him when I came up town with the butter." "I still don't want any kittens," I said. "I *can't* drown them," she said. "Elinor! Their eyes aren't open yet!" "Their eyes don't cut any ice with me," I said. But before I could stop her, she had untied the sack and rolled them out on the floor where they promptly made a mess—all eight of them. But they were cute. "All right," I said, "I'll take that one. Now you go right straight and do your duty by the rest of them." She packed them up again and headed for town. The next time I went to the beauty parlor I found out that seven more of the Armstrong's butter customers had baby kittens too. Not that they were any too happy about it, but she had persuaded them.

"I know you," I said, next time she was at the house. "I did what I promised," she said. "I threw the sack in the creek." "Mighty lot of trouble over a sack," I said. "I thought I'd better do that," she said. "Why?" Lance asked her. She sounded so serious. "Because if Kinloch finds out about it, it will probably be me he'll put in the sack and drown." What made it so funny was that that's exactly the way Lock is; not that bad, of course, but she hit the nail on the head just the same. "Drown you in the creek, huh?" Lance would laugh and say every time he saw her for the next two weeks. If he said it once he said it a thousand times. But after that I quit worrying about how they would make out. (How *they* would make out, hell. Who told you you

189

were Little Orphan Annie, Mrs. Lance Gerrard? Mrs. Lancelot Gerrard. Yes, Lord. . . .)

But I did start worrying again. I started worrying after that one hell of a night when we had the wreck. Because she wanted to tell, she wanted to tell right off. She's like that deep down and I guess that's another score for her and Kinloch if they can sense that in one another and know it's a likeness. Oh, she comes to talk to us by the hour because the way we live is the nearest thing in Tarsus to the way her folks used to live. Not that she doesn't like Lance and me. But let something like that Ben Gardner thing come up and it shows you where her heart is. It would be hard for her to put that into words, I guess; to say, Mr. Dan and Kinloch are the people I long for, not you and Lance.

But by the time we had argued for thirty minutes and all got back to the house and Lance still said, 'No, don't tell,' she got confused and wasn't sure any more. The nearest she could come to explaining her confusion was to ask me what she should really do, and when I said, 'Leave it alone,' she finally agreed because for some ungodly reason she counts on me. But I'll always remember the way she looked when I said it, the strange second glance she gave me, some sort of disappointment, almost shock, in her eyes, that faded slowly back into the other, the still surface. She's had that still look too often ever since. She was glad to see Scott in a way, I suppose, but it takes more than the elegant Mr. Shaffer to touch her, even if he is her brother.

I guess I ought to have kept my mouth shut. I guess her conscience wasn't any of my jurisdiction. But, hell, what justice would you get by getting justice? It was Lance and Justin's doings and she would suffer. I started to talk to her about it once, but she changed the subject. Then I was glad I didn't go on, because it's over and done with now and there sure-God is no going back to it. Well's to forget what you can't help. You pay by the pittance anyway, if you don't pay by the pound. No you don't either. You pay by the pound or not at all. There's not much to this conscience business. This world and one

190

more, as Daddy says, and then the fire works. Of course, there's always some more whisky in this world if Lance doesn't drink it all. . . .

When she came out of the kitchen with the drink in her hand, Lance was saying, "Hush, there's the car." He motioned Elinor to stop, and they listened for the sounds above the slow rain. Then there were the steps on the porch, the man's voice and the girl's. Elinor still stood in the doorway between the hall and parlor. Then Justin entered, cast a glance into the living room where Lance and Simon turned to peer at her around the sides of their chairs in simultaneous action like a pair of mechanical figures. She looked next and with heat at Elinor before she veered toward the kitchen from which she presently emerged barefoot, carrying an enormous sandwich. She curled into an arm chair and with a lithe movement of her legs that amounted to a gesture, kicked her wide skirts well above her knees, and commenced to eat.

"Home early, ain't you?" Lance inquired, eyeing her.

"Up late, ain't you?" she returned and took another bite of sandwich.

They might have known, Elinor thought. Waiting around for a scene, forgetting she's one of them too. They might have known she's not going to let it touch her.

"Did you see Ruth?" Elinor inquired.

"Ruth! Why in the hell should we go to see Ruth?"

"I thought you might have stopped by. I just wondered how she's feeling."

Simon wadded his newspaper, heaved himself straight and batted his daughter's bare feet. "Where you been, honey? Out of town to the picture show?"

"We didn't go very far," said Justin. "Not that far."

But farther than you'd care to admit, thought Elinor. I'll lay money on that.

"That boy nice to you?" Simon went on. "Anybody not nice to you, just let me know."

"Oh, for God's sake, Papa," said Justin.

"Going to miss old Scott," said Lance. "Scott and Ruth, too. It's going to be lonesome down at the house, specially without Ruth dropping in."

"I don't see how you're going to tell whether Ruth's down there or not," said Justin. "She thinks about something else half the time and doesn't open her mouth."

"Honey," said Lance, "on the day you wake up looking like Ruth Armstrong, you can give up talking for the rest of your life and it'll be all right. Come to think of it, it'll be all right anyway."

"That Armstrong boy's wife? Old Dan'l's daughter-in-law?" Simon said. He batted Justin again with the paper. "Pretty as my baby? No."

Even Justin giggled at this, but Elinor laughed a shade longer than Lance.

"Eavesdropper," Justin said to her. "You didn't want to miss a trick, did you?"

"Hell," said Elinor, "I just happened to be standing there. I couldn't tell you a word you said. It made me so sick I forgot it."

"You'll remember enough of it to write it to Ruth," Justin said. "You and Ruth. You made sure how it would turn out with Scott and me."

"Lord, child," Elinor drawled, "I hate to disappoint you, but Ruth never said two words about you and Scott. You got nobody to blame there, baby, but your own self. It's like I told you the other day."

"You're mighty proud of how you always know what's going to happen before it happens. You had to wait around here, didn't you? You had to say I told you so."

"Hell," said Elinor, "it was Lance wanted to stay. I been ready to go home for three hours."

Simon and Lance exchanged glances. Lance shrugged. "Wimmen," he commented.

Nobody said anything. Justin finished off her sandwich, then picked

192

Elinor's half-full glass from the table and drank it down.

"When's Ruth coming back, Elinor?" Lance inquired conversationally.

Before she could reply, Justin brought the empty glass down heavily on the table. "Ruth, Ruth, Ruth," she cried. "It's all I can hear, day and night. If anybody says Ruth to me one more time—I'll, I'll—" She cast about for a phrase, failed, jumped to her feet and walked angrily toward the hallway, her bare heels thudding.

"You'll what?" Elinor murmured. As barely audible as her words were, intended principally for her own satisfaction, Justin heard. She wheeled in the doorway, flinging her heavy hair back dramatically.

"I'll say that Ruth Armstrong is a murderer," she said. "I'll say she drove Ben Gardner's car into the gully and killed him—killed him— killed him—"

Her last words were shouted, half-sobbed on the stairway, for Elinor and Lance had sprung to their feet after the shock of her first utterance and rushed toward her together where she stood in the doorway, for a moment defiant, her face contorted with shock at what she heard her own voice utter and the tears of hatred and heartbreak rushing full and over-due into her slate-colored, expressionless eyes, until seeing Elinor's hand raised to strike her across the mouth, she dodged and ran for the stairs. Barefoot, she took the steps four at a time, the familiar ground she had run since childhood, while Elinor caught her high-heel in the rug and half-fell but did not stop, as Justin's crying, "Killed him—killed him—" rushed on now without volition or control, like a mad dog that must be shot to stop him running. It continued in sobbing, muffled inarticulate noises, the rhythm of the phrase without articulation, even after the bolt was shot on the bedroom door where Elinor stood and beat her fists against one side while Justin stood and beat her fists against the other.

Below stairs Lance, who had stopped in the doorway after the first dash that Elinor inspired, leaned lazily against the door jamb and peered after his wife and sister. He started suddenly. There was

Simon, standing just at his shoulder. He had not noticed his father move from the chair.

"Is it true?" Simon asked. "Dan'l Armstrong's daughter-in-law? Is what the child says true?"

Lance nodded, "We were all in the car," he said. "Ruth was driving."

"Yeah?"

"We didn't see any reason to do anything about it; probably cause a big trial, waste a lot of money. It was pure accident."

Simon grunted. He stretched and shook a long audible yawn out of his heavy frame.

"You ought of told me about it," said Simon. "I ain't got any reason to do nothing about it either."

"Well, you know now," said Lance.

"I'm going to bed," said his father. In the hallway above, Elinor still pounded on the thick, oak-paneled door. Simon turned on the stairs. "Son," he said, "I'm too sleepy right now and Miss Elinor's in such-and-such a temper. But you might drop by the store tomorrow afternoon and tell me all the de-tails of this."

Lance thrust his hands in his pockets and stared at the toe of his shoe. "Just leave it alone, Papa. There's been enough said now. Just leave it alone."

"I aim to leave it alone," Simon said. "But there ain't no harm in finding out what all I aim to leave alone, is there?"

"I guess not," said Lance.

"All right then," said Simon. "You coming over tomorrow?"

Lance thought a minute, then shrugged, looking up to meet his father's eyes. "All right," he said. "I'll come."

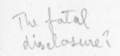
The fatal disclosure?

FOURTEEN

O N Monday morning when the blue coupe bearing Ruth Armstrong and Scott Shaffer was scarcely fifty miles along its journey, Miss Cherry Bell LaGarde died. Her death occurred within forty-eight hours, almost to the minute, after she learned that her old lover's parting gift to her—a gift large enough to set before the eyes of all Tarsus the sign of his defiance—was mysteriously missing from below her window. Randall Gibson, who was beside her constantly, was moved to considerable inward philosophizing when he noted that the burden of her half-rational complaints was directed not against whoever had taken her treasure from her—a fact which never became clear in her mind, nor did he try to make it so—but was bitterly turned on whoever had *allowed* this to be done. She accused the living and the dead. She railed weakly against him, against his father and mother, against people whose names he had never heard, against poor Kinloch Walston himself, but more often than all, against a group designated simply as "they."

Whisky and all the drugs that Randall and Dr. Moore could muster afforded no relief, probably because her system was long familiar with them, so that she was more or less already in the state they were supposed to produce. All, that is, except sleep. She did not sleep. Be it to Randall's credit that he did not sleep either for the two nights and days that he sat beside her, sending the colored girl for anything she wanted and patiently answering the same questions a thousand times, until on Monday morning she turned her head in its dainty lace-trimmed cap away from the window, asked her last question—"Is your mother *ever* coming to see about me?"—and died.

Be it also to Randall's credit, though no one knew for certain, that he was genuinely grieved, perhaps more genuinely than most in bereavement because his grief carried no feeling of his own loss, but only sorrow for her and the course of her life for which his mind supplied many adjectives.

Yet he had lost something, he realized, after the funeral was over and he came back to the empty house where no one called down the stairs to him and he knew that when he walked up town tomorrow no one would stop him to inquire of poor Miss Cherry Bell. He realized that, for all his harangue to Kinloch, she had been the one thing of Tarsus that was peculiarly his own. "In sickness and health, for better or worse, till death do us part," he repeated sardonically to himself, and forthwith began arrangements to make his departure.

Be it also said for Randall that he himself packed for safe keeping the small articles in her room which she had treasured: the gilt-encrusted souvenirs of the St. Louis Exposition, her letters from Kinloch Walston, the little blue French-heeled slipper from which a Memphis beau had once drunk her health in champagne, and other such like.

So a week after her death, he came down into the hall where the auctioned furniture was huddled, jammed sofa next to dresser on top of bed, with delicate fingers picked his hat off the top of a china pitcher trellised in pink roses and went to ride with Kinloch to the station.

"Where will you go, Randall?" Kinloch inquired.

"Where I have no identity, Kinloch."

"What I mean is, what does your ticket say under 'destination'?"

"New York. But no, no, no! Do not give me Ruth's address. She is a vision of delight and if I look up someday from behind my newspaper in the park and see her passing, I shall thank whatever gods may be for letting her be there, but I shall not go and speak to her. And if she comes too close, I shall hurry away muttering something to a near-by cop in an authentic Bronx accent. The last thing I want to see on the face of the earth for ever and ever is somebody from Tarsus. I inevitably shall, because they are everywhere, but when I do my every effort will be directed toward dodging away before it is too late, before the eyes glow in sadistic recognition and the voice says, 'Well, I declare, if it isn't Randall Gibson!' You know, Kinloch, in a big city they do everything to identify you. They name the street you live on by a number. They put another number on your house. They reach you by a number in a telephone book. They number you at work, for taxes, for social security, for the proper table in the restaurant. They pin you to earth with numbers like Gulliver among the Lilliputians. And yet you escape. It is a marvelous thing. I shall be down in the whole world's books, yet I shall be free. And if I choose to roll an old rubber tire down the middle of the street someday, as we used to do when we were children, nobody will say, 'What on earth is Randall Gibson doing? He's crazy, I tell you. Mama, I've always said he was crazy. Haven't I?' Yes, Kinloch, you sweat it out here in the self-importance of your little private battle, but do not think about me too much when you grow discouraged. You may decide on going away, too, but if you should, in heaven's name, I ask you as my last request, my death-bed plea as far as you are concerned—don't ever look me up."

"I'll miss you, Randall," said Kinloch. "We all will. More than you know."

Randall's pliant, mocking lips grew sober. Clad in the assembled phenomena of a new hat, a coat and pressed trousers, he looked so incongruous to his usual self as to be almost comical. An old-maid look, that was what he had. An old-maid-school-teacher look. "Thank you, Kinloch," he said, and even his emotion was disciplined and prim, something he had probably thought about ahead of time and decided to keep in hand.

"Randall," said Kinloch as they stood on the slate-covered gravel beside the tracks, while the freight and baggage wagon ground into position, tugged along by a sweating Negro boy. "Randall, I've been in the court house the past few days."

"Reading court records," said Randall with his old gossipy promptness. "I've seen you slip in and out, skirting Gerrards. So I figured. So I figured."

"There was a Dr. Derryberry," said Kinloch.

"Exactly," said Randall. "I've got a conscience, Kinloch. I've got no business pushing the very button of the violence machine."

As mournful, urgent and unarguable as time, the train whistle blew.

"When you said that Father and Felix McKie were planning a new trial, you couldn't have meant just reopening of the same case. Because they had a good idea of the evidence Aunt Cherry Bell could have given, yet they did not call her as witness. And since they had knowledge of that evidence at the time, they couldn't change their minds and open the trial again on the strength of it. And from the tale as you told it, there was no other loophole."

"Ah," said Randall. "You have also been reading law."

"Yeah, and when I came across that I knew where you had misled me. You slurred over it. Yet you have a law degree. There, I said. There is what's wrong."

The tracks clattered, the drivers rolled, pounding. Tall, great and black, the engine surged ino Tarsus.

"Oh," cried Randall, as white steam hissed at the hot, untroubled calm of the little station, "to think that I leave still untied the biggest string on God's little surprise package, Tarsus. But if I stayed to watch that there would be others, always others."

"I've found out that Dr. Derryberry lives back in the hills, about thirty miles beyond Keystone Bottom, way back in that God-forsaken country where the Gerrards came from in the first place."

"In the beginning," Randall said, "one sometimes finds the end."

Back of them, a fat colored woman toting her dinner in a grease-spotted shoe box labored into the first coach behind the engine. Before them, a thin white woman of patient expression was aided up the steps. She clutched a mixture of green plants, wrapped round the roots with a wet newspaper.

"All abode!" the spruce porter called.

198

"Wait!" Randall called. "Hold it a minute, boy!"

"Boss," said the Negro, grinning. "We's on time today. Mos' any other day we's late and he don' care, but when we's on time, hit puts de bee on him." Then he called generally, as though a great crowd waited: "All abode!"

So, with a quick shake of Kinloch's hand, an anxious trying to get another word in, a calling back that was forever lost in the renewed hiss of steam, a struggle of big black-shod feet and big black suitcase through the narrow entrance, Randall Gibson left Tarsus.

And Kinloch Armstrong stood watching till the biggest part of the noise was gone; then he gave a pull to his hat brim, wheeled as the last whistle sounded at the crossing, walked back to his dusty pick-up and drove away toward town.

A stalemate in prospect between what Kinloch knows about Generals and Generals know about Ruth?

Part Three

AUGUST in Mississippi is different from July. As to heat, it is not a question of degree but of kind. July heat is furious, but in August the heat has killed even itself and lies dead over us.

It was strange then that right in the dead center of August, Kinloch ran head-on into the time that was alive.

When he first sensed it, a little way off from him yet, he thought that it had to do with his having the crop in hand so that a day or so away wouldn't hurt. But he had known this about the crop since mid-afternoon, three hours before that moment when he stood on the gallery washing his hands.

He had to wash his hands a second time to get the pitch off. One of the Negroes had come riding in on the mule just as he had got cleaned up for supper and he noticed the gob of blood in the fresh track and how it lay on the dust refusing to mix. If it had mixed, he might have thought it was just a splash of water in the dust, but this way he saw the color and knew the mule was hurt.

"Hey!" he called. "Hey, Gold!"

"Suh?"

"You sidling up to that barn mighty fast. How'd you hurt Bob?"

"Suh?" Gold was all pain and surprise. "Bob hurt?"

Kinloch jumped down from the gallery. "Cut himself on the plow. I told you to watch him about that. Not bad. Go get that can of pitch for me and go on, go on to town where you're heading, but next time this happens and you don't let me know—"

"Yes, suh, Mist' Kinloch. Next time I sho goin' notice."

He examined the cut which had laid the tendon bare just above the off hind fetlock; said, "Whoa!" and daubed it; let the mule into the lot and slung the harness into the barn. Then he was on the gallery again, sloshing water into the pan, for though they had put in plumbing when Ruth came, it was hard to change habits. He saw Gold come out of the wood below the lot, cross the lower pasture and crawl through the barbed wire fence instead of using the gap (and he was going to ruin that fence, too, crawling through it). Gold entered the wood again, going home where he would not stay very long.

Kinloch took in all this as he reached for the towel and then he stopped, his dripping fingers extended, because the pasture where Gold had just been, the lot where the mule was eating now, the barn where the harness lay crumpled, and the pan which held the dirty water—all had changed into something different.

Later he had reason to wonder if all those concerned in the events of the next two days had not also been stirred at this moment.

He ate supper hurriedly and just before it got good dark he was back on the gallery by the bucket and wash pan again to see how things were and things were still different. Sometimes you just get winded or have too much sun and things cut-up like that, he thought.

He watched the bronze light fade from the clouds that lay in the northeast. Right in there somewhere, he thought. Right in there and it's time to go see. The crop's in hand and this has come over me strong as preachers lay claim to and it's time to go see.

When dark had descended completely, he crossed back through the house to tell his father. In the room, the warm sweet scent of Ruth was threaded into the darkness. Nearly four weeks now she had been away. His heart ached, for he felt that all was not well and had not been since the night they had quarreled. Once before she left he had determined to cast aside long enough to speak with her about it, the feeling that she had betrayed him, but there was such a look of dread about her at times that he was sure again that he was right in what he had thought and he would not bring it up. Then she was gone and there was nothing to say, for he expressed himself but poorly in writing and her letters were worse than his. She kept saying she would stay a few days longer.

204

Then he went on across the room. Wait? he thought. Why, I will do well to wait for morning.

"I'm going fishing with Thomas T. tomorrow," he told his father.

"So?"

"Leaving before day."

"So?"

"I may not be back till Friday."

"What's today? Wednesday?"

"Wednesday."

There was a long silence out there on the front porch in the numb, thick darkness. Knows as well where I'm going as if I'd shouted it, Kinloch thought, and between exasperation and humor, his pride was melting fast and he might have spoken if Dan Armstrong had not at that minute begun to sing. He sang loudly, beating the chair with his walking cane, about Ole Dan Tucker (he got drunk, fell in the fire and kicked up a chunk); and as soon as he finished that he started on Cotton-Eyed Joe and then Rachel, Rachel, I Been Thinking and The Broad Missouri. Kinloch sat with the song like a wall between him and the rocking chair, trying to probe the enigma of it. Maybe he's just singing to be singing, he thought at last, going into the house. I'll tell him about it when I get back.

He drove out of town early the next morning on dusty roads, but by ten o'clock he saw that there would not be dust for long. There would be mud, and what mud, he thought, for the road lay so deep in dust that to a watcher the pick-up must seem a black speck chased forward by ballooning yellow clouds. The road tunneled narrowly into the hills. Sometimes its channel was cut full fifteen feet downward to the bed. The high roadsides had eroded inward from their crest where oak sprouts clung and grass lay whitened from the drought and elderberry vine hung round white blossoms myriad-eyed in the dust.

On roads like this when the dust sealed off a backward view, a driver saw only the rise or descent or twist of the way ahead and if another car met him and the two happened to avoid collision, he must stop, draw far over and creep past, two wheels in the ditch like as not, while the pursuing dust sprang hungrily from both ways, whirling and boiling into nose and eyes, leaving its dry coat on the sweaty skin.

But Kinloch met no cars that journey. At intervals the hills would break and the road would run level with the fields and then he would watch the clouds. They were piling high in the east and they hovered and circled just out of his vision as though they gathered strength to close in on the sun.

If it rains, I'll never get out of here, he thought. I ought to turn around and get on home fast as I can. But he went on.

The farther he went the more he marveled at the deadness of the whole scene. Randall Gibson had been right when he said you could ride out here for a whole day and never see a house. Kinloch had touched the area himself, quail hunting in the fall, but that would be after cotton picking when things would seem barren anyway. Now not even a strand of smoke floated upward from the hills to reassure him. What little cotton was planted had not grown tall and bloomed half-heartedly, while in wider fields thin weeds grew over the shallow ridging of old rows.

Between such a field of cotton and such a field of weeds, beside a fence bending under the weight of jackson vine, in the middle of the hot sun, the pick-up jerked and went dead.

If the Gerrards had to come through this when they headed for Tarsus, it's no wonder they won't be prized loose, he thought.

An hour later he shut down the hood—the metal so hot it burned his hands, mopped off the sweat and some of the grease and observed how the clouds were swift now in the sky, how their motion increased the fixation of vine and tree and field, but he knew that before long these would writhe together when the wind struck, like the feathers of a dead bird blowing.

Soon's I find me a place to turn around, he thought.

He found the side road to turn, but he found also the fresh marks of a wagon and team going north between two fields, and instead of turning around, he followed.

Dust whipped before and behind in the wind. Midday light streamed down the clouds and flooded the scrubby horizons, like a sudden color-shot in a black-and-white movie. Then the clouds made their move and the sun went out. But Kinloch's heart had quickened again. If I can follow these folks home, they might lend me a mule, he thought. I can still get there today, if I can just get a mule.

He lurched at high speed over the rutted road, so sure that his pick-up and perhaps the wagon were the only things on it that he almost ran down the man on the calico pony. All he could see for a minute were spotted belly and frantic unshod hooves; then the pony came down stiff-legged and flat-eared and the limber sallow-faced young man in a golf cap leaned toward the window and said in a voice that was like a rifle bolt sliding home:

"You foolin' with me?"

"I'm mighty sorry," said Kinloch. "I didn't see you till it was too late. I was trying to locate a house up that hill yonder."

"No house there."

"Then where's the nearest house?"

"Go back to the big road and on about five miles." He clicked to the pony.

"Hey!" Kinloch yelled.

"Yeah?"

"Where 'bouts this road go then?"

"Peters out, stranger. 'Bout a mile the other side of that there hill."

"Listen here," Kinloch said. "I got a gas line in this engine held together with tape that ain't going to last five miles even if I could go five miles and that I can't, because this flood is going to break in the next five minutes. And if there ain't any house on that hill up there and if this road peters out in the next mile, where in the name of God are those fresh wagon tracks going?"

"Listen, stranger," said the limber young man. "I got seven miles to ride through wood and hollow with nair a cast of road broad as this here. I got bridges to cross what have been known to bust out so clean and go so far that one time my grandpappy rid over in the Delta in ginning season and seen something laying up side of a cotton house and said, 'There's that-air bridge washed out last June.' I'm riding a hoss that's hell bent and mortal touchy about getting his feet wet. And I don't see no wagon tracks noway."

"You foolin' with me?"

The young man shut his loose-lipped mouth quick, like a dog snapping flies. He began to grin.

"The Guptons live on top that hill yonder," he said. "Follow the road, stranger, and it'll take you there. Mind you holler from the front gate, stranger. The Guptons got no use for a stranger."

The first thunder broke as Kinloch pulled out before the low, white-washed house. Through the unnatural darkness, he could see two men running about in the side yard. They were hurling harnesses into the wagon which sat under an open shed, while a third, a boy, was dragging the team through the lot gate. Chickens flew squawking across the front yard, their feathers blown backwards in ruffs, and a woman held the front door open and pointed out across the hill, shouting. He looked behind and saw where the rain fled toward them in a high white wall, and he ran for the porch. The two men ran in from the side yard at the same time and they all three rammed into the door together, until the woman heaved them through and banged it shut behind them. In the space of silence with the wind closed out and the rain not quite there yet, the two men stood off together and eyed him. They were very tall men with exceptionally long arms, so long it seemed that when they walked their knuckles would bump their knees. He turned and saw a stumpy, muscular, middle-aged man, who stood in the doorway, eyeing him also.

"For pity's sake," the woman said quietly, "I told him to come on in." The rain struck the tin roof. "He was going to get drownded!" she shouted.

"What you want, stranger?" the stumpy man inquired.

"I got a way to go, rain or not," said Kinloch. "I want to borrow a horse or a mule."

"I ain't got hoss nor mule," said the stumpy man.

"I'm in a big hurry," Kinloch said. "My wife's low sick. I got to find a man name of Dr. Derryberry."

"You ain't from out this way," the other returned. "Ain't there doctors where you come from?"

"For pity's sake," the woman said. "Get inside with your talking. I'm going to fix dinner."

The stumpy man debated this advice, then he stepped aside and motioned Kinloch and the two tall men into a large square room with a double bed on each side of the door and some chairs set around an enormous swept fireplace.

Kinloch waited to be offered a place and then went to a chair without being offered it, and he and the three men sat down together in a friendly sort of circle, Kinloch thought, considering they made him feel like they were three rattlesnakes arguing about which one was going to strike him first. There was a small clucking noise behind him, but he did not turn. They evermore don't like strangers, he thought.

He heard the woman talking to somebody in what must be the kitchen and then he saw the girl. She came across the dusk of the room toward them, her steps and motions all silenced under the storm and he started up from his chair with a cry.

She stopped still at the sound, as rabbits do before they run, and her wide eyes cast up to meet his.

"Excuse me, ma'am," said Kinloch. "You looked so much like my wife I thought for a minute it was her."

"Well, she ain't yore wife," said one of the tall men, who sat between them. "She's my wife."

209

She set the lamp on the table. Her hands, cupped around the lighted match, showed big and calloused. But with the lowering of the chimney, the light climbed to her face and again he was startled to see the leaf-like brown eyes, the clear skin and dark hair, and in addition to feel again that manner that had struck out at him across the breadth of the room, a quality of perpetual evasion along the very path of longing. Then she looked at him again.

"Well," said the stumpy man. "Go on. You was saying Doc Derryberry cured somebody come down with this same thing your wife's got. How she took?"

Kinloch improvised a long list of symptoms.

"Sounds bad," remarked the stumpy man.

"That's how come I got to get to him right away," Kinloch said.

The stumpy man sucked his teeth and thought about it. "Still, it's funny I ain't never heared tell of it. If Doc's done cured a woman out here took with the likes of it, folks would of heared tell of it. You children heared aught of it?"

"I ain't," said the girl's husband.

"I ain't neither," said the second tall man with the inflection of getting done with it.

The three of them eyed him again, seeming to say that they had dismissed the question and that whatever happened now was up to him.

Then the girl spoke. Her voice was breathless, as though she had run a long way to tell them. "I heared tell of it."

The three men whirled to look at her as if she had never spoken before and they did not know until now that she could talk at all.

"Hit was over in Egypt," she informed them. She leaned forward, speaking only to Kinloch. "Egypt is where I come from." She jerked her hand. "Way over yonder way. I ain't been over here for long." This was some pride. "Hit was a woman down with pain in her chest and all that in late summer like this here and quinine didn't do no good, but Doc Derryberry he come and cured her. I don't know what

210

he done, but he cured her."

"What was her name?" the stumpy man asked from behind her.

She jumped, like the rabbit again, but she held ground. "Miz Barker. Ned Barker's wife. Ellie Dosha she was."

"You sho now?" asked her husband.

"I'm sho, Les."

"I'll pay in advance for the loan of the horse," Kinloch said. "You know good and well I'll have to come back to get my truck. That ought to do you for security."

"Se-currr-i-ty! Se-currrrr-i-ty!"

The hair prickled from his scalp and he sprang to his feet, wheeling toward the unearthly sound. A make-shift cage, square, like a miniature prison cell, sat on a shelf in the corner and there the parrot swung with cocked head and breathing, mocking beak half-open.

"Se-currr-ity!" the bird drawled again, then rapidly: "Hello stranger come speak to Joe you like it here plenty good whisky plenty good come speak to Joe. Pooo-ooor Joe! Se-currr-ity!"

The stumpy man rocked backward and forward; he slapped both his thighs and burst into a whoop of laughter. He got to his feet and repeated this process, rolling his shoulders in laughter. Suddenly, all in the room that had been threatening and close-packed under the beat of the rain, now broke exuberant from the shell. The two tall men shouted with laughter and beat each other staggering blows on the back. Les caught his wife and swung her about the room, his heavy shoes beating out some accurate rhythm he carried in his head. The parrot laughed louder than them all.

The man who started the uproar took it upon himself to quiet it also. He picked up the poker and struck the floor systematically until they sobered. Apparently he kept the poker near him for this purpose because the floor was scarred. He was as gruff as though he had never laughed at all, as though laughter was something he disapproved of by nature.

"Tobe," he said, "go saddle Betsy. This man wants to get along.

211

Won't stay to eat. Will you stay to eat, stranger? See, he won't stay to eat. Now if you're sho enough looking for the Doc, I'll tell you, you go right up yonder till the road forks. . . ."

Tobe brought the little red mare to the front steps. Kinloch went to mount, but Tobe had exchanged some form of communication with Les and he jerked the mount back into the rain. "You ain't leaving no *keys!*" he exclaimed to Kinloch, aggrieved.

"Ain't leaving what?"

"You leaving that-air truck, but you going off with the *keys*. Look ahere, Pa. He's going off with the *keys!*"

"It's his keys," said the stumpy man from the doorway.

"But Pa—"

"You, Tobe! You heared me. He's done paid for the loan of Betsy. It's his keys."

Kinloch moved toward the mare again.

"Oh, mister?" This time it was the girl.

"Ma'am?"

"You—?" She lost heart, forgetting; then she remembered and said it all at once, like one word. "You come from *town?*"

"Out from town. From right near Tarsus."

"Oh." She turned her face aside. She moved over to Les, standing very near to him with her arms dangling, not quite touching him.

Kinloch rode off into the rain. "Thank the Lord I'm shut of them," he thought, and not a mile along the way, coming through a second-growth stretch of woods, he made a sharp turn where the brush was heaviest and there they were, Les and Tobe, one behind the other astride a big black horse, like children out for a lark. Except that the back one, Tobe, was carrying a shot gun.

"Pa done changed his mind," Tobe said. "He done decided you better leave them keys for us to look after."

"Get out of my way," Kinloch said.

"We asking peaceable," said Les. "We ain't aiming to hurt nothing."

A fever of impatience, at odds with his usual deliberate nature, had been building in him steadily since he first looked at the sky and saw the clouds, and it was in cold fury that he struck the rain out of his eyes, and rode the mare straight forward, scorning them and the shot gun too.

Because I did not really believe in them, he afterward reflected, crawling out of the tangle of mud and wet leaves while his fingers explored his damaged forehead. I did not believe that if I touched them I would feel anything.

"I told you about them Guptons," said the voice.

He looked up into the face of the limber young man with the jack-knife features and the kind of golf cap city men wore before the depression aslant over his eyes. He was holding the two horses, Kinloch's and his own calico, and he was sitting patiently on a stump.

"Where are they?" Kinloch inquired, long past surprise.

"I run them off. I been hanging round here waiting to see what they was up to. I took to a hollow waiting for the rain to slack and when you rid by I started to call."

"Why didn't you?"

"Got too much Old Nick in me. I says to myself, I says, 'What them Guptons mean, having kindness to lend that man a hoss?' Then I seen Les and Tobe coming along on the other hoss, and I says, 'That man just ain't got no sense leaving that '33 pick-up where them Guptons can get aholt of it.' So I burnt the road through the short cut and doubled back and then come nigh to getting here too late. I let fly two shots and the second one blistered the hoss's tail before they could get down. Then was gone before they could say howdy, let alone goodbye." He jerked at his cap brim and laughed.

"They wanted my keys," Kinloch remembered. He felt in his pockets. The keys were still there. "Set on it, like children. Just like children, wanting something so bad they can taste it."

"They do love to drive a car now," the young man said. He was as philosophic in the middle of the downpour as if he sat under a shade tree with the sun shining. "They had one, you know."

213

"No. I didn't know." He mounted.

"Sure." The young man flipped the reins over his pony's neck. "Busted it up on the side of a hill one night here not two weeks back. Not a form thing in sight and the moon high. Driving full of that likker they make. It will confuse a man, I'm saying. Their feet been itching for a speedometer to shove ever since."

Kinloch rode on ahead. The young man trotted behind him. "Stranger," he called, "I'm just hoping there ain't no way them Guptons can find to start that car without the keys. They'll do it if they can."

They came out of the woods and the path broadened. The limber young man rode beside him now, and the sharp, sallow, laughing features, cut in two by the cap brim just at the bridge of his nose, sailed along beside Kinloch's shoulder in the comfortable camaraderie of the road, the astute hitchhiker who asks no questions and pays for his ride with a handful of amusing stories, well-told.

It seemed he had no notion of parting. Since he had done the favor and it had come off well, he took Kinloch over as his personal property. He had also an extra quality about him, something that the isolated country and his familiarity with it provided. He talked of his travels with pride and a touch of shyness. You didn't expect to find the likes of me out here, he seemed to be saying.

He had been up in Memphis not so long ago, working at a filling station, the biggest one on 70 going out towards Arkansas this side of the river, and there was a girl in Memphis, a blonde. He talked about her.

Then there was the time he went to Chicago and got a job as chauffeur for a wealthy lady who was a lot older than he, but still not what you would call old. She made love to him and let him borrow the car whenever he wanted it and he would go to see a red-headed girl that clerked in a store down town, one of those tony stores. That was all right till the rich lady found out about the red-head. Then she squalled and screamed and told her husband he'd been stealing the

214

car. But he never told her husband how she had acted behind his back and when the husband was fixing to have him charged with theft, he came back to Mississippi. "I come on back here," was how he put it, jumping over what kind of escape and chase Kinloch could only imagine.

"But sho enough, stranger, I never heard tell of folks acting like them two Chicago folks. Mean and low-down for no reason, but by nature. Her in her big fine fur coat squalling like two cats fighting. My gal showed her up she did and she didn't have no fur coat. And them acting like big shots. Have you ever knowed such folks?"

"Yes, I've knowed such folks."

They saddled along through the steady rain. "That Doc Derryberry, he's a funny one," said the limber young man. "Got a gold medal long years ago back in school, they tell me, but we never thought much about him. Just old Doc Derryberry, you know. I dropped the name oncet to a doctor in Memphis and right off he knowed all about him. He writes up things for doctors all over the country to read. I didn't think nothing about it then, but after I got back from Chicago, I got to studying about it. If Doc is all that much, what's he got in mind living all his life back here in Dark Corners? I tell you one thing, mister, a man has got to get out in the world. Soon's I feel the time loosen, you know where you'll find me?"

"Chicago?"

"I hadn't got it all studied out yet. But I know where you won't find me."

"Happen to know any folks name of Gerrard living out this way?" Kinloch inquired.

The jack-knife face tilted quickly toward his own and he got his first glimpse of the sharp eyes. "You looking for Gerrards?"

"I used to go to school with a boy by that name. I have heard they came from out this way."

Of course, he thought. They would have a name out here too. Else why would he look at me so?

"There's some around these parts, though you might be riding wrong if you aim to find them."

"I don't aim to find them. The only man I want to find is Dr. Derryberry."

"Then you got your want," said the limber young man and pointed.

Down an eroded slope of field so matted in weeds it looked at first glance like a sweet potato patch, at the foot of a steep wooded hill opposite them, the level of earth lay flat and brown as a piece of cardboard. Just back of the center in this area, as exactly as a child might have placed a sand house on a space of his own sweeping, was fixed the square, one-room cabin. A shed room jutted off at the back. Twin rows of cedars, set with the same exactitude, formed a path to the door. The cedars were white-washed an even distance up each trunk and these with the whitewashed cabin stood out solid and clear as a child's careful drawing, while all about them sky and wasted fields and dull woods mixed fluid together under the rain.

"Hope your wife gets all right," said the limber young man.

"Hey, wait a minute!"

The young man drew rein and turned.

"If it hadn't been for you chasing Guptons off me, I don't know what would have become of me. That and showing me the way here. I want to thank you."

"Why sure, stranger." The young man flipped up the brim of his cap and grinned all over his pliant features. "Sure glad to be of help."

Kinloch found himself smiling back. In the pleasant give and take of their talk, his impatience had slipped from him without his noticing; he would miss this boy. Impulsively, he rode forward, holding out his hand. "My name is Kinloch Armstrong. If ever I can help you, you got nothing to do but come to Tarsus and ask for me."

"Oh, I doubt I'll be wanting nothing," the young man said, shaking hands. "But do any Chicago folks driving a long black car come a-wanting me, you might just let it drop easy-like, how I done skipped out for the Ri-yo Grande. You just tell them that."

216

"Asking for who?"

"Tom," said the limber young man, flipping down his cap brim. He wheeled the calico pony smart as a circus cowboy and clapped his heels in. "Tom Gerrard. That's me."

He was gone in a gallop, over the rise and down the slope beyond. He disappeared inch by inch so that his horse seemed to be galloping on one spot where the earth sank magically, claiming elbows, swaying shoulders and last of all, the jaunty cap.

The pony had thrown a splash of fresh mud on Kinloch's cheek. And I was thinking how I might look him up to go hunting with me this fall, he sat saying to himself more than once.

The gritty feel of the mud recalled him. He rubbed it away. He did not decide to go on, he just went on anyway without thinking about it; he was going ahead on something he had already decided.

He dismounted and knocked at the door.

"Come in!"

There was no knob, he gave the door a push that was too hard and it slammed back against the wall. He stepped inside. The cabin was one large dim room. Opposite him, the door into the shed room stood ajar, so that he could see the furnishings of the doctor's office; a cot, a table where a black bag rested, a dentist's chair and shelves piled with thick drab books. It was hard to make out the objects in the larger room because the wooden shutters were closed. There was a fireplace, swept and cold, an iron bed, and over in one corner a neat little coal-oil stove with pots and pans hanging in graded rows above it.

But when he turned toward the reach of the room upon his left, he discovered furnishings of less severity. A pillowed couch, books and an Aladdin lamp upon the table, and back of these, there by the one open window, a little man nestled in a great armchair like a child. His thin hands rested upon a book which lay open on his lap and he was watching Kinloch with an interest both intense and undisturbed.

"Come in," his high voice commanded for the second time.

217

Kinloch closed the door and approached. The little man leaned forward and held out his hand. Kinloch started at the contact; it was the hand of a child not ten.

"Forgive me for not getting up. He has come a long way, I told myself, and with some trouble—" He regarded the swollen bruise on Kinloch's forehead. "Yes, with some trouble. A long way, with serious intent and trouble. If I had stood to greet you—well, we both might have felt a little foolish."

Here he did rise, and Kinloch saw his meaning. He was impossibly short; he would have had almost to stand on tiptoe to reach his visitor's shoulder.

"Sit down, Young Armstrong." He resumed his own seat, tucking his legs under him.

"You know me?" Kinloch cried. "Who told you I was coming?"

"There now," said Dr. Derryberry. He pulled at a goatee which, together with his sparse untrimmed locks of reddish gray hair, made him look like a miniature diplomat out of a high school history text. "Nobody told me you were coming, Young Armstrong. It has been in the back of my mind for some thirty-five years—thirty-six, to be exact —that something like you would come tramping in one day. You look a great deal like your father looks or used to look. Tell me, is he still alive?"

"Yes, he's still alive."

"And he sent you, did he? He thought better of it at last?"

"No. No, he didn't send me."

"No? Then why do you deny it so quickly?"

"I didn't come to find out things about myself," Kinloch said. "I'm not interested in that. I'm interested in finding out things about you, doctor."

"I know, I know." The doctor spoke with precision, yet there was a drowsy quality beneath the surface of his voice, something of the complete self-interest of the person who wishes to go to sleep. "You won't have to threaten me. I shall tell you whatever you wish. About

218

me, about Dark Corners, about medicine—"

"About a trial?"

"Of course. About a trial, of course."

"Now that I'm here at last, I don't see quite what you wanted so much as all that, doctor." He noted again the ascetic nature of the room. "God knows why you'd want money or what you'd do with it after you got it."

"Then you were telling me the truth, were you? Your father didn't send you after all."

"I wouldn't lie to you." His mouth twisted a little on the ugly word.

Dr. Derryberry smiled dreamily. "Neither would you spare me."

"Not money then," Kinloch continued, "but something you wanted worse than money. The lie you told back then might have got you what you wanted at the time, but it got you what you didn't want, too. You didn't plan it this way after the fine medical school record and your name a sign of promise all over the state. You didn't plan to spend a lifetime out here in the woods."

"I was born here."

"You like it here?"

"I have grown to like it. I hated it once—for many years."

"Then what made you do it? What made you swear to God before a courtroom that a lie was the truth?"

Dr. Derryberry set the fingers of his hands together. "A lie is a bad thing, eh, Armstrong? We start with that, the axiom, the given symptom. A lie is bad. So we proceed towards truth. But here we strike the first obstacle. In order to proceed one must go backwards. Do you want me to proceed?"

"Whatever you've got to say, backwards or forwards, I came to hear it."

"I got entangled," said Dr. Derryberry. "That was it. I was entangled." He paused, as though sampling the validity of the statement he had made.

"What do you mean, 'entangled'?" Kinloch asked.

"It will surprise you to know," said the doctor, "that I am as anxious to tell you as you are anxious to hear. Have patience.

"For one thing, my mother was a very religious woman. For another, I have always been excessively small. My mother took me as a child to all-day revival meetings. I heard the stories of the man who tried to get away with something or other and do good without repenting, but this evil he had done caught up with him without fail. Also the stories of the man who tried to do evil and get away with it without doing good, but when he came to die he would remember his mother and Jesus and repent, so that this also caught up with him without fail. All around me, something of this nature was happening to people I knew, and on several occasions I remember well, many of them shouted or knelt or ran up to the platform or prayed aloud or cried. Also, I learned when I was not at revival meetings that I would always be small, and that I would never be able to compete. Laughter is too loud here, families are too large, trees grow to great height— or did before the lumber men invaded us, and men shoot thunderous shot guns. Most of them would seem to be all of one husky size, though by an actual survey of this I have proved it untrue; but they are so sure of their majority in this matter that they will undertake to call the fat man Fatty, the thin man Skinny and the little man Runt. I could never deal with them.

"My record in medicine at the university has been called phenomenal, but this term is incorrect. The record is merely the outward measure of my inward wish to escape. Most men, I suppose, find their religion in life and their superstition in medicine. I have reversed this order. Medicine became my surety, and life my superstition. A superstition, I may add, is not at all false to the man who holds it. He calls it by its true name only when he is with others. When he is alone, it casts its shadow on him and he feels its power.

"I had not been home in six years when I received word that my mother was dying and that I must hurry to reach her in time. This came just as my plans were complete to open my first practice in

Birmingham. I told myself that I would go to her, but that I would not hurry. Yet the revivals had done their work, I found. I did hurry against all my will and better judgment. I arrived just in time for her to extract my promise: I was to take care of my sister and my sister's child until they could find a place elsewhere. If I had not hurried, I would have arrived and found that relatives or friends had taken charge of this matter and I would have been pushed aside. I made the promise and I kept it, but I did not wish to live with them. I moved into this cabin and during the ensuing weeks my first patients began to arrive. Shortly after, my sister went away to look for work and the child came to live with me.

"I had wished to live alone and with this event I began to be afraid. My sister left with the intention of sending for the child within a matter of weeks. Of that I am sure. Her letters came often. It seemed that every responsibility would soon be off my hands, and yet I was afraid. If you ever want anything to happen, Armstrong, begin to fear it.

"As the months passed, I grew fond of the child, a pretty, blonde-headed thing like my sister, but young, scarcely fifteen. The very prettiness that made me so fond of her, so avid to see her when I returned from a call, to love her finally as if she were my own child—this very quality also carried its own fear. Others would notice that she was pretty too.

"She came home one morning after spending the night with some friends over the hill from here. When she entered the room, I observed her features, her way of moving. I knew that it had come about."

He looked toward the door. He pursed his small wet red lips, from which the short correct words dropped one by one like pellets being counted into a bowl. Kinloch also turned toward the door. The young fair-haired girl, eyes shining, light on her feet as she closed the door behind her. . . .

"Not long after that I saw the man. He came to bring her home from a chance meeting, perhaps, perhaps from a rendezvous. She was riding sideways before him on the pommel of his saddle and he held her close to him, riding boldly to the very steps where he lowered her, then cantered away. I was peering through a window, but I dared not come out. From that time forward I was dragged forward from event to event. All my fears appeared before me one by one, embodied, along with much I had not thought to fear. I warned her of him, that he was past forty for all his fine looks and that he was up to no good, but I could never deal with her as an authority in such a thing, as I might have made her stay in bed if she were sick. I would tell her that he only rode out here on Sundays to impress his kin and that there were pretty girls in Tarsus he must know, but she would ask me if I thought they could be as pretty as she, and I had to give in. She kept it all on the level of 'courting,' teasing, blushing and so on, as the other girls would do with the younger suitors.

"Not long after she met him, early in '98, I stopped hearing from her mother. I wrote frantically, then in something close to panic I rode into Tarsus to send a telegram. There was a doctor in your town I knew—old Sheridan, dead now. I called on him while waiting an answer to the wire. That was the day then, that I was later supposed to have gone to Walston Cedars and examined Kinloch Walston. I played well into their hands, for I had told my business to no one, yet there were those who remembered my visit well enough to swear to the exact date.

"The telegram was not delivered. No one by my sister's name lived any longer at the address. You in your town, Armstrong, can you conceive how large to one here in Dark Corners the outer world can loom when it presents a mystery? I went to Jackson. Those who remembered her had some notion she had gone to New Orleans to take a new job. I went on to New Orleans, but there the faint track faded. I could not find her and no process, no method of what next to do came to relieve my mind. Since the whole question of the girl's safety had now become entangled for me in the question of finding the mother, I came home a defeated man. I ceased trying to enforce my will on her. I tried instead to make myself dear to her. No grandfather could have treated her with so little criticism or with so much care.

"When I saw my next fear come true, I tried again to take some action. It was the fall of '98. I waited for Young Wills Gerrard in the woods he always passed through going home. I accosted him. I remember my fear of the meeting. Had some injury made it necessary, I could have amputated his leg without a tremor, but I labored under this mission. I had wished for no such thing as this. Also he was tall and big. He had large features, I remember. His was a brutal face, a brutal man. He thought over the marriage I insisted upon. He laughed at my threat to protect her. 'I could knock the head off your shoulders with this whip, doctor,' he said. But he hinted that we might make a bargain. There was a trial approaching in Tarsus. He was interested in the outcome. The evidence of a doctor was of prime importance. It was necessary, he said, for his future. He made his offer—an offer that demanded my profession, my way, my religion, if you please—and I wandered home along the big trees in a daze.

"I entered the house and saw her. We had never spoken of her condition. But she was shamed, pitifully shamed, before me. She was preparing to leave, to run away. Where would the child go? The sight of her few possessions brought out and laid together on the bed was too much for me. I gathered her to me. I reached up and stroked her blonde hair. I told her that I had managed everything. That Young Wills would marry her soon. She cried with happiness and relief. I have re-lived that moment many times, Armstrong. I felt then for one short moment the joy the good provider for his wife and children must feel often within the walls of his home. You have a wife, Armstrong?"

"Yes, I have a wife."

"And children?"

"No children."

"Ah. Then of the trial you already know. He had a suspicious nature, this brutal man, so that he would not fulfill his bargain until I had fulfilled mine."

"But Simon Gerrard, doctor! He swore he went with you to the examination that you never made."

"Simon? Oh, yes, the young one. He was anxious that all should come out well. He insisted to his brother that since their part in the case had been kept secret—it was ostensibly, I believe, a battle between the relatives and the heirs—Simon insisted that he swear that he had accompanied me to the examination. It would have been a natural thing. I knew his people. They have lived out this way for many years."

"He got anxious," Kinloch repeated. "He wanted to make sure."

"Young Wills thought the move a dangerous one, but he was willing to let his brother do it instead of himself."

"However you look at it, the facts remain," Kinloch said. "Simon did it."

"Two nights after the trial was over," Dr. Derryberry continued, "Young Wills came riding here with the preacher and a witness. As it turned out, this was the day before his death. He gave the girl to know that night that he had been forced to marry her in order to gain things much dearer to him than she was or ever had been. I understood then how sweet it must be to murder.

"The girl was stricken. She loved him, or fancied she did—it is the same at the time. The child was born a few hours later, in the early morning. I delivered it, a poor thing, two months premature. The girl grew hard after that. It was a great burden to me, a constant pain. She was no longer the light-footed pretty child who had seemed, for a little space, like my own daughter. I am almost sure there were other men. Her baby—a boy, Young Wills Gerrard's son—lived to be around ten. I cared for it as I had cared for her. She left me years before, going the way her mother did before her, to some town to work, though not in the good way her mother went. Whatever course she

224

took, it was not what her mother chose, I am certain of that.

"By then I knew that I would be here always. My deed at the trial had canceled my last hopes of some day becoming a great leader in my profession. But by then I was inured to the thought of staying. I do a great deal of work in this area; I visit houses in a radius of twenty miles, and the next doctor is twice that far away. It is the most I can do: attend to my work, write a few medical articles and keep my house swept.

"When the boy died, I sat here alone for the first time in fifteen years,—I who had intended to carry out a promise to my mother and spend a few weeks with my sister. The next step was before me; I saw it plainly. The next fear had already formed. I had done an evil thing and it would catch up with me. Someday, I said, when I am coming in from a call there will be a man waiting for me on the steps; or while I sit here reading at sundown, a knock will come at the door. You see now how it has been. Now that you are here, Young Armstrong, what do you want me to do?"

"Perjury," said Kinloch at last, half to himself, as if by naming the technical name he could somehow compress or cancel all the circumstance of its performance.

"Perjury," repeated Dr. Derryberry, as though he named an obscure disease.

"For Simon Gerrard who swore he went with you, but unfortunately for you too."

"Simon Gerrard and I. Yes."

"I had expected," Kinloch said, "to find a man who did wrong with a wrong intention, but you—you are a victim like all the rest of them. You did the best you could."

"Goodness has little to do with outcomes," said Dr. Derryberry. "Evil is different. Doing evil will catch up with you, whatever excuse you had, and it is hard. I know. But it is a thousand times easier than trying to undo evil. You will find that out."

Kinloch flung his head like a goaded animal. "I can't waste time

225

this way!" he cried. "It's getting late and I can't waste time. If you start fumbling and fooling around in a mess of words, first thing you know you've got the devil on the throne of God."

Dr. Derryberry nodded slowly, smiling with some private understanding. "I see the difference now. I had wondered what it might be."

"What difference? What do you mean?"

"In the late evening of the very day the trial was concluded, I looked up from where I am sitting now and saw your father standing in the door."

"My father? Here!"

"Here for the same reason you have come. He came in much the same way, on a spattered horse through mud and rain. He threw the door back hard just as you did. It was mid-winter and quite cold. I was a young man then, of course, and the girl was asleep on the bed. Until just now, until the minute you said that you could not waste time, those few things were the only difference between that day and this. . . ."

When Kinloch rode back early the next morning, there was a new batch of Guptons sitting on the front porch. Night had come on before he had finished his mission with the doctor and uncertain of the way back, he had consented to sleep there. He rode toward the Guptons with some caution. The stumpy man was on the porch and the woman who had let him into the house, but the others were children of all sizes, dressed in overalls and gingham in various conditions of repair. They were everyone of them shelling butter beans. Innocent as a basket of kittens, Kinloch thought as he flung the reins over the gate post.

"Howdy," said Mr. Gupton peaceably, as he mounted the steps.

"Howdy," said Kinloch.

"Stomp your feet on that-air crocker sack if you don't mind, stranger," said the woman, also peaceably. "I done swept three times already."

226

The children surveyed him and went on shelling butter beans. It was implicit in everyone's manner that the storm was over.

"You find Doc all right?" inquired the stumpy man.

"There stands your horse," said Kinloch. "I'm much obliged. Now if you'll just tell me what you've done with my pick-up—"

"Sorry as I can be, stranger," the stumpy man said. "Les and Tobe done gone for a little ride this morning. They ought to be back long about now."

"A ride!"

"Well," the other reasoned, "you was gone on one hoss, the other hoss is stove up, a mule is a off-an-on critter to ride and they had to git sommers faster than the wagon could go."

"Like knocking me over the head wasn't enough, you've got to go do this."

"Knocking you over the head!" Mr. Gupton brought his feet down on the floor with a thud from where they rested on a wash tub of petunias. "Them wildcats. They going to git me in trouble yet."

"I swan," said the woman. She got up and funneled an apron full of beans into the bucket. "I knowed they was up to something. Mind Rosa don't hear you."

Her words were scarcely out before the pick-up came roaring up the hill, spewing mud like an outboard motor. Les and Tobe regarded Kinloch with some disappointment. "Done come back," they remarked to one another.

Mr. Gupton did not say anything. He went into the house and presently emerged carrying a heavy black buggy whip.

"If they come for you this time," he informed his sons, "I'm going to turn you over to them without batting an eyelid. Helling through the mud in that man's car and telling me that hoss slipped and rammed on a stump when it's a bullet done it plain as the knot on his head." He pointed the whip at Kinloch. "I told you to go ask him for them keys, didn't I? If you're bound and determined, go ask him one more time, I said. I didn't tell you to maul him." He snapped the whip on the floor. "Git to the post. You first, Les."

Les stepped forward, abashed as a child at correction before company. He wrapped his brawny arms about the post, nearly reaching the roof and hid his face against his shoulder. The children cleared away.

"What I really need," said Mr. Gupton, rolling up his sleeve, "is a stouter whip." Then he had an idea. "Don't you move," he said to Les. He went into the house again and came out with a package wrapped in newspaper. He gave it to Kinloch. "Damages," he said, swinging back on the whip again.

Kinloch heard the blows begin to fall as he got into the pick-up. When they had failed to get the keys they had ripped out the wires back of the switch, but he was on to that trick. The mystery to him was the gas line. What the boys had done to it, he could never quite make out and neither could the garage man back in Tarsus, but whatever it was, it worked.

Was that the shrill laughter of the parrot he heard behind him?

He swung the long way around on his return trip, keeping to graveled roads, and that was how he came to pass through the little village of Bobolink where two men ran out into the middle of the street to stop him. One was the marshal and this one leaned through the window already talking.

"I always been friendly to you boys," he was saying, "and it ain't the honest trade I'm objecting to, but I done told you before you ought to stick to wagons because tearing through folks' front yards and driving down the sidewalk at four o'clock in the morning ain't nobody's idea of peaceful business. They're on my neck about it and I'm here to tell you— Hey!" He turned to the other man. "It ain't them."

The other man spit tobacco. "Any fool can see it ain't *them*."

"I mean," said the marshal, "it ain't either one of them."

"It's the car," said the other man.

"How you know it's the car?" asked Kinloch.

"Mister," said the man, "that car you're in run down a trellis of my wife's rambling roses and turned around in her petunia bed and busted two pots of maiden hair fern half in two and stripped the petals off every last zinnia she's growed, with me there yelling and her at home crying till this minute and the flower show next week and you ask me how I know it's the car."

good

"Did you get the license?" asked the marshal.

"License? What do I want with a license? That's the car."

Kinloch leaned out of the window. He picked up the parcel Mr. Gupton had given him, and passed it to the man with the grievance. "Damages," he said.

The man chewed tobacco a while, then he reached out his hand. "Okay."

"Lawd," said the marshal.

Kinloch touched his hat and drove away.

Grabs ahold of you like a suction pump, he said to himself, and don't want to let you go. It was Dark Corners he was thinking about, that place where by the side of the road lives the man who hits you on the head, where your blood enemy saves you from harm, where the pawn in the whole game puts you up for the night. The place where his father had come before him.

He knew one missing scene already; through Dr. Derryberry's meager phrases he had seen the whole event in all its strange detail.

"He came much as you came just now, on a spattered horse, through rain and mud. He threw the door back hard just as you did." And there sat the miniature mockery of a man, who knew he was a mockery, huddled head down and anguished in his big chair, his two tiny hands clenched between his knees. And there the girl lay, sleeping on the bed, and smiling, because she had gone to sleep knowing that Young Wills was coming to marry her soon now and everything would be all right.

Dan Armstrong took the scene in one glance from the doorway and after that one glance he no longer had to ask the question that had puzzled him over the long, muddy ride from Tarsus; he had only to answer it. "Young Wills' child!" he said, turning to confront Derryberry, who nodded silently, then broke down and told him everything. He told the truth because he really did not know anything about lying at all and the lie he told the court—the only one he ever told perhaps—was too big for him. It was crushing him already when Dan Armstrong came. It continued to crush him while Dan Armstrong listened. He told the truth because that was the only thing he could do, and oddly enough if he had schemed ten years for the meeting he could not have hit on a better thing. The girl slept through it all; they hushed their voices to keep from waking her.

"Very well," Dan Armstrong had said, "the child shall have a name then. I can wait for that."

"What are you planning?" Derryberry asked in resignation. "What can I expect?"

"As light a sentence as they can arrange for you, I hope," Dan Armstrong told him. "A sentence for the boy Si, too. And Young Wills, grand rascal that he is, will have not an acre to his name. The court will rule against him when the truth is known that the will is valid. The scoundrel can come back here where he belongs and look after his family. Tarsus will have no more of him when it all comes out. But like as not he'll be here with the preacher pretty soon. I'll be getting along, doctor." And he rode away.

Yes, "getting along," Kinloch thought, driving out of Dark Corners. Getting along back to town and what did he find there but January 20, 1899? Young Wills and Ole Tuck and Jeems dead and Felix blind. Then did he just give up? Or were there other scenes, scenes now in the mind, way down deep like a well where you have to wait to hear the stone strike the water you can't see, so deep that this long after he would start singing to block off having to explain or give an answer if I asked, "Did you just give up?" And what if I had asked? He would only have said it again, as he said it the night I accused him: "Si Gerrard just followed Young Wills; he was just on hand."

Rainbent grass and vines and muddy roadside sloshed past in empty monotony.

He could not hush the riot in his mind at any place except one, and he came on that place unexpectedly, for the road was strange. He crossed a rise and looking down he saw level after level of farm land break clear and unwooded toward the creek. Beyond the creek rose the water tower, the Methodist church spire, a smudge of train smoke climbing in the hot air (it had not rained here), and jutting in at the left, one corner of an ornate turret.

Over the ragged familiar topography, his thoughts shaped and quieted gratefully, as cover settles over a sleeping body.

I got what I went for, he thought. Never mind the rest.

The dust whirled up beneath the tires as he sent the car hurtling down the narrow grade, flinging himself toward Tarsus, toward the old condition like a thirsty man toward a spring.

SIXTEEN

O N the same night that Kinloch determined to make his journey, Ruth walked out of the apartment house where she was staying with Scott and, hailing a cab, gave a distant address. Arriving, she searched out the proper room number in the lobby and climbed the four dingy flights of stairs without hesitation or haste. But when she came to the door itself, she stopped and listened to the rapid beat of her heart, wondering if she would indeed lift her hand to knock.

All the way through the city, sitting in the cab, holding the address in her hand, she had thought that it would be quite in the order of things for her to find that the person she sought had moved, leaving no word, or at the most, was gone out for the evening. But here she stood, and light came narrowly out from around the door into the dark hall. From somewhere in the house a baby wailed on one note like a mechanical toy and in another sector a man and a woman wrangled at one another. She knocked at the door.

"Come in."

She turned the knob and stepped inside.

The man she had come to see lay on a rumpled day bed; the metal lamp that had once adorned his room in Tarsus was aflame beside him, and he was reading. He did not look up at once; it was as though he finished a paragraph. Then he lowered the book and the deep eyes below the forelock traveled slowly upward from the toes of her shoes, at last to her face.

"As long as anything that has ever seen Tarsus has legs to walk," said Randall Gibson, "it will seek me out."

"Kinloch sent me your address," she told him. "He said he would feel better about me if he knew—if I knew—that someone in the family—from Tarsus—"

"Except for one noted occasion, Kinloch has never paid the slightest attention to anything I ever said. The most singularly stubborn man I ever saw. Also he is unpardonably slow."

She reflected that Scott had angered her to tears not three days before when he made a slurring remark against Kinloch, but now she smiled.

"Not that," said Randall, observing her smile. "I am not concealing any heart of gold. I wish with all my soul you were not standing there. I am actually up here, you understand. I actually left. I wasn't being coy. Kinloch must have bribed Miss Mary Sue at the post office for that address."

"He did."

"I could wring his stubborn neck. After all I said to him. Well." He rose, towering improbably in the dim bare room where books leaned together on the shelves with the appearance of not having settled yet, and he dragged a chair out of the shadows for her. "Sit down, Cousin Ruth. I am not trying to say that I am not glad to see you. That is the trouble, you see."

She sat down. "I only smiled because I knew that in spite of what you said, you love him too."

"Of course," Randall said. "There are always two sides." He thrust his bony fingers through his hair in exasperation. "But try and tell Kinloch that. He goes through life the same way he would plow up a field, straight down the furrow with his eye trained on a fence post. How did he get my address? Why he went and demanded to have it, and in spite of my explicit instructions to Miss Mary Sue, he got it. He made you come away, didn't he? You got in the path of the plow and you saw it wasn't going to stop for you and you got scared—"

"You're going to say I ran away. I guess I did. I was afraid. He is concerned about something and I can't tell what it is, except that I think it is all my fault and—I thought if I left—"

"All *your* fault!" He stared and laughed and stared again. "Okay, okay. I'm just beginning to see the point about Homer being a woman.

Inter esting genesis of The Iliad.

Nobody but a woman could possibly imagine, much less state as sober fact, that ten years of war, the destruction of a city and twenty-four books of epic poetry were all the fault of a woman. On the other hand, maybe Homer was a man and a woman confronted him with the story. He saw there was just enough truth in it to make arguing with her practically impossible in such a small space—just twenty-four books—so he did the next best thing, he let it stand exactly the way she said it and went on with the story which—"

"Oh, Randall, hush, hush. I'm the one who hasn't got space to argue. It doesn't seem like much that somebody else caused a war when you've got one man's blood on your hands."

He pulled up short, rich hair and eyes slanting up at her under the lamp. "You *what?*"

She nodded. "Ben Gardner." The name had struggled darkly within her for so long that when she freed it at last she felt a warm, comfortable exhaustion and she closed her eyes, leaning back in the chair, and told him everything.

"Good God!" Randall cried. He had taken her hand to encourage her in the telling and now he dropped it almost roughly and lunged to his feet. "You don't know what Kinloch's up to and he doesn't know what you've done. Who in the name of God struck you both tongue-tied?"

Next page

"We quarreled," she said. "It got all mixed up that way and afterward—I was more afraid than ever. I don't know what to do. You've got to tell me, Randall. What am I going to do?"

He leaned swiftly and caught both her wrists together in one long hand and pulled her upright. "Now you tell me, Cousin Ruth," he demanded of her, "what *are* you going to do?"

She drew back from his abrupt grasp, his reversal in manner, flaring before she knew it or could think about it, saying the truth: "I am going home to him, of course."

"Right away?" he pursued, thrusting his face forward, the questions hurled at her. "Answer. Decide. Right away?"

She shrank. "I don't know. I've stayed too long now. What is it, Randall? What is on his mind?"

"He'll have to tell you that. Lord only knows what's happened by now. Somebody is going to get hurt; maybe the whole business will de-rail—"

"What is it, Randall? If only I knew. That's been the trouble all along. What is it you're trying to say?"

"That Kinloch needs you, Cousin Ruth. That you've got to go home and tell him at whatever risk, with whatever fears. Oh my God, don't you know that I understand how it is when one is not accustomed to act? You stood at the door just now for a while before you could knock. You might have just gone away. It is always a fifty-fifty chance that you might not do what is to be done, and then again you might. Still, you are better off than I. I have no chance at all. I was born at dead center where I remain, cross-legged as Buddha but I can't ever keep quiet about it . . . Yes, I said he needs you. And you must go home. Isn't that right? Isn't it?"

"Yes, I must."

"Right away? Tonight? You must."

"Yes, tonight."

"Good. It's done. There now. Don't let me frighten you. If nobody ever demanded anything of you, ever set you going the right way, you might stay up here four years instead of four weeks. Isn't that right?" She held on to his arm and he patted her shoulder with awkward kindness. "Don't worry, Cousin Ruth. What he will do when he finds out, I do not know, but he will not desert you. And do not be impatient. When you have lived there ten years or so, you will perhaps come to understand how it is next to impossible to put Tarsus and Old Daniel and Kinloch and Simon Gerrard into words, and when that time has passed and you go calling upon some newcomer who wants you to answer a thousand questions, you will find yourself shaking your head and saying that you have to get home and see about the children. But all you can do now is go back."

235

"I will, Randall."

He crossed the room and searched through the table drawer for a sheet of paper. "You know, Ruth," he said, writing, "I used to sit in the Melrose Cafe and watch you pass and wonder if the day would ever come when you would look me out and talk to me. I had decided no, and I believed no, and the knowledge rankled a little—vanity perhaps, perhaps some sense of incompleteness, something that would gnaw at me distantly and set me to wondering, Now what, What's wrong. But one has only to wait. Now that you have come and things are complete somehow, I will find that worrying me too. Here, give this to Kinloch. Remember now, he needs you without delay. No, don't thank me. When you know it all, you'll see how much is your fault, how much mine. Go on now. Tell me again. When are you leaving?"

"Tonight," she said, at the door.

"Good. Tonight. And don't stop to have things out with your charming brother."

"He doesn't know—anything."

"Of course not. He was a convenient spring board for getting away. Right?"

"Yes."

"Tonight now."

"Yes, Randall. I've said so."

He opened the door for her. She caught his hand. "Thank you, Randall."

"Lord, Cud'n Ruth," he said sincerely, "don't be thanking me."

She put her hands on his shoulders and tiptoed to kiss him on the cheek.

He smiled one of his rare, genuine smiles which no one in Tarsus would have recognized and in which there was more than a touch of shyness.

He saw that there had returned to her eyes an old look that he had missed that night—a confidence both appealing and very nearly pathetic, he had often reasoned, since it was based on innocence of things that were false. Then he felt the light pressure of her hands slip from his shoulders.

He stood in the lighted door and watched her go down the dim hall to the stairs. Somebody ought to go with her, he thought, because Lord knows if she'll get there. Like leading a heifer with a rope and pulling and tugging her until you get right up to the lot gate and then you look back and at the last minute she's slipped her horns out and all you've got is rope. I reckon that would be true if it was just duty and not love, too. But I reckon it is love, too. And I reckon she'll go, all right.

She turned at the head of the stairs and her trim figure, her natural grace of motion put the whole cheap building to shame, as she called back, "Randall? Randall, come go with me."

In the silence that followed her voice, he became conscious that a weakening pang was large within his breast. But on the moment that he realized this, he stiffened and reached to close the door. "No. There's nothing I can do. Nothing at all. Ever."

Then she vanished and he shut himself in, because it seemed that with the dying of her footsteps on the stair she was back in Tarsus already, walking down the street before the Melrose window, and that here alone, engulfed in the heart of the city, for all his boasting when she first entered, he would never be sought out by anyone again.

Which was what I wanted, he thought sardonically. He removed his toothbrush from an unwashed glass and poured himself a drink. He returned to his book, pushing down within him the dissatisfied feeling that it had been a very little visit she had paid him and that he could have dragged it out longer, much longer, talking, discussing. But there is reason for haste, he thought, and it is Kinloch she really needs. Kinloch who will stay there with it and do the thing wrong maybe or right maybe—but do it anyway and she will love him in whatever case. While I am gone, cut off, forever unable to take up the hand that in Tarsus I at least had the honor of consistently refusing. Gone; neither one place nor the other; just gone. Which is what I wanted.

The scene à faire.

SEVENTEEN

KINLOCH did not take time to go home on his return from Dark Corners; instead he drove directly to Walston Gap where Elinor Gerrard came out to the pick-up.

"Sure, Lock," she said, thrusting elbows and head into the window of the truck. The long summer had drained her face; her black hair was pulled straight back so that the bones stood out beneath the flesh with the old persistence of the skull. "Sure, if it's important. I'll go get Lance."

"Is Justin here?"

"Oh, Lord. Eternally. You want her too?"

The three of them crowded into the cab beside him. Justin sat on Lance's lap and wriggled, querulous but interested. She had been discovered in the back yard taking a sun bath, and refusing to dress, she had thrown a dirty shirt of Lance's over her halter and shorts.

"Is Ruth home?" Elinor inquired.

"Not that I know of," he said. "I haven't been home myself since day before yesterday." He touched his unshaven cheek absently and they did not ask him anything more, though Elinor did remark that if he wanted Miss Henrietta she was probably at home with a sick headache.

"She doesn't count," he said.

"Oh, I see."

"Then you're a hell of a lot smarter than me," Justin said, scratching.

"Aw, shut up," Lance told her, but Kinloch said nothing.

He herded them before him through the dim cool concrete aisle of Simon Gerrard's general store, toward the narrow steps in the back. The office hung above the store like a scorekeeper's box; it was close to the ceiling and small, hidden from the eyes of clerks and customers

238

by a wooden lattice work so that Simon could look down upon his business, but his business could not look up on him. A black double-doored safe occupied a quarter of the floor space, challenged in bulk only by Simon himself, who weighted the last squeak out of his swivel chair and bulged in rounds of solid flesh through every crevice.

He was there behind the desk, flanked by long rows of musty tan ledgers and files, faced by odd packing boxes and pop cases for his tenants to rest on, sweating, solemn-breathed, aging, powerful and alone.

He began to rumble as Elinor, Justin and Lance appeared, but as he saw who followed them his tone changed. It bloomed, mellow, indulgent and cordial upon the name: "Kinloch Armstrong!"

"Afternoon, Mr. Gerrard."

"Well, pardon *me*. I thought these scallawags had just come up here to dun me. Have a seat there, son. It's right funny you dropping in just now. I tell you for a fact, Kinloch, not five minutes ago I was setting here thinking how if Dan Armstrong don't get himself into town where I can see him, I'm going to have to take a chance on catching him at home some Sunday. Ain't it funny how things will happen like that? Who would have thought that not five minutes later you would come up the steps? Tell me about Dan. Hot enough for him?"

"He stays right close to home most of the time," Kinloch said, fanning himself with his hat. "I think he feels the heat less out our way than in town."

"Worse summer I can remember," Simon pronounced. He mopped his face. "I tell you what I got, though, Kinloch. How about an ice cold coke around for everybody? Just let me holler to Bub—"

"No, thank you," Kinloch said. "Not today."

There was a pause. "Well, now," Simon went on. "You young folks must be planning a trip or something, eh?"

Justin giggled. "We might be, Papa, for all we know."

"Eh?" Simon repeated.

"Lock brought us here," Lance explained. "Some business he had to discuss, he says. We don't know what the score is."

Simon leaned across the desk. "I tell you now, Kinloch, if it's some matter of business, you'd do just as well to talk to me and not bother the children. Lance, he's junior partner, but I—well, you know how it is, you get in the habit of tending to most matters yourself. And Justin. The child—"

"Well, what in God's name—?" the child began.

"Yeah," Lance seconded. "What *is* it?"

"He can tell you," Kinloch said, pointing to Simon. "As good as I can."

Simon stared at him, then laughed. "Maybe you know what you're talking about, son, but I'm just plain lost."

"Then why is your hand trembling, Mr. Gerrard?"

Kinloch walked to the single narrow window that overlooked the square.

"I saw your face when I came up the steps. It brought to mind what another man said: you been knowing for over thirty-five years that something like me would stand in your door someday."

He had touched the switch. Behind him where the hawk came down, the silence swelled monstrous, reeling above the calm store where a clerk sold rice and overalls, snuff and thread to a colored woman who kept her shopping list hidden from sight and asked for each item as though it were the last.

Simon said: "Your father and I have buried the past. Don't forget that."

"I do not believe that it is the past at all," Kinloch returned. "It is the present. That is why I brought your children."

"There are those who would shame to call you Dan Armstrong's son," Simon challenged.

"That is hardly for you to judge," Kinloch said quietly.

Simon turned slowly in his chair, the whole mass of him swaying with the movement, like an elephant turns, seeming half-asleep in the

240

grand finale of the big show. Then he woke up. "All right! All right! Lance, Elinor, Justin, child, this man wants to talk business. I'm going to talk business, but you all are going straight home. I won't—"

"Oh, Papa!" Justin cried. "I've never been so excited in my whole life! You *can't* send us home now!"

"Whatever he's got to say," Lance broke in, grimly, "I want to hear it. You might need us here, Papa."

"I've got a story to tell," Kinloch said. "I don't think they've heard it before."

"Lance," Simon mused, "you may be right, son."

There was another silence, but this one was different and when Kinloch turned back from the window, he knew that it was Simon who made the difference. The big man was smiling softly to himself and his pen staff tapped the open ledger before him.

"Tell your story then. You can't make a dent in this crew of mine, did you but know it. Maybe we'll all tell stories today. But you first. By all means, Kinloch, you go first."

Justin sat down on a coca-cola case as he talked; she buried one hand in her heavy hair and her dull eyes grew bright with interest. Elinor's look was burning and intense, but it was Simon Kinloch fixed on: Simon who smiled with superior ease and sank his head farther down between his massy shoulders and seemed to sleep, like the elephant again, but for the tapping of his pen staff against the ledger. Kinloch began to think in the mind back of his own voice, If I can stop him tapping that thing. He got to the trial and the tapping stopped but the smile was still there. He skipped the doctor's story on purpose thinking, Now I'll get the smile, and he went on to the death of Young Wills and the smile faded, but the tapping resumed. He told about the night on the bridge and the smile faded again, but the pen staff struck harder, impatient; and then he said 'Dr. Derryberry,' coming around the corner fast on the name, and the smile collapsed, the pen rolled across the desk, and Kinloch smiled himself and went on straight to the end.

At the fall of his voice, came Lance's sharp intake of breath. His face was drawn. "It's not true?" he whispered, turning helplessly to Elinor, who confronted him stolidly, arms folded. He stepped toward Simon. "Tell him he's a liar. Tell him, Papa, tell him! By God, I'll— Is it true; Papa? Is it true?"

"No, son," Simon replied. "It's not true."

Elinor was to wonder for many years why Simon said that, just as she had puzzled often to know why he had married Miss Henrietta. She laid a hand on Lance's arm. "Of course it's true, Lance." She spoke quick and low. "Oh, don't, honey, don't. Look at it. Of course it's true."

Simon did not once raise his eyes to his son. "There's too much of his mother in him," he remarked, half to himself. "Always was."

Lance wheeled away as from a blow. He faced into the shelf of ledgers; his hand rested for support on a corner of the safe.

It was Justin who directed the first question to Kinloch. "You mean if Papa lied about something on the witness stand, then this long afterwards they can still send him to the pen?"

Kinloch nodded.

She thought a minute, then her eyes fixed upon him and narrowed. "But how can you prove it?"

Kinloch drew out the doctor's confession. "Here. I've got it here."

Quick as a cat, Justin leapt at him. Her fingers grazed the paper. The lattice shook.

Simon caught her arm. "Baby, baby," he reproved, smiling. "We don't need to do that. Think, child, think. And now, sir. Have you finished?"

"No," Kinloch said. "I've only just begun."

"Finish then."

"I came here to offer you a choice, Mr. Gerrard."

"You think you can wave that paper under my nose and I'll sign away my land to you?"

"I'm interested in justice," Kinloch said. "Not land."

"Justice! The court has ruled already."

"But it can rule again where you're concerned, Mr. Gerrard. If you want to take your chances, that is. Knowing the doctor as I do, I don't think you'll get very far. I never saw a man so relieved to get a thing off his conscience. That's one choice. But I guess I'm a pretty dumb man, Mr. Gerrard. I don't know as I'm easy enough with the law to think there aren't ways to get justice quicker and surer. I offer you the chance to publish a statement saying that Kinloch Walston was never insane and that all your property was therefore obtained on a false basis. You need not be afraid because I will not pursue the case if you will then proceed to offer your land at auction, *all of it*, so that not one acre of what was once Walston can ever be Gerrard again. That's what I want."

"Why?" Elinor inquired, speculatively. "If you don't want the land back, Lock, then why? I'm not objecting, I'd just like to know."

"Because me and a lot of other people live in Tarsus," Kinloch said. "Because I for one have felt every day I can remember that something was wrong here and that I couldn't live here right until it was gone. Because I've felt what was wrong for a long time. Because now I know what's been wrong. Because I hate every damn one of you. And I pray the day will come when you'll not stir the dust here any longer and when the very memory of you is something people get vague about. I offer you the choice, Mr. Gerrard."

The smile was back. "Suppose I ain't interested in neither one of them choices? Suppose I don't want to buy one today?"

"I don't think that's up to you to say."

Simon struck his palm on the desk, printing it with his moist fingers. "And who are you to say, either?"

"I don't understand."

"There have been things, Kinloch, and I want you to know it—there have been things I been kind enough to ignore for the sake of friendship."

"What do you mean?"

"Where is your wife?"

"What about my wife?"

"Oh!" Justin exclaimed. She began to laugh. "I forgot all about it!"

Elinor jumped to the floor. She blazed at Simon across the desk. "Oh, no, you don't! You shan't do it, Simon! You do and I'll—I'll show you! Lance, Lance!" She pulled at his sleeve.

Lance's eyes were clouded, fluid and unfocused as though he had waked in the middle of the night. "What? What's the matter?"

"We promised, Lance! You remember, don't you? We promised!" She shook him.

Justin was laughing harder. "I forgot about it, Papa. I forgot all about it. You could have gone to Parchman, while I—"

Kinloch was among them suddenly. "What's this about? What are you talking about?" He seized Justin by the shoulder and jerked the laughter out of her in an instant. He leaned into Simon's face, clinging to the desk because he dared not risk himself to touch the man. "*What about my wife?*"

"Watch out!" Simon cried, recoiling from him. "Hush there, Elinor, Justin! Folks will hear us. There. That's better. Now, Lance. It's time for another story. Or have you waked up yet?"

Lance's eyes went from his own hand where it rested on the safe to Elinor's hand upon his arm, then slowly over her head to his father's face. "I can't do it, Papa. Let it alone. Elinor . . . Ruth . . . Oh, Lord! Just let it alone! Let this alone, Lock, you too. Trouble . . . you have to . . . don't you see how you have to . . . ?"

"By God," observed Simon. "Did a man want to tar and feather you, Lance, you'd soften up the tar for him and go kill your own goose."

Justin gathered the tail of the big shirt into a firm knot across her stomach. "Never mind, Papa. I'll tell."

"There's my girl," Simon said. "Come here, baby." He put his arm about her. "Some things are bad but they're necessary. You tell that to Lance."

"Good *night*, Papa," Justin grinned. "I'm big enough to talk now."

"Before you talk, Justin," Elinor broke in, "there's one thing I want to do." She stepped over and slapped the girl across the face. The blow popped loudly in the little room. "Six years I been wanting to get that done," she resumed her seat, saying with a hard tension that brought her voice almost to a whisper: "All right! God damn you, Gerrard, Gerrard! Talk then!"

Kinloch had never thought much about Elinor before, except to catalog her as one of them too, but now as Justin's story of the ill-fated June night was finished, he instinctively met Elinor's eyes.

"Is that the straight of it?"

"I'll swear it's a lie from New Orleans to Memphis, Lock. You can count on me."

"But is what she said straight?"

Her eyes lowered. She did not have to answer.

Kinloch turned his back on them and looked out the window. He had not asked if the tale were true, because like the day in the Melrose when Randall Gibson first told him about the land, he had no need to question; both had the crooked, careless way of truth which shoots at something else (or pretends to) and hits you. . . .

"Elinor" Simon was saying, "you're a fine girl and I couldn't think more of you if you was my own daughter, and that's a fact. You're a straight-thinking girl and one for my money. In fact, there ain't but one thing you ain't ever squared up with, honey."

She matched him look for look. "What's that, Simon?"

"You ain't ever come to admit the side your bread's buttered on, nor who's been spreading it for you all these years. Lance there, he knows, and I'm fixing to prove it to you, by damn. By God damn. Justin child? Here's pen and here's paper. You write it out here, brief and to the point: 'On the night of June 6, 1935. . . .' That's right, honey. . . ."

. . . Through the window, out in the square, the sun did not fill the early afternoon any more than water fills the ocean because without water there would be no ocean and the sun was the afternoon. Between him and the statue in the court house yard, a little boy was riding a Shetland pony around in a circle. The pony trotted fast; his feet moved like a sound (peck-peck-peck), but there was no sound. A second boy waited beside the fence. He stretched out his arms eagerly and caught the pony's head, the reins. He sprang on just as the first boy went off, so that their four white legs turned past each other like the spokes of a wheel and the pony did not miss a step of his circling, feet chopping the dust like a little clock ticking, and still no sound. . . .

The pen scratched while Simon prompted. "That's right, that's right. Now. Sign it, baby. There. Lance! . . ."

. . . It did not once occur to him to think of her as separate from himself; to him the death of Ben Gardner was something he himself had done and simply lost from his mind. It belonged to him, at least, and if the burden of it landed on his back at the wrong time, that was his hard luck. Yet think of her he did, as though she were an unexplained part of his own nature that he did not understand and could not control, and exasperation and compassion, that sharp mixture, flooded together into the hollow of his chest, and within him, too, as on stage, the little boys were riding the pony and the pony went round and round in ceaselessly receding dimension in the afternoon which was the sun and was within him too, and he felt that he was drowning, wanting to gasp for breath but knowing the disaster of it. . . .

"Yes sir," Simon was saying, "if you have to do business, Kinloch, you better do it business-like and that's how I'm aiming to do. You got a paper; now I got me a paper. Lance!"

"I can't sign it, Papa. It wasn't her fault, Lock. It was our fault. We told her not to tell anybody. We made her promise. She didn't know what to do. She just didn't know. You got to believe me, Lock. If I'd have known anything like this would ever come up, I—well, I wouldn't—"

246

"Lance." Simon had risen to his feet and he waited behind the desk, swaying a little, holding the pen and paper forward to his son. "You set on playing the fool? You want to see me and your mother and sister talked about, your family turned into a laughing stock before this whole town? You know how folks are. Let this get out—"

"But you said—you said it was a lie, Papa—you said—" Kinloch turned from the window and the four of them watched Lance while the last admission that it was not a lie spread whitely across his face. At last he raised his eyes to Simon again. "You're trying to tell me that if I sign this, it won't ever need be known. Our name—it's for our name—?" He groped, taking the pen.

Elinor said: "You sign that, Lance, and I'll leave you."

"It won't be the first time she's talked about leaving," Simon said.

Lance shot Elinor a resentful glance.

"Good guessing, Simon!" she snapped. "Now he thinks I've talked behind his back. I haven't, Lance, and what's more you know that what I'm saying now I've never said before. Not to you, not to anybody. I mean it, Lance. You know I mean it."

"You can fight that out later," Simon said.

"You'll never get my name on that thing," Elinor told him.

"It doesn't concern you," Simon answered, "as Lance well knows." Then with a curious deliberation, his gaze caught up Justin and Lance and seemed to draw them physically near to him in a bond of flesh and blood which was not love, affection or loyalty as the two who watched thought of those things, but which was a quality both shared and potent, though no one on earth, not they themselves, could have named it. "Lance."

Lance took the pen and signed the paper, and the strange tie snapped, hurled aside as no longer useful. Simon waved the paper in the air again, drying the ink.

"No good to ask you, huh, Elinor?"

"I reckon there's been enough wasted breath in the world without that, Simon."

He chuckled and leaned back. When he spoke, the bloom of strident indulgence was in his tone once more. He leaned his elbows on the desk.

"Kinloch, I've knowed you ever since you were a little thing in knee britches running around scrapping with Lance here as boys will do. I've knowed your daddy before you. The last thing I'd like to think would be that Dan Armstrong sent you here today." He waited. It was half a question. Kinloch did not answer. "It might come closer to say that old man Felix sent you back into Dark Corners. Eh?" Kinloch said nothing. "Let bygones be bygones, I've always said. Why, I been proud to call Daniel Armstrong my friend, Kinloch, my friend. But here you come up with this paper and much to my dislike I got to get me a paper too. Now we each got us a paper. Kinloch, I'm going to do the best thing I know how to do. You give me a choice; I give you a choice. You turn that paper over to me and I'll turn this one over to you and we'll shake hands on it and nobody in Tarsus will ever know the difference. How does it strike you, huh?"

"You know," Kinloch replied, deliberating as he spoke (and he was quiet now, his heart beating strong and steady against his ribs), "it was a funny thing that when I left Dr. Derryberry's house early this morning, I said to myself that I had uncovered the last. The last one in a trail of crimes and cheats and blood. The last name on the list; the tail end. You almost had me there for a minute, Mr. Gerrard. When I heard what you had ready to spring on me, I almost started to beg you for the very thing you're offering me now. Then when I thought about it, I saw all at once that Derryberry, he wasn't the last one at all. Who was the last one? Why, me! It's me you're striking at now, same as you struck at the others, every one, you and Young Wills, getting them to protect what they love by giving you what you want. Reminding them of honor when honor means nothing to you; reminding them of home and family and loyalty and love or a woman's name, with your hands out to catch whatever they might drop when they ran home to see about things. Reminding me of my wife

248

and her not even here to say a word. Well, I'm not quite ready to drop everything and run home. I've got as far as this office today and jarred you up in the saddle all because I haven't acted like all your other victims. You might be a little different this time yourself, Mr. Gerrard. Shake hands, you said, for instance. Shake hands with you? You been living in this town so long and seeing decent men shake hands over a deal so many times, you think you're one of them? Shaking hands don't mean a damn thing. It's who you shake hands with that makes the difference. And for you and me to shake hands! It ain't even right to call that useless, Mr. Gerrard; that's just plain silly."

"I warn you," Simon said, "I won't stop until you do."

"The truth is," Kinloch returned, putting on his hat, "you'll never stop until I make you. And for that privilege, Mr. Gerrard, and no handshaking done now or ever, I think I'll stick around for a while."

He nodded to Elinor, walked down the stairs and was gone.

A few minutes later, he climbed wearily from the cab of the pick-up, mopping his sleeve across his brow. He had reached the gate before he saw her and then he did not recognize her, but paused, frowning through the glare at the disheveled travel-stained girl who was standing on the steps, her hands extended before her as though she walked in her sleep. Then he cried out, he cried her name, running.

He saw the frightened appeal in her eyes as his arms went round her. "I've come back to tell you—to tell you—" she began.

"I know already," he said. "I just found out. It's all right. Don't worry. It's going to be all right."

He felt her cling tightly to him, thankful, loving and completely his own, and he heard the first low sob she gave, beginning to cry. Here was what he had often wished from her, the absolute unthinking trust whose absence had gnawed at him since he had first loved her.

But even as he soothed her and talked to her, he looked out over the top of her dark head where it lay against his shoulder and he thought, involuntarily, but not without craft: "It might be all right now, sure enough. It's a good thing I held out against Simon Gerrard."

EIGHTEEN

ELINOR moved about her room, hurling dresses, cosmetics and lingerie into two large suitcases she had bought for her wedding trip and had scarcely used since. Junk, junk, junk, she thought, looking in the closet at the discouraging multitude of dresses. Lord, it looks like all I've done for the past six years is buy clothes. Well, Justin can have most of 'em with my sisterly blessing.

Then Lance hit the door, running, but it was locked and he must have fallen back twenty feet the way it sounded, like the disaster of a character in a movie cartoon.

"Good-bye, Simon," she had drawled there in the office after Kinloch left. "I lived to see the day you got good and scared and for that I praise the Lord. Maybe you're running low on luck, Simon. Reckon?"

She had not waited for an answer. She passed by Justin like she was dirt in the road, going to Lance whom she regarded reflectively for a moment, then kissed him on the mouth. "Poor baby. Good-bye, Lance."

He had called after her desperately. "Elinor! Elinor!" and followed, but for all that she had beat him back to the bungalow. She had started out walking and on the edge of town Mrs. Peterson, who was going to the missionary society, picked her up and drove her home. Lance must have waited in town for a ride. Yes, she had lived to see Simon's bluff called, but to see the day when Lance would walk home from town, that was too much to hope for.

"You can't leave me now," he pleaded at the door. "Now that I need you so much, you can't, you can't—"

The telephone was ringing. He went to it. "For you, Elinor."

"I can't come," she answered. "Unless it's Ruth come back."

251

"I think it's Ruth," he said.

"You're lying."

"All right then, it's Jessie Mae."

"I can't come."

He returned to the phone; she heard him talking. He came back to the door. "Jessie Mae is getting married tonight up in the Methodist parsonage. To Roscoe Wright. She wants you to come. You and 'that nice Mrs. Armstrong' if she's here."

"Tell her I won't be there. Tell her I'm going home."

"I *can't* tell her that. You know what a gossip she is."

"Then make up your own lies. Don't worry me."

Jessie Mae. A husband killed in June. Deserted by a lover in July. Married again in August. She sat down on the edge of the bed.

"She says she is all excited, and she wonders if you think people will talk—?" He was back at the door. "Don't cry, Elinor. Oh, Ellie, Ellie, if you'd only let me in. Darling, I— Don't cry, don't cry."

"Lance, you silly fool, I'm not crying. I'm laughing." And that was true.

But I could cry, she thought, stirring about the packing again. God damn it, I could cry a week, thinking about Daddy (about Amos Anderson Dudley, 'Mister A. A.') who's going to ask me a hundred questions so that I won't have to answer any of them; cry for Ary Morgan Dudley, for Mother, who won't ask me anything at all; for both of them when I tell about it and for their never once saying, I told you so; and for the reason why Lance can't break down the door and horsewhip me if he wants me to stay so bad, like he broke my riding crop that day when I hit him, broke it in front of everybody and marched me out and said, "You're going to marry me."

But I won't cry. Let Ruth do my crying for me. She's got the shoulder to cry on. And if you haven't got it any more, you haven't got it, and if you never had it, you never had it, and to hell with it, Elinor Dudley, because it's just Elinor Dudley, like it always was and that's all you can make of it, Lance.

"Now you know how it all was," Kinloch said to Ruth, "and why I was mad at you and what I thought, and I know how it was with you."

"Now we understand," she said, and she heard her own voice as if she sang.

They had sat talking on the steps for a long while and now a breeze blew and they spoke of it gratefully.

"And I came back," she said. "I came back to you."

He turned to her smiling, loving her in his smile, and she caught his head between her hands and pressed it against her.

"You never meant to stay away," he said.

"I never meant anything. I just drifted. Randall set me right." But quite as that person himself had known, there was no thought of Randall in her eyes when she looked at Kinloch and smiled and kissed him. "Scott said you were stupid," she informed him.

"And what did you say?"

"Oh, he was drunk, but I took up for you. I said maybe you were stupid, but then I was stupid too."

He laughed drily. "That was fine taking up for me."

She moved away from him suddenly and gathered up her bag and gloves.

"Leaving so soon?" he asked, but she was grave now.

"I've got to go into town, Kinloch. It's what I decided, long before I got back here, while I was on the train. You must take me into town and I've got to tell them, whoever I'm supposed to tell, at the court house, I guess. I've got to confess it now. I've got to have it all put down in writing so everyone will know."

She saw the pity and dread for her cross his face and she knew that he had been thinking of this very thing. She stood up, holding out her hand. "It's the only way," she said. "Isn't it, isn't it the only way? You and Mr. Dan—I saw him just now, he was here when I came, and I knew it more than ever—and his father in the picture in the hall and your mother in the picture on the dresser and your grandmother. Oh, no, Kinloch, I couldn't go through the door again. He asked me in, but I couldn't go in. They would look at me, he would look at me, you would look at me and know, and so it's the only way until it's done I can't go inside and say I'm home."

He nodded. "It's the only way. You're right." And then he said, deeply moved, and she would never forget it: "You are very brave."

She stretched out her hand again, but he caught her to him instead, holding her against him fiercely for a moment in the shadow of the porch before they went out into the sun toward the dusty pick-up.

Kinloch stopped a moment with his foot on the running board. "Father?" he called toward the silent house.

"He was here just now," Ruth said. "He talked to me about how hot it's been."

Kinloch called again.

"He must be out back," she said.

Kinloch shook his head, hesitated, then got into the cab.

She sat close beside him on the way, fanning the dust with her hand. "This is what you want, besides, isn't it? When I've done this, you can go on against Simon Gerrard?"

She saw the line of his jaw tighten and in the small motion a gap cleft between them like the stroke of an axe. He did not reply. She felt suddenly timid and small, for she knew that he had stopped thinking of her when she said that, and he must think of her now. He must think she was brave, think it, think it hard, or she might stop being brave. She laid a hand on his arm.

"Kinloch. Oh, darling, are you sure you want this—this revenge. Oh, are you sure? We have each other now. Isn't that enough? I won't go there any more, I won't even speak to them any more—"

He gave a short laugh. "That will cut them deeply, I'm sure," he said.

"Don't speak that way," she begged. "I feel so as if it's all my fault. I didn't understand, that's all. But now I understand, and I—"

"No," he said. "You don't understand. You just know, that's all, you

254

don't understand."

She was silent again. On either side now, in dusty hedges and rough sidewalks and houses low and high, Tarsus rolled past. There was the filling station where they had first talked, the dust had smelt of autumn then, keen out of memory she smelled it and she felt her breath would not come; but he was not seeing the filling station nor the court house beyond, where they were going, but was staring at the empty curb before Simon Gerrard's store.

She remembered the note and pulled it out of her bag, and handed it to him. "What is it?" he asked absently.

"Randall Gibson said give it to you."

He glanced at it hastily and thrust it back in her hand. He pressed the accelerator and the truck wheeled past the court house in a spray of gravel. She watched, puzzled, while he circled past Simon Gerrard's house. His face was knit with alarm.

"What is it?" she cried.

He made an unexpected loop in the center of the street and she fell back against the door.

He caught her shoulder and shook her. "Father? Did he say he was going anywhere?"

"Why, no. He was at home. He's still at home, I'm sure."

"Not when we left. He wasn't there. I know the look of the place and he was gone."

"What is it then? What's the matter?"

He jammed to a stop before the Melrose Cafe.

"Listen, Ruth," he said, leaning toward her. "I haven't time to explain this and I hope to God I'm wrong, but I've got to go and see about something. Go inside and wait. I'm going with you to the court house, but you must wait a few minutes for me. Understand?"

She had no time to agree; he was gone in whirling gravel and dust, striking a deep rut head-on, so that the wheels jumped spinning from the road, gaining frightful speed in mid-air.

She walked inside and sat down dully. Joe-boy Snell came and flicked a cloth across the table. "Nothing," she told him. "I'm waiting."

The note lay crumpled in her hand. She opened it and read it through.

"I send you back a lady with my compliments. She would have returned to you at all events because one of her names is Milly Cabot, poor child, and the other, as I have tried to indicate to you, is Ruth. I have exercised myself to the extent of cheating a little as in Blind Man's Buff, of turning her in the right direction and saying, 'Now walk.' I am glad to do this, for it is a common failing among us to think that guilt may be expiated, wrong undone and tragedy turned inside out during the last act. This is false and I am not deluded, yet I do seek a little credit for her return, I do wish you good fortune, I do turn my back when I think what may be happening now and say, 'Maybe not.' Forgive me some day, Cousin. In your ponderous way, it may take years, I know, but get to it at last, I pray you. Lord, I just remembered the summer we worked at the gin. For God's sake, burn that address. Randall."

Me too.

She read it twice, but she still saw nothing but a piece of paper. She folded it carefully and put it back into her purse. It was growing late.

She got up and walked across the street to the court house alone.

NINETEEN

Simon Gerrard sat for a long time in his office above the store, but he no longer tapped the pen staff against the open ledger, nor did he smile. The shadows were lengthening in the square outside when he got to his feet with a grunt. He took out a large handkerchief and swabbed his neck far down below the shirt collar, exposing the line where the sun-reddened flesh divided into whiteness. He mopped his bald head and smoothed his monkish fringe of hair. At the top of the steps, he paused and walking to a cracked mirror strung to the wall on an enormous nail, he buttoned his collar so that his thick neck bulged enflamed above it. He slipped his blue four-in-hand tie firmly into place. He rolled down his sleeves and buttoned the cuffs. Then he picked up his hat and passed down the stairs and through the store.

"Mist' Gerrard?" the young clerk said by way of greeting.

"Evenin', Bub. Hot enough for you?" said Simon Gerrard, and went out to his big black car.

When Felix McKie heard footsteps approaching him across the back yard, he laid aside the length of plank in his hand and stood in the middle of his own darkness, inquiring twice to the sky, as though men were giants: "Afternoon, friend. Who is it?"

Then he heard the heavy breathing and perhaps his senses brought him more mysterious evidence, for he tilted his slick, unwrinkled face higher yet to the light and said: "Si?"

"The same."

Felix grunted. He had been wanting a talk with Simon for some time. Since he was here alone, he had no means of grading the high bluff that separated his hilltop from the Gerrard land, and he knew

257

that every rain was robbing him, and for Felix it was a very easy step to equate the rain with Simon. Insult had turned to injury when after a downpour in June, an inlet of ground had undermined and dropped out below the fence, leaving a stout bordock post to swing uprooted in air. For two months now the sinkhole, shaped like an inverted keyhole, the round lobe extending inward toward the house, had lain untouched in Felix's back yard. A note to Simon had brought no reply; he was too proud to send another, and last night Felix's old nightmare—that of walking off the bluff into high water—had recurred. Unease dogged his footsteps through the morning; he found that if he was to do any work in peace he would have to lay planking over the danger spot. Later, some night soon, he would get down in there himself, down there at the bottom of the narrow deep drop, and he would fix things the best he could. So he was planning when he heard the car ascend the hill, heard the knocking at the front door, and at last footsteps moving toward him over the grass.

"It's about time you came to see about this bluff," said Felix. "Nearly all summer gone since I sent you word. If this keeps up you'll be tending my grape arbors on your own land and I won't have stick nor stone—"

"You can stop that act right now," Simon broke in. " 'Justice,' you sent that boy to say to me. I saw through that before it was good out of his mouth. I know you, Felix McKie. I know what you want. I know you don't forget."

"I don't know what you're talking about," Felix said. "But if you ain't come to do your duty by this gully, you can get your meddling feet off my land." He struck the ground before him once with his strong hickory cane.

"You better hear me," Simon said. "It's your meddling that brings me here."

"Meddling! Ha! You see here? Your confounded meddling gully is washing my land out from under me with every drizzle that falls. You see that hole? Thirty feet deep if it's an inch and ready to cave back farther with no more encouragement than a heavy dew. Weaned on meddling, you were, and now you say 'meddling'. Get off my land, what measling trifles of it I got left to me. I got work to do."

"Listen, old man," said Simon Gerrard, and for some reason he had raised his voice, though Felix's hearing was acute. "I been looking for this day to come and I knowed well as my own name in what quarter it would rise. I come to say, 'You call that damn fool boy off me or I'll set worse than that loose on you.'"

"Boy? Boy?" Felix said, and struck the ground twice. "You keep saying boy. What boy?"

"Armstrong's boy, that's who. And it was you that sent him, talking about justice."

"Young Kinloch, eh? So he's up and at you, is he?" Felix laughed. "How come you laying this to me, Si?"

"He got a shove from somebody," Simon said. "And Dan ain't got the guts to do it."

"I hone for the day you'll stand before Dan and say, You ain't got the guts. There was the day when the mention of his name would send your knees bucking."

"That's right. Go back to when I was barely grown to dig your dirt—"

"Now you think you're grown up, is that right, Si? It don't make no difference, Si. You think you're Young Wills, but you ain't Young Wills and no amount of money and big houses can turn you into Young Wills."

"Listen here—" Simon Gerrard began, but he could not go on because Felix McKie was laughing. The laughter was too shrill to let him go on and he could only stand waiting for the man to stop while above the sunken eye sockets the thin blue lids quivered as though they were about to open.

"You in the room at the old Davis place where you all lived then, and dresser, bed and easy chair all piled before the door—" He cackled. "—and little Henrietta Mathison not married a month, here she

come, rap, rap, rap, toting food—" And he cackled. "'—It's me, Simon. Don't shoot, Simon. It's me.' Not a white man could come up
the walk, no, nor nigger nor hound dog to the back without you was
sprawled out on the floor, hanging on to that shotgun like them boys
fighting Germans—" The laughter stopped. "—knowing well, Si Gerrard, that should Dan Armstrong come to the door and say, 'Come
out of there, Si Gerrard. I'm waiting for you, Si Gerrard,' that you
would pull down the barricade piece by piece and come out same as
Young Wills came out, oh, he came out, he did, right into the court
house hall—"

"To be murdered."

"Murder! I'll say murder. He came out with the blood of that
good old darky on his boots and it was murdered blood."

"I wouldn't say murder so loud. There's a murder charge been
hanging loose around Tarsus for a long time and there might be a
witness or so left to back it up."

"So you come to threaten, sure enough," Felix said. "That boy of
Dan's, he must have shook you up, Si. Why don't you run along home
now, and hide?"

"I came to discuss this, sir, but I see you're getting too old to talk
sensible."

"I'm sensible to them that deserves sense," Felix returned. "And
as for old—" He doubled his iron fist and shook it. "—there's strength
left in this arm yet, enough to send you into the middle of next week."

On his sinewy, bowed legs, Felix moved a step forward and the
fist went before him, shaking in air. Simon started, retreating a step
or two, and Felix heard him retreat and cackled louder than before.
"An old man, you say! For shame, Si. And me an old blind man. Will
you run from a blind man, Si?"

He rocked back and forth on his bowed legs in high humor. He
paused suddenly, turning his head a little to one side and listening.
There was someone coming out of the path from the wood. Maybe
Dan, he thought; I'll show him now, I'll show him how to deal with

Si Gerrard. And he doubled up his fist again and began to laugh again and move forward slowly behind the fist and the laughter, for all the world as if he were trying to play bogey-man with a little boy.

"And old blind man can make you jump. Oh, you still know who your betters are, Si Gerrard, and anything named Armstrong, Walston or McKie can cramp the space the Lord designed for the guts you never had." He bent low to his fist, coming on. "It don't take nothing more than an old blind man to send you home running—"

And then his fist struck flesh, the flesh of hate that goes wilder with the touching than the flesh of love.

"I came to reason—!" Simon cried, but at the same time his arm flayed out as though moved by a sense of its own and the heavy hickory can in Felix's hand swung upward until arm and cane pointed straight to the sky and there Simon caught on, wrenching at the cane and the iron arm so that the two clung swaying together, panting so fiercely that not even Felix heard the rapid footsteps come upon them, and neither saw the second cane come down.

It did not descend in a blow. Instead the crook of it hooked neatly about Simon Gerrard's neck, and weight was thrown against it so immediately upon this contact that the big man had no time to resist but was yanked apart from Felix, and floundered in the sudden release.

Simon turned, reeling and astonished, and found himself face to face with Daniel Armstrong. Dan's shaggy white eyebrows were raised high in full appreciation of the ludicrous nature of his tactics and Simon's wild surprise.

Dan now looked with interest toward the sinkhole which lay like a shadow or like spilled black paint on the green grass. "That's a mighty lot of lumber for such a little old washout, ain't it, Felix?"

"It may be little now, Dan, but it don't aim to stay little."

Simon stared at the two old men, first one, then the other. His hand was still clutched to his throat and he coughed. Fear and rage were

261

both strong within him. He did not understand them. It was as though they played foil for one another, shoving him about a stage, and then turned audience as well to laugh at him. With this procedure they had baffled him, the two of them, and others in Tarsus—but it was especially Dan Armstrong—ever since he could remember. Not all his energy, his getting, could lay hold upon this maddening elusive quality, which would not acknowledge his existence, much less his victories, which peeked out at him from behind whatever countenance they presented, and winked and slipped away.

Here before he could stop coughing was Dan Armstrong speaking to him, though there was nothing of humor in the voice. "Ain't square to pick on a blind man, Si. If you bound to be picking, pick on me."

Dan held his cane by the wrong end and now, standing there in the late sunshine, tall and calm, he lifted his arm to let the cane slide down his fingers to its proper position again; but on the motion, Simon's eyes bulged, his lower lip jutted and he lunged. His shoes bit into the soft grass and his hands came down together with all ten fingers wide in grasping for the stick.

Dan moved, intending to let him stumble past, but he was not quick enough and under the sheer weight of Simon's body, his knees buckled and he felt his joints stab together all over him as though they had turned to knives. He heaved forward, trying to keep his feet and to unbalance the drag upon his arm and shoulder. "Feared I was going to hit him," he thought, as the man clawed up him, like a panicked cat, and he heard the words come halting out of the throat that he had bruised: "I—should of—brought me—a walking cane—ganging—up on me—when I come—to talk—"

The two staggered forward. Dan felt his face grow red as brick and his breath came labored out of the constriction that gripped his whole frame. He felt the clotting of his throat as though it must be hawked before he could speak, before he could say, "Just turn me loose, Si. I don't aim—" But he could not get breath to hawk with his blood pounding so and the weight bearing on his arm so, until with

262

sudden temper at everything that dragged upon him, weighing him—age, weakness, Simon Gerrard, and the long heat—in one supreme surge he flung his head skyward, flung his limbs upright and straight, and shoved the miserable weight from him.

"—to talk—business—" Simon said as his hold broke.

Black spots rimmed with fire rode swiftly, wheel on wheel, before Dan's vision as he sought to shake himself together, like an old horse shaking a heavy mane. Then he could see again, but still he could not speak to cry "Watch out!" to Simon Gerrard, who had stumbled backward to the rim of the sinkhole. There the big man stood, thrashing his arms to keep balance, while six inches before his feet the ground was dividing slowly. Dan could hear the breaking of little white roots as the dirt severed softly with the sound a plow makes sliding into the new furrow.

"Oh, Dan, Dan!" It was Felix calling from somewhere off to the right, but Dan was already moving forward, his hand stretched out. He could not move very fast, because his joints were still trembling so badly that the few paces between him and Simon seemed quite a journey and on the journey he reflected that it was a nuisance and a shame for old men to be cutting up this way, and he was impatient with Felix and Simon both for starting such a to-do.

And just then Simon Gerrard fooled him again. He did not reach for Dan's outstretched hand; he dodged it, ducking, and with this motion, the width of grassy earth parted beneath him and dropped him chin deep downward into the narrow hole. But there were depths beneath him yet and whatever root or ledge of earth supported him was already slipping. He seized grass that gave way and clods of dirt that crumbled and his eyes were not on the things he grasped for he still looked fearfully at Dan Armstrong. The same eyes, Dan noted, they had not changed, they were the same eyes that had looked up into his face through the flickering torchlight that cold night when he stood in the wagon bed beside the coffin and slapped the pistol against his strong thigh and shouted, "Why aren't you home with your dead?" The same eyes, quavering, inferior, afraid. "I put the fear there," he thought, with a wrench at his heart and all the years that were in it, and the wrench flowed smoothly into the actual pain stabbing at his joints until his blood went thick as molasses. "But why in Father's name don't he quit looking at me and grab ahold of that fence post behind him?" Just for an instant then, Dan's voice came back. He thrust out his cane. "Hold on!" he shouted. "Take it and hold on!"

He saw the eyes change with understanding. He braced himself for the strain and pulled. Felix, Felix, where was Felix to help? His voice was gone again and the black, fire-rimmed wheels came back, larger now, dipping out of the sky. The eyes on him were filled with the dumb helplessness of a dog that you drag out of deep water. Side to side, slowly, like a long dream, they swung above the narrow pit, while Simon sought a footing and the loose earth crumbled, scattering over his big face, his heavy limbs.

There was a big wind blowing from somewhere. It seemed to Dan Armstrong that he had been hearing it for a long time now. A big storm blowing up, maybe, a wind anyway, blowing strong and wild and free. If it would only strike, cool him off, give him more strength. He looked away from the trusting terror in the eyes of the man at his feet and lifted his face to search the sky.

But what he saw was not sky.

Later by a matter of minutes, Kinloch broke from the wood into the yard, running. He had driven the shortest possible way, bursting down the plantation road to the Ole Tuck pasture where he had left the truck, and then scaled the high bluff to the path, running the path where leaves and brush lashed out to hold him back. All the way from the courthouse square to Felix's back yard, he heard two voices alternate, their deliberation of tone untouched by his own haste. All the way Dr. Derryberry put his fingers together and knit his little brow and said: "Simon grew anxious . . . he had to make sure . . ."

And Simon Gerrard shifted in the chair behind the desk and said: "It might come closer to say that old man Felix sent you back into Dark Corners. Eh? . . ." Then he saw the empty house again, the empty hill, as they were when he got into the truck with Ruth, knowing the house and hill were empty even then. The doctor again; Simon; the empty house. . . .

He was mid-way across the yard before he stopped. At first he saw no one but Felix, walking about near the farther side of the house and he stood panting, waiting to get his breath and laugh at himself for such a foolish mission. Then he ran again.

When he looked up at last from the tall body on the grass where he had worked and called vainly, he knew that he had seen this all along, seen it in the yard just now when he stopped and denied, seen it back at the empty house and denied, seen it the night they had quarreled and he had denied then also. For how far back had he denied? He put his hands to his eyes to blind them from the sight of his own guilt, for his whole life seemed about to be swept away into it.

Simon, he thought, lowering his hands from his face. Where is Simon? I will find him, make him confess, kill him. And he looked again about the yard. But in this he knew better also; he turned quite naturally to the sinkhole and gazed into it without surprise.

In spite of the long dry spell, the earth there at the bottom was soft and lay in chunks like broken cake. It had yielded to the fall of Simon Gerrard's body so that he rested half-buried and seemed a part of that which had originally collapsed when the secret water, working inward and inward through many a long slow rain, had at last had its will. Kinloch could see dimly, far down in the deep rank-smelling hole, how the man's head lay at right angles to his body, like a plant broken at the stalk. One eye was buried in the earth and one stared upward toward the grass-fringed sky.

"Dan? Oh, Dan?" He had thought all the while he heard the calling that it was inside himself, but now he heard the pecking of the cane and saw Felix McKie approaching. He went to him. "Dan?" The smooth brown hands touched his shirt, his arms and face. "Are you hurt, Dan?" Felix laughed. "I got all turned around, Dan. All turned around in my own back yard. Are you hurt, Dan?"

"It's not—not Father, not Dan, Mr. Felix. It's me, Kinloch. I came too late. Here, let me take you to the house. They're both dead."

Then he was thinking, as he carried his father's body home through the woods, he was thinking or saying: "Father, I was trying—I was trying—"

But he could get no more words to form beyond that and his feet went on, step at the time, printing the dim trail, with "Father, I was trying, I was trying—" until as he descended toward the branch even these words left him. He became conscious that in the hot wood where the dew was rising, the late shadows of trees and brush fell so thick about him that it seemed they traveled with him, crowding just out of touch behind and before. When he crossed over the branch he happened to look up the little hill ahead and there he saw It.

It was crouching where the dim light broke through the trees, there where the path crested. He stopped, watching It, gone cold with fear and no longer able to cover his eyes because of the burden in his arms. Nor would covering his eyes help, he knew, because here was no vision leading backward into his own guilt, but Something ahead toward which he must go, or turn back. Later he wondered if It was not a Creature of his own death, or rather of the death of his hate which had grown so large as almost to become himself.

He did not think of that at the time. He stood trying to measure It, to reduce It to words, but in this It refused him, and so he knew only that It was there, that It was acutely aware of him even though It was not looking at him.

So he could say nothing to himself about It, whether It was God or ghost; and though he saw that It took occasion for Its stance on the spot where the shadow of a man carrying a man fell far ahead in the late afternoon light, It was more than a shadow, nonetheless. He knew this without reason but beyond doubt, in the same way that he

266

knew that It had the power to destroy him utterly. His fear mounted terribly. He still stood in his tracks, but he longed to turn and run as he had never longed for anything in all his life.

"Is This what I was trying to find," he wondered, "and didn't know it? Is This what I was moving toward all along?" He did not know, but on the thought all notion of turning back left him and he walked forward, straight toward the enormous, sprawling, vaguely bestial Shape that turned slowly to face him as he came.

But stand and kill him It did not; It receded before him: at first he felt accusingly that It had failed him. He did not yet know whether It was fierce or pitying or devoid of emotion, and the only proof he had of Its forebearance was that he did reach home at last.

Then It left him. It left him in the bare, uncarpeted room where he laid Daniel Armstrong's body on the bed; It crumbled away among the scattered shadows of bed and wardrobe and chest of drawers and wash stand, or went into the mantle piece where beside the carved oak clock with the yellowed face, a white starched collar had been left lying.

He straightened from his work beside the bed and looked around and It was not there anymore and he was as empty as the house he stood in.

He tried to sit down and be still but he kept staring at his hands, vaguely concerned that there was no blood on them anywhere. Nothing on me but a piece of paper, he thought. When he thought of the paper in his back pocket, it weighted on him like a chain. He got up and went into the kitchen where he turned up a few live coals in the bottom of the fire box and tore the doctor's statement to pieces and nursed it to thin black ashes, striking no match.

TWENTY

O N a chill, clear November afternoon in 1936, Kinloch Armstrong put on his leather jacket and drove to Walston Gap to see Lance Gerrard. The two had not encountered one another except in passing since the inquest of August the previous year. For they did get to the court house after all, he and Ruth, Kinloch reflected as he drove by the square white-painted brick building where about the steps the old men sat and did not move except to brush the whittling out of their laps, and audibly resented everything that existed in Tarsus, even the cold that was soon to drive them across the street to the iron stove in the drug store.

But that August day they had moved of their own accord; they had come with the rest of the town to crowd the court room upstairs where the inquest was held. There it was Felix McKie they heard principally, his voice rolling and the burr of old Kinloch McKie traced faint across his phrases, as he told how the events of the past and present had at last terminated in the deaths they considered that day. He drew to a close. He raised his fist to the sky.

"I always said, 'There's a temper in you yet, Dan,' and right I was proved to be. Eighteen-ninety-nine or last week, what is the difference now? God's just will does not reckon time—"

The young lawyer interrupted. "Are you implying, Mr. McKie, that the late Mr. Armstrong deliberately killed the late Mr. Gerrard as a result of this quarrel you have just related?"

"Aye, Dan would kill, in defense of a friend as I am proud to name myself his friend. There was strength in Dan to do right. Went against it once, long ago, as I just now told you, but not twice, not Dan—"

"Mr. Webber?" Kinloch was rising.

"Yes, Mr. Armstrong."

268

"I suggest that this testimony is only Mr. McKie's own desire of what should have happened and is not necessarily to be taken as evidence. I suggest that when my father—when Mr. Armstrong said, 'Hold on,' he did not give warning, but advice. Mr. Gerrard was found holding on to the walking cane my father carried. He had not been struck by it."

"The boy don't know," Felix interrupted. "He come running after it was all over. He wasn't there to see."

"Neither," Kinloch reminded him gently, "were you, Mr. McKie. Mr. Webber, I urge, I insist that Mr. McKie's belief bear no weight in determining the cause of Mr. Gerrard's death. My father—" His head was high; he did not tremble, yet within him he felt his breath tighten upon the words. "My father was a plain man, as you people in Tarsus know, and because of this I think it seemed that he was also a simple man, but this was not true. He had a delicate decision to make once; you have just heard about it. To some people the decision made him look like a shirker or even a coward, and he was man enough to know this and still go on. I was closer to him than anyone alive, yet even I— I shame to say it—have doubted him and accused him. And being a plain man, he could not put into fitting words why he did what he did and neither can I, now that I think I understand better. All I can tell you is: my father having made a decision was not one to go back on it. He did not cherish hope of revenge. He did not die in such an act."

Mr. Webber leaned across the desk where he sat, below the empty judge's stand. Behind his thick glasses, his eyes were meditative. He was new in town, but already given to a great cumulating interest in all its doings.

"But the very provocation of this disastrous quarrel, Mr. Armstrong—wasn't it your own desire for revenge?"

"You may say I killed them," Kinloch replied. "You may say I killed them both."

But the coroner's jury declared, with medical assistance, that Daniel Armstrong died of heart failure and that Simon Gerrard died of a broken neck due to an accidental fall.

"It is no difference," Felix complained to Kinloch as the crowd filed out. "God works—"

"However He works, Mr. Felix," Kinloch said, "my father knew better than you or me either one." He spoke sharply; beneath his sun-browned skin, his face was worn and tired. Ruth slipped her hand into his and at the touch he spoke more kindly. The old man's grief had been genuine and deep. He would not outlive it and his lonely afternoons there on the steep hill would attest to it daily when the time for Dan Armstrong's visit would roll round and pass into sunset. "We'll drive you home, Mr. Felix," Kinloch said, taking the blind man's arm.

As he and Ruth and Felix McKie faced the door, Lance Gerrard slipped from the back bench and down the stairs. He was alone, for Elinor had carried out her plans and Justin was even then preparing to leave and seek her fortune in New York. And take her chance on finding Scott Shaffer again, Ruth had decided when Justin asked for his address. Perhaps she would get him after all; her vitality was superior to his. But no news of her had been circulated around the town in the months that had passed; only the old men who sat by the court house steps were heard from time to time remarking on her more obvious charms in a way that was at once elegy, insult, and praise.

Here now a year later, Miss Henrietta had moved back to the Mathison place to live with her old maid sister. There the talk of Colonel Mathison and his great score of slain Yankees continued unabated, though Miss Henrietta's Garden Club activities stopped abruptly, her church work died a lingering death, and the U.D.C. was the last to go. She paid fewer calls and received fewer callers; her sister said that her headaches were worse, but whatever it was, she spent a great deal of time in her room. Perhaps she was re-reading her favorite book, *If I Were King* by Justin McCarthy, whom she had mistaken for a woman and so had named her daughter; and perhaps

270

when her eyes tired, she looked up from her reading and removed her nose glasses to regard her favorite picture, that of Galahad in armor, him she had mistaken for Lancelot and so had named her son. Neither Lance nor Elinor nor anyone else had ever had the heart to inform her of these errors, but Justin had learned better when she went to the university and for once had been eager to get home in order to break the news. The kindness of the others had apparently been in vain; Miss Henrietta either did not believe Justin or she forgot about it.

Soon after the inquest the Gerrard house had been sold to Halpin Bramlett, a grocer who also dealt in real estate. But the house was empty still, Kinloch noted as he drove by, and in front of its silent, turreted bulk, the graceful outlines of Miss Cherry Bell's little minstrel stood and mocked its ugliness before all the world.

He found Lance in the living room of the bungalow, surrounded by stacks of papers, soiled dishes, an empty, smoked coffee pot, bottles, and a thousand cigarette butts. Kinloch could see through the window that he sat at a desk with his head buried in his arms. He came to the door and his eyes were red and swollen though he had not been drinking. Crying? Kinloch wondered with the unease of a man who has always thought only women and children cry.

Lance's welcome was one of genuine warmth. He resumed his place behind the desk where he fiddled nervously with a letter opener designed as a small dagger, hurling it time and again so that it stuck in the wood before him.

"I heard you were selling off the land," Kinloch said, sitting down.

"Yeah, Lock. Yeah, I am. I got no reason to keep it. Mama's in good hands and Justin—Lord knows if she wants you she'll find you, come hell or high water." He did not mention Elinor, though they both thought of her as he paused. "You know, Lock, I just thought the other day, every one of the things you said you wanted to happen has happened. Old man Felix told all that about the Walston fellow at the inquest, how he wasn't insane at all, and now I'm selling off the land,

271

and we'll not stir dust here any longer. Yeah, Lock, that's how it is."

Kinloch nodded gravely. Lance's manner of speaking, not accusing, free of the old careless mockery, but toneless and slow, drew them together in a strange mood as though they were old men meeting after many years of divergent path.

"Not saying there's satisfaction in it for me, Lance," he replied at last.

"No. Not thinking you're satisfied. I never got to tell you, Lock, but you were right in what you said at the inquest. Old man Felix was off on the wrong foot. Everybody in town thinks so, too. They knew your father." Before Kinloch could reply, Lance looked up and smiled. "How's Ruth getting along?"

"Fine. A month more to wait. I declare, I never would have thought she'd be this crazy for a son."

"A son, eh?"

"Oh, sure." They laughed.

"Look here, Lock, I don't want to get personal or anything, but for a long time I've been wondering. What fine did the court give Ruth on Ben's—on the manslaughter charge?"

Kinloch told him.

"I always felt more to blame than anybody," Lance said. "Lock, you'd be doing me a big favor if you'd let—"

Kinloch shook his head. "I raised it, Lance. Good crop last year and this too, but even if the crops hadn't been good, I would have raised it somehow. Thanks, though."

"I meant that."

"Sure, Lance. Thanks a lot. But no. No, I came to see about buying that little strip of land between my lower pasture and the branch. It's been on my mind for years now. Fence has to cross the branch twice, you know, and what with children wading and cows coming down to water, it's hard to keep up. I figure the old line went along the branch way back yonder, but the water switched course."

Lance scrambled among the papers and dragged out a map. "Sure,

I see where you mean." He bent over the map, thinking. "Lock, listen to me this once more. I know you must feel rotten over all this business and how it was from the beginning and how it turned out, but God only knows the torment I've been through. Thirty years of not a worry in the world, and then it all hit, and, Lock, it hit hard. You want this little piece of land. Take it, Lock. Just take it and let's don't speak about the money at all."

Kinloch sat with his gray eyes fixed thoughtfully upon the hat in his lap. The old difference was there between them again; he saw it and thought about it and said: "No, Lance. Thanks again, but no. I reckon that won't do it. And I reckon too, I made a mistake ever to come thinking I'd buy that strip of pasture. I changed my mind. I don't want it."

Lance toyed with the letter knife. "I see what you mean, Lock, and I'm sorry. But grant me this: you'll never know what it is to have to find out that your father was not an honest man. Justin didn't care—Mama never registered—Elinor left—and I—I've sat days and nights thinking there ought to be something I could do. Something. I think if you'd have taken that little piece of pasture just now, I might have offered you the whole damn plantation."

Like putting windows in church and like great big funerals, Kinloch thought; like they say some folks wear holes in the carpet praying for the dead.

"But I see that maybe you feel the same way I do," Lance went on. "Like you never want to set foot on any of that land again, much less own it."

Kinloch looked up in surprise. "I do feel that way. Just then when I said I didn't want it after all, I felt that way about it, too."

"And that the only thing either one of us can do," Lance pursued, "is go ahead the best way we can without too much mention of the land or of the things that have happened and gone."

Again surprised, Kinloch nodded in agreement. So he had told himself.

"What are you going to do, Lance? I heard you were planning to leave."

"I've got that much figured out, enough to know I can't stand the sight of this town any longer. Soon as I get this business finished off, I'm going west. Mama's brother is out in California. Fruit grower. I ought to have left years ago, but somehow you get in the habit of being where you are. I'm going to learn the business out there if I can, try and get in with him. And then—" His face softened and he hesitated.

"Then what?"

"It's too far ahead to say now. But there's Elinor, you know. You can't ever tell. Maybe if I can get things moving out there, she might not be too sorry to see me coming up her Daddy's front walk some time." He hurried on. "I'm actually getting a little excited about clearing out of here, being on my own for a change. I've been looking around Tarsus these past few months and thinking, My God A'mighty, how could I ever have thought it was all right to stay here? No business, no energy; why it's all but dead and don't know it. You see that too. You must. I've been thinking maybe you and Ruth might be making plans to move on after the baby comes. What about it, Lock? Why don't you think it over?"

"I thought it over once a long time ago," Kinloch said. He rose, putting on his hat and buttoning his jacket. Lance followed him to the door. "But some things seem right and others don't. I don't know why. But I reckon I aim to stay on. It seems right for me that way, that's all."

"New country!" Lance was saying. He leaned back against the door jamb, his eyes growing brighter than Kinloch had ever seen them. "New sights to see. People who don't know anything about you and care less. From what they say it's big as all outdoors. Easy going and friendly, too. Have you ever been there?"

Kinloch did not answer; he had hardly heard. He was thinking of a young man who rode a calico pony, a limber young man whose head was full of Chicago and adventure and the Rio Grande, whose name was Tom Gerrard.

It seemed to him ever since he had come that there was something more to be done and now he knew what it was.

If he had wanted to he could not have kept back the warm smile. He held out his hand. "Good luck, Lance."

Though there was a long moment while Lance stared hesitant with surprise, Kinloch did not lower his hand until he felt the other clasp it, or turn away until he heard Lance's voice: "Same to you, Lock. Same to you."

Too pat an ending —
deaths, hand clasps and
all — to the tale.